P9-EKY-727

CALGARY PUBLIC LIBRARY

JUN   2016

DESERT BOYS

DESERT BOYS

CHRIS McCORMICK

PICADOR

New York

This is a work of fiction. All of the characters, organizations, and events portrayed in this book are either products of the author's imagination or are used fictitiously.

DESERT BOYS. Copyright © 2016 by Chris McCormick. All rights reserved. Printed in the United States of America. For information, address Picador, 175 Fifth Avenue, New York, N.Y. 10010.

Selections from this book won Hopwood Awards at the University of Michigan.

"Habibi" was inspired by Anton Chekhov's "Gooseberries."

The following stories first appeared, in different forms and under different titles, in the following publications:
"The Tallest Trees in the Antelope Valley" in *The Southeast Review*.
"Shelter" in *Flyway*.
"My Uncle's Tenant" in *Fiddleblack*.

picadorusa.com
twitter.com/picadorusa • facebook.com/picadorusa
picadorbookroom.tumblr.com

Picador® is a U.S. registered trademark and is used by St. Martin's Press under license from Pan Books Limited.

For book club information, please visit facebook.com/picadorbookclub or e-mail marketing @picadorusa.com.

Designed by Steven Seighman

Library of Congress Cataloging-in-Publication Data

Names: McCormick, Chris, 1987– author.
Title: Desert boys : fiction / Chris McCormick.
Description: First edition. | New York, N.Y. : Picador, 2016.
Identifiers: LCCN 2015044337| ISBN 9781250075505 (hardcover) | ISBN 9781250075512 (e-book)
Subjects: LCSH: Boys—Fiction. | Young men—Fiction. | Male friendship—Fiction. | City and town life—Fiction. | Mohave Desert—Fiction. | San Francisco (Calif.) —Fiction. | Psychological fiction. | BISAC: FICTION / Literary. | GSAFD: Bildungsromans.
Classification: LCC PS3613.C38267 D47 2016 | DDC 813/.6—dc23
LC record available at http://lccn.loc.gov/2015044337

Our books may be purchased in bulk for promotional, educational, or business use. Please contact your local bookseller or the Macmillan Corporate and Premium Sales Department at 1-800-221-7945, extension 5442, or by e-mail at MacmillanSpecialMarkets @macmillan.com.

First Edition: May 2016

10 9 8 7 6 5 4 3 2 1

For Mom, Dad, and Madelein

Do I stay or do I go?
And do I have to do just one?

—Jackson Browne, "The Fairest of the Seasons"

CONTENTS

———— ✤ ————

DESERT BOYS

MOTHER, GODFATHER, BABY, PRIEST

———— ❧ ————

N ot long ago, three desert boys built a paintball field in the middle of nowhere. The idea came to Daley Kushner after his mother, a severely cautious Armenian immigrant unwilling or unable to differentiate between simulated violence and the real thing, refused to pay for her only son to be hunted down "like a mule" at the professional field in Acton. Daley didn't bother informing her that nobody, not ever, had hunted a mule. He just took his idea to the other boys, who immediately agreed to the plan. Dan Watts, whose parents owned a landscaping business, offered to borrow the necessary equipment, and Robert Karinger—whose dad had fought in the First Gulf War—had the idea to call each other by last name only: Kush, Watts, and Karinger. This gave an otherwise fun project the heaviness of what Karinger called "a life-and-death enterprise."

"Why Kush," said Watts, "and not Kushner?"

"Kushner sounds too much like my name," said Karinger. "We'd confuse people."

Nobody, Kush knew, would ever confuse him for Karinger, and

what people there were to confuse, Kush couldn't say. He was just grateful to have a nickname, and ready to get to work.

This was the summer before high school. The boys biked from town to the Antelope Valley's uncultivated desert, working long days so they could get the most use out of the paintball field before classes started in the fall. The dirt from newly dug trenches and bunkers established rings of three-foot-high passageways and walls, which Karinger called "bulkheads." From time to time, they ventured farther into the desert to find and collect abandoned furniture: a plaid La-Z-Boy sofa—orange foam innards jutting from its arms—made a quality barrier along the north section; a large brass-framed mirror, cracked in places and fogged by the remnants of old adhesives, provided an interesting *Enter the Fist* effect from an otherwise blind trench. Other objects, including many of the shredded tires lining the nearby 138, were sorted into tall wobbling piles. After weeks of shirtless, blister-forming labor in 100-plus-degree weather, the three boys flexed and compared their newly shaped and sun-soaked muscles. Then they rode home to fetch their guns.

Karinger was the only one to bring along any armor. He owned a face guard designed to look like a World War II–era gas mask. He never wore it, though, and simply carried the mask under his arm in the desert. Holding the mask seemed to give Karinger an indisputable authority, which he used to set up the rules of the game.

"Since there's three of us, we can only do one of two things—every man for himself, or two-on-ones, rotating the lone wolf."

The idea of being ganged up on had always frightened Kush, but not badly enough to consider inviting one of the sisters—Karinger's or his own—to even the teams. He suggested they stick to every man for himself. Then, suddenly afraid, too, of never having a partner: "Or two-on-ones, if you guys want."

Karinger pressed the tip of his gun against Kush's chest. Kush hadn't read Freud yet, but he still felt a kind of thrill.

"In war," Karinger said, "indecision means death."

Watts, half-Mexican, tanned while the others burned. He offered his suggestion coolly. "Let's do every man for himself, see how it goes, and then reassess."

"Right," said Karinger. He aimed his gun a few inches from Kush's foot and fired three shots at a rock the size of a coyote's skull. He told Kush to pick up the rock and toss it to him.

"This," Karinger said, holding the paint-splattered rock in front of him, helmet still under his arm, "is the Stone of Victory. Be the first to take the Stone back to your starting point without getting hit, and you win." He placed the Stone of Victory in the crook of a Joshua tree's arm.

The three stood back-to-back-to-back and, as directed by Karinger, took one hundred long steps each in his own direction. Then they waited for Karinger to fire his gun in the air—the designation of the start.

Also not long ago, though more recently, I got an email inviting me to a baptism that would take place in my hometown, the Antelope Valley.

The baby to be baptized was a boy whose father happens—or happened—to be an old friend of mine from childhood. The boy's mother sent the invitation along with an apology for not sending a hard copy. She didn't know my physical address, she explained, and I wasn't on any of the social networks. After a bit of investigation, she found a blog I'd contributed to, and an email address. She signed off:

Hope to see you,
Jackie (Connolly) Karinger
☺

For some time after reading the message, I wandered around my apartment, thinking of little else. This was the second piece of news I'd heard about my old friend Karinger in as many months, after a gulf of communication between us that lasted over five years (and never, finally, resolved itself). The other bit of news being that he'd been killed in Kandahar, Afghanistan, in November. Another friend from that time, Dan Watts, with whom I'd been in slightly better touch, called in January to tell me. At one point in the conversation, Watts said: "I always imagined those soldiers using paintball guns, that the war was just a large-scale version of what we played as kids." I confessed that the same thought had occurred to me.

Still, I couldn't focus on much in Jackie (Connolly) Karinger's message other than the strange addition of the smiley face. In bed or in the shower, I'd find myself ascribing to the face some meaning, a hint at something larger, something Jackie (Connolly) Karinger might have wanted to say to me, but could not.

One day in February, I decided to take a walk to mull over the invitation. Even on sunny days, Oakland at that time of year was mysteriously wet and chilly. A used bookstore stood ten blocks from my apartment, and I didn't realize I was heading there until I was drying my shoes against the mat out front. Lloyd Alcero, an old classmate of mine at Berkeley, greeted me from the register at the center of the store. The place was small, and I could see I was the only customer.

"Hey," I said. The sound of my voice came out tinny and weak. I hadn't spoken to anyone in days. I cleared my throat and moved toward the back of the store, to a section I'd been interested in some time ago, but not so much recently: GLOBAL TERRORISM. Someone had placed a sticker of W's face on the label. Neck tilted, I scanned the spines along the shelves.

Lloyd Alcero came up behind me. "Doing research for another prize-winning essay?"

There had been an essay contest on campus a few years earlier for English majors. My submission was a piece about the effects of past wars on American fiction (specifically, Salinger's), compared to the inability of our current wars in the Middle East to produce similar results (due, according to my thesis, not only to the lack of a draft but to an anomalous combination of what I called "unwarranted-ness and apathy" as well). I didn't—and don't—know if I believed that, but the essay turned out to win the top prize: publication in Berkeley's alumni magazine, *California,* along with a check for five thousand dollars. Naturally, the only people who remembered I'd won were other participants in the competition, including Lloyd Alcero, who brought up the topic every time we spoke.

"No," I said. "What about you, Lloyd? You writing anything?"

Lloyd was one of those young gay men whose outlandish flamboyance and energy, inextricably linked, seemed to exhaust and straighten other gay men who came into contact with him. He was wearing a white bandanna over his forehead, and a tuft of dyed-green hair sprouted like a small artichoke from his chin. He stopped fussing with the books, happy to hear the question. "Just my novel," he said, shifting the bandanna. "It just keeps growing and growing—it's up to, like, twelve hundred pages now. My ideas keep feeding off each other."

At this point—maybe he noticed my boredom—he pulled from the shelf a book whose cover showed the burning Twin Towers. "Can you believe this September will be ten, as in one-zero, years?"

I did the math; we'd been in high school for less than a month.

"I didn't even know what the World Trade Center *was,*" he said, laughing. "I spent most of that morning asking people why it was such a big deal. It wasn't like Britney Spears died or anything. Needless to say, I was not a bright kid."

I actually felt relieved. To this day, I cringe when I think about how nonchalant I'd been, how casually I'd treated the news. I told Lloyd so.

"Well," Lloyd said, getting back to the books. "We were just kids, you know? We were children. On the other side of the country, no less. What can you do?"

Choosing a few slim books at random, I stacked them on my arm. I felt a strange, patriotic obligation to buy something.

"You should come in more often," he said. Again he adjusted his bandanna, which I guessed was a nervous tic.

I wished him luck on his novel. "Let me know when it's ready for another pair of eyes," I said.

You could see how long he'd been waiting for someone to say that.

They were only kids, sure, but some of them dealt with the circumstances with more gravity than others. While Watts and Kush, happy to be out of class early, joked about how terrorist attacks should happen more often, Karinger focused on the long-term consequences.

"Maybe we'll get a world war," he said.

Since school had started up again, they'd gone out to the paintball field only on the weekends, and went that Saturday after the attacks. The mood was different this time—no one seemed to be having any fun. At one point during the game, Karinger, who'd Scotch-taped a miniature American flag between the eyes of the mask under his arm, started walking, without urgency and without aiming his gun, directly at Kush. Kush was so confused by Karinger's nonchalance that he hesitated to shoot. And then Karinger did what he'd never done before: he put on the mask. The gas-masked figure kept approaching at this slow, haunted pace, and

Kush began to doubt the person behind the mask was Karinger at all. By the time Kush lifted his gun, he felt the sharp blast of a paintball against his right biceps. He dropped his gun to grab at the wound with his left hand, where a second tremendous pain began to grow. Karinger continued to shoot from a few yards away. He wouldn't stop firing. Kush dropped into a ball on the dirt, at which point, the popping sounds of released carbon dioxide and ammunition stopped, at least for a moment.

Watts came over, yelling at Karinger. Kush tried, and failed, to hide his crying. After a while, Watts offered his hand to help him off the ground.

Karinger said, "Why the hell didn't you shoot me, Kush?"

Watts said he'd had enough for the day. He was going home, and Kush wanted to join him. But as Watts got on his bike to leave, Karinger told Kush to stay for one more game.

"You're going to win," Kush said. "Why would I even play?"

"You've got to start thinking different," Karinger said. He'd taken off his mask now and was jabbing his fingers into the side of his head. He had the bright blond hair of an albino, and he'd recently had it shaved to military length. Sometimes Kush imagined Karinger with blue eyes, but now that Karinger was staring directly at him, lecturing him, they were clearly hazel. "Stop saying everything that goes through your head, Kush. The first step in being tough is convincing people you're tough. Including yourself. You've got to pretend you're tougher than you are, keep some shit to yourself. This is what not being a pussy is all about."

He went on to explain the rules of this new two-person game: essentially, chicken. They'd each get one shot at the other person from a certain distance before taking a long step closer. Then they'd shoot again, and step closer. And so on. The first person to quit the game lost.

"Thanks for the pep talk," Kush said. "But I'm going to pass."

"Fine," Karinger said. "You can get two shots for every one of mine. You want to get me back, don't you?"

Gingerly, Kush rubbed the welt on his hand and thought of how gratified he'd feel to give a matching one to Karinger. So he walked to his spot in the desert, thirty feet from where Karinger stood. Then he hollered, "Are there any rules?"

"You shoot twice, I shoot once. No need for masks"—he tossed his aside—"because there's no face shots. And no ball shots. Cool?"

"I won't aim for your face, but you should probably wear your mask. I can't promise anything."

"No masks," Karinger called out. "It'll force you to focus your aim."

Kush tried to swallow, but his mouth was dry. The heat had the back of his tongue scaly. He aimed his gun and shot, missing wide left. His second shot missed high.

Karinger's first shot hit Kush on the left wrist.

"Shit!" Kush said, grabbing the pain.

They stepped closer. This round, Kush's first shot missed again, but his second hit Karinger in the right shin.

"Good," Karinger called out, shaking his leg.

By the time they were standing ten feet away from each other, Kush had stopped feeling the pain. He found himself laughing wildly every time he was hit, just as Karinger did. As they stepped closer together, Kush imagined their bodies merging. The silly idea had an odd heaviness in his mind, and allowed him to feel a tickling pinch where the pain ought to have been.

When they got within point-blank range, they aimed at each other's chests.

"It's a draw," Karinger said, still laughing. "See, man? It's a draw."

Their laughter quieted down. For three, four seconds, their eyes met. Then, at the same time, they pulled their triggers.

There it is, Kush thought, doubled over in the desert. There's the pain again.

They hadn't merged after all.

I still hadn't responded to Jackie (Connolly) Karinger. Her email stayed open on my computer—I must have read it thirty times. Looking around the room, I saw on the edge of the coffee table the three books I'd impulsively purchased from Lloyd Alcero. In an effort to buy more time, I went over to inspect them: *Understanding the War on Terror, After 9/11: America's Global War, The Muslim One: A Memoir.*

I turned the third book over. The author's black-and-white photograph: a young woman wearing a hijab. Chin down, she looked up at the camera. Her thin eyebrows tensed, giving her face the severe expression of a distraught mother, but she couldn't have been much older than I was. Seeing her photograph reminded me of someone I'd known ("known" is a strong word) in high school. For all I knew, she could have been the same woman. Upon checking the bio, however, I learned that the author was raised not in California, but in Florida, where she'd foiled her uncle's plot to set off a car bomb at an amusement park. Still, I couldn't shake the feeling—due, I suspected, to the timing of it all—that this author happened to be someone whose life was perpendicular to mine, and that, if I were to read her book, I'd learn something about myself at that intersection.

She'd written the memoir, strangely, in the third person. It began: "For the first sixteen years of her life, Adila Atef spoke with a throaty, confident voice." By the time I reached the epilogue, I'd forgotten the book was not, in fact, a novel. The veracity of the story was re-revealed to me in those final pages, where the author converted to the first person:

Contrary to the beliefs of many—friends included—I
wrote this book in the third person not for its therapeutic
or distancing effects, but because it represents more ac-
curately the way in which I remember these events un-
folding, more like a film than a diary. The *I* can't exist in
more than one place at a time, and I am here, now. Who,
then, was that other Adila?

Nowhere in her story was the experience of the girl I'd been
aware of in high school. She and the author were not, I accepted,
one and the same.

Of hundreds of girls at Antelope Valley High, only one wore a
headscarf.

She was two years ahead of Karinger, Kush, and Watts, and so
they rarely crossed paths. The only reason they knew of her was because, after the terrorist attacks, she'd been harassed in the main
quad at lunch, and the local media came to produce a special report. Peter Thorpe, local newscaster, along with a microphone-
tethered cameraman, interviewed students on campus. He asked
questions some in the community later agreed were loaded, including whether or not this girl's wearing a headscarf to school was in
any way disrespectful, "considering the circumstances."

Kush and Watts—along with about fifty other kids—vied for
a spot in the shot's background, making faces and flipping the
camera the bird. By the time they realized Karinger was being
interviewed, Kush and Watts had missed the entire conversation.

"He took my name, age, and class," Karinger said when he re-
joined his friends. "I'll be on TV at seven o'clock tomorrow night."

And so they made plans to watch the special at Karinger's place,
a brand-new two-story tract home on the west side of town. His

mother, Linda, had won the house in a lottery, one of a thousand she entered every year. She, along with Roxanne—Karinger's twelve-year-old sister—joined Kush and Watts in front of the TV, between multiple roaming cats. The three boys sat on the center couch. Linda took the love seat, and Roxanne, stomach and elbows down, lay flat on the carpet in front of them, chin on her hands. She wore a pair of little denim shorts, fraying at the ends. More than once, Kush caught Watts following the thin white lines of her legs to their meeting place.

The show started. Peter Thorpe spoke to the camera, live in-studio, against a green-screened photograph of three women in burqas. Kush looked to see that everyone's attention was on the screen. When it was, he studied the bottoms of Roxanne's big toes, which were only slightly larger than paintballs. His own sister, Jean, had just moved away for college, and he rarely saw her. He rarely saw *any* girls—definitely not the bottoms of their toes—so he studied Roxanne's with the unsexed air of a paleontologist.

The segment shifted to an exterior shot of the high school. A voice-over informed the viewers that he (Thorpe) had recently had the opportunity to speak directly with students. One after the other, kids began making their on-screen claims. ("I have Trigonometry with her, but she never really says anything"; "She seems nice enough, but you never know"; "I'm sure it's hard for her to be the only one, but her being here is hard for everyone else, too, you know?")

Finally Karinger, with his white-blond buzz cut and matching, furrowed eyebrows, appeared on the screen, much to the elation of his mother, who placed her hands over her nose and mouth, speaking into them: "My man, my man!" Roxanne turned her neck to look at her brother on the couch above her, as if checking for similarities and differences between him and his on-screen counterpart.

On-screen Karinger began:

"At first I was kind of—" He looked to Peter Thorpe for approval. "—pissed." He leaned into the microphone. "She definitely brings up a lot of stuff you don't want to be reminded of." Now he turned to look at the camera. Kush wondered how many times Karinger had practiced this before—he was a natural. "But that doesn't mean she can't wear whatever she wants to wear," Karinger continued, "because that's what my dad fought for." The kids in the background thrashed each other for attention. Kush, meanwhile, looked at Roxanne. He didn't feel what he thought he ought to feel; he found himself thinking of the shape of Karinger's legs, trying to remember if they belled out in the calves the way Roxanne's did. Then he turned to Watts, who looked up from Roxanne's legs, too, and gave Kush this look, eyebrows-up, that said, *I know, huh.*

Linda reached out to her son and put her hand on his knee, saying something about the future president. Everyone congratulated Karinger on his performance—even the cats, swarming, seemed pleased with him—because he really did represent how the community felt, disturbed but principled. A bit self-righteous, Kush might've added, but at least *humane.* On their bike ride home that night, Watts and Kush talked about how proud they were of Karinger, admitting surprise. Kush hoped Karinger's speech would inspire the rest of the school to leave the Muslim girl alone.

Unable to sleep that night, Kush got out of bed and found a pen and a sheet of paper with two lists he hadn't updated since middle school: one list, "Foster," for people he admired and another, "Pester," for people he felt he could do without. On the "Foster" side of the paper, which he'd go on to fold and carry in his Velcro wallet for a number of years, he wrote beside Karinger's name: *As a kid, you like your friends because you have fun together. As you get older, though, you start rooting for them. You want to be proud of them.*

Five days after Jackie (Connolly) Karinger's invitation, Dan Watts called me.

After high school, Watts was the only one of us to stay in the Antelope Valley. While Karinger joined the marines and I moved to Berkeley, Watts worked his way through an EMT program at the local community college, passed the National Registry examination, and now worked as a paramedic. We blamed his schedule for how rarely we spoke (a few times a year). His voice had a coarse, sleepy quality, which some of his recent acquaintances must have mistaken as a consequence of his rigorous job. The voice was, however, the voice he'd always had, and hearing it this day came as a warm comfort.

He asked whether or not I had plans on the eighteenth of April, the date of the baptism. When I told him about Jackie's email, he sounded relieved: "I didn't want to bring it up in case you weren't invited."

"Wait," I said. "What would you have done if I didn't know about the baptism? What if I'd asked what was so important about April eighteenth?"

"Huh. I didn't think that far ahead."

I asked about him—was he going to be there?

"Believe it or not," he said, "I'm the godfather."

A strange, embarrassing jealousy came to me.

"What about you?" he said.

"I don't know," I said. I told him I changed my mind every hour. "I can't get the thought out of my head that he wouldn't have wanted me there."

Watts laughed. "Probably not. But isn't that your cue?"

"Do you remember that Muslim girl in high school?" I said. "The one they did the TV special on?"

"Yeah, for sure. Did you guys meet up? Wait, are you with her *now*?"

"No, no," I said. "I've just been thinking of Karinger's interview. Where he shocked us with his sheer humanity. Remember that?"

"Yeah," Watts said. "Too bad it didn't make a difference."

I'd remembered Karinger's self-righteous but heroic speech, but I'd forgotten the rest of the story. Less than a week after the televised special, the girl in the headscarf was enjoying the lunch her mother had packed for her that day (a peanut butter sandwich, of all things), when she was pinned down by a group of six female seniors, who proceeded to spray-paint her white scarf red and blue. She rolled up to avoid both the fumes and the beating she presumed (understandably but incorrectly) was coming. According to Peter Thorpe's follow-up report, she elected to be homeschooled for the remainder of high school. The six girls, who'd each been handed a five-day suspension, were initially also banned from attending senior prom. After a community petition gathered enough signatures, this additional ruling was reversed.

"I really believed Karinger's speech was going to convince everyone on campus to leave her alone," I said. "I went home that night and wrote this extremely sentimental note about growing up. About being proud of your friends, as opposed to just enjoying their company."

"Sounds like you," Watts said. "You still carry that note around, don't you?"

"No," I said. "I'm not *that* sentimental."

The truth was, of course, I'd been even *more* sentimental. Years after I'd written it, after what turned out to be our last conversation, I slipped the note into Karinger's backpack. My hope was that he'd stumble upon it after I'd gone home, understand its significance, and return to me, his best friend, inspired to make me proud again.

"I don't know," said Watts. "I bet you still have it."

"Tell me about the baby," I said. "Tell me about your godson."

But then my phone pinged, and I saw the name—LLOYD
BOOKSTORE—on the screen. I told Watts I'd call him back in a
few minutes, but I ended up talking with Lloyd for a long time, an
hour and a half, and meeting up with him that night at a bar, and
by the time I got home, Watts may or may not have been at work or
asleep, and I didn't want to bother him either way, so I turned off
my phone and went to bed.

For the boys, there had never been in their midst a girlfriend—a
young woman with the power to transform the priorities of a young
man fundamentally—until Jackie Connolly pressed her cornsilk
lips against the forehead and cheek and mouth of their friend Karinger. This was their junior year: the rattle of 2003, as Karinger
would say, the fangs of 2004.

That Karinger, the only one with a girlfriend, was also the only
one of the three who had a car seemed to the others not to be a
coincidence. Earlier that year, Linda Karinger had purchased for
her son (and, she specified, for her daughter to inherit) a royal blue
1988 Ford Mustang. If it weren't for the daily rides to and from
school—not to mention the joyrides on the weekends—Kush and
Watts might have resented Karinger for his "sick ride," as they, without irony, called it. As it was, Karinger's successes felt entirely like
theirs to share.

Until, of course, along came Jackie Connolly.

She was beautiful in the way people call the desert beautiful,
which is to say that although some people actually believed it, most
of the time it was said in response to someone else's denigration
of it.

Her blond hair, invariably tied back with a red headband, was
as thick as the tails of the horses she tended to on her parents'
farm in Quartz Hill. Regularly she came to school smelling like an

old haystack. Although she was thin in the face, arms, legs, and chest, her hips spread against her like the San Gabriel Mountains. They'd had a class together here and there since freshman year, and Kush had met her during a brief stint with the Future Farmers club. But it wasn't until Karinger, Jackie Connolly, and Watts all had junior English together that she became Karinger's girlfriend and therefore part of the group. The schedule had it so the end of that particular class meant the beginning of lunch. Kush, enrolled separately in Intro to Literary Criticism, had to cross the width of campus to meet up with the other three, who, by the time he arrived, had invariably begun eating already.

Maybe all young people in love think about their relationship in the future tense, but Karinger and Jackie Connolly *vocalized* their future. Earlier in the year, the launch of the new war in Iraq promised Karinger at least some action, and he and Jackie constantly hypothesized on their capacity to be a military couple, to have a military family. They even talked unabashedly about money. Getting married before shipping out meant higher pay for Karinger, and possible wedding arrangements were tossed around in the lighthearted, creepy tone of the clinically deranged. They were proud to kiss in public—never raunchily, mouths always closed—and held hands any time they were in reach of each other. Nobody but Kush seemed to mind.

Because she shared the class with Karinger and Watts, Jackie Connolly seemed to think of Watts as Karinger's best friend, not Kush. (In Kush's mind, their friendship was an equilateral triangle—a generous thought, since Watts was the newer addition to the group.) Kush would watch Jackie laugh after Watts made a joke, and she'd go on and on until she snorted and—in some particularly egregious cases—cried. Meanwhile, after Kush told a joke of similar quality, she'd offer only a bit of flattery, this eyes-averted chuckle and smile. He found himself simultaneously jealous and contemptuous of this girl—this pallid, manure-shoveling girl.

Once, on a violently windy Saturday afternoon in November, Karinger backed out of plans to head to the paintball field, citing Jackie as his reason. Instead of riding in the smooth royal blue Mustang the way they'd envisioned, Kush and Watts pedaled their bikes side by side like children, struggling to push forward into the gusts. At one point, Kush confided in Watts his secret hatred of Jackie Connolly.

He said, with effort: "Don't tell Karinger, but I want to rip that red headband out of her hair and throw it at her stupid face."

Watts, who was in better shape and full of breath, said, "Why would I tell Karinger that?"

It occurred to Kush that maybe Watts *was* the better friend. They didn't say another word on the subject until Watts brought it up again a few minutes later.

"You got to admit, though," he said. "She's got an amazing ass."

They pedaled their undersize bikes like bears at the circus, and the wind carried their laughter.

Lloyd paid the eight dollars for the pitcher of beer between us, so I felt obligated to answer his question—"What've you been up to?"—honestly. I told him I'd done nothing for two days but read and think about an old friend named Karinger.

"What kind of name is that?"

"A last name," I said.

"What's his first name?"

"Does it matter?"

"It'll bug me."

"It was Robert," I said.

" 'Was'?" Lloyd asked. When I didn't say anything, he ordered a second pitcher.

I told Lloyd about the invitation to the baptism and about the last time I was in the Antelope Valley—the previous Christmas. I'd taken my mother's car to drive by Karinger's house. He was a month dead, but I hadn't heard.

Even as the sun was setting, I could see Karinger's house had been repainted a kind of pastel green. The small town I grew up in had become a relatively large suburban city—empty stretches of desert had mostly been replaced by fast-food restaurants and shopping centers. But it was the paint on Karinger's house that seemed to me like the greatest change. Every other detail—the motion-sensor light fixture on the garage and the royal blue Mustang in the driveway—had remained the same. The perfect sameness of the house had been ruined by an ugly coat of pastel paint. Pulling up closer, I noticed another change: the Mustang's license plate frame had been replaced with a pink camouflage one labeled USMC GIRL. Karinger's mother had kept to the deal—this was Roxanne's car now.

I kept telling Lloyd the story: I drove in the direction of our old paintball field, far enough out of town to be left undeveloped for now. The dark was setting in, and no streetlamps lined the road. I was the only driver in sight, so I took my time. I flashed my high beams at the desert shrubs, searching for the old paint, which must have come off by now in the rain and wind. When I reached what I remembered to be the right place, I pulled the car to the side of the road and felt the sand settle underneath the tires. I left the engine going and kept the headlights on, but got out of the car. A realty sign I'd once shot at still hung there, though nothing had been purchased or built. That far out, the wind came at me in sprints. The chains of the realty sign clamored, and in the east, stars began to show themselves. Across my stomach, I held my arms to stay warm. A scratching noise came over the sound of the engine; a wide and squat tumbleweed had nested under the front fender. "Shit," I said, getting low to clear it.

Lloyd, born and raised in San Francisco, couldn't believe I came from a place with tumbleweeds. "In California?" he said. "The next thing you'll tell me is you've got a cowboy hat in the closet."

"No," I said dramatically, "just skeletons."

"Hey," he said, "Wasn't that the original title for *Brokeback Mountain*? *Skeletons in Spurs: My Closeted Life on the Range*."

We laughed. Somehow I was having fun talking to him about the same material I'd been agonizing over on my own. The bar lights weren't dim, and I wasn't very drunk. The difference had to be Lloyd. I found myself looking for details in his face and throat, the few curls of hair reaching out from the collar of his PUNS ARE FUNS shirt. He was a dork. I hated his green goatee. I liked him.

"I've had a crush on you for years," Lloyd told me once we'd gone back to my apartment. He spoke a lot during sex. Once he'd fallen asleep, I made my way out of bed and to the computer, where I typed the following email:

Dear Jackie,

First: Sorry this has taken so long.

Second: Congratulations on your baby—Watts told me when you first got pregnant, but I haven't had the chance to congratulate you directly. You always struck me as someone who would be a great mother. Maybe it was how I always imagined you taking care of those horses—I don't know, I just felt that way.

Third: Last time I was home, I drove by Karinger's place. This was the day after Christmas. I knew he wasn't home. I just found myself sitting in my mom's car out front, staring at his old Mustang in the driveway. I don't know why I'm telling you this. I guess it's just to show that the timing of your email was uncanny. I've been thinking about the old days a lot lately—about the guys, about our last few days together. I always sort of hoped things would return to normal after we all grew up a bit.

That being said, I will try my best to make it. April 18 at Sacred Heart, 1:00, right? This is the church by the old library? Suddenly I'm really excited to see you again, and everyone. I can't wait to be back home.

Daley (Kush) Kushner

Every morning when they were picked up for school, and every afternoon when they met in the parking lot to go home, Kush and Watts slid into the backseat of the Mustang. They didn't do it to treat Karinger like a cabdriver; the passenger seat was already taken. Roxanne Karinger, suddenly thirteen and a high school student herself, sat quietly in the front, hugging the unmistakable freshman mark that is an overstuffed backpack. She rarely spoke, and when she did, she had a soft voice that was overwhelmed by the engine or else the tires and shocks doing their work. For this reason, Karinger, Kush, and Watts hardly noticed her.

Or, at least, that's what Watts told Karinger. Watts told Kush the truth.

The truth: Watts looked forward every morning to that switch—the car pulling up outside his house, the perfect royal blue door opening, the girl stepping out to let him in. He'd sit directly behind her. Through the space between the headrest and the seat, he'd stare at her white-blond hair and watch the tiny, wild strands of it dance above her head. Later, when the weather turned warm, her sundresses and shorts and tank tops augmented the impact she had on him. But even in those cold mornings of the school year's middle section, when she'd have on a baggy sweatshirt, maybe, and a pair of dark jeans tucked into boots, just the simple motions involved in her transition from a seated position to a standing one were enough. To young Watts, they seemed to be a characterization of sex itself.

"Plus," he told Kush, "she's got an ass almost as nice as Jackie's, and Jackie's ass has *years* on Roxanne's."

There were certain moments when Karinger seemed to notice Watts's attention. Sometimes, while Roxanne worked the lever to unfold her seat, Kush caught Karinger staring at Watts from behind the wheel, as if daring him to leave his eyes in the wrong place for even a second.

Then there was the time The Police's "Roxanne" came on the radio. Naturally, everyone looked to the girl in the passenger seat. When the chorus hit, the three boys sang along, laughing as they tried to reach that raspy high note. During the last chorus, Watts— caught up in the fun—put his hands on the shoulders in front of him, leaned in, and sang the girl's name directly into her ear. They were stalled at a red light. Karinger turned and looked straight at Watts. Kush, meanwhile, homed in on the beautiful new dimple in Karinger's locked jaw, which he'd never noticed before. For his part, Watts did the only three things he could: He removed his hands from the girl, leaned back in his seat, and looked to Kush for help. The light changed, but Karinger didn't move. He just kept staring at Watts. In her softest voice, Roxanne told her brother to go. He didn't move. A driver behind them honked his horn. It took another "go" from his sister before Karinger turned and put the accelerator, finally, to use.

Kush was still thinking of that dimple when he took a seat in his favorite class, Intro to Literary Criticism. Dealing with "advanced" students as she was, Ms. DeGroff felt free to curse in her lectures, speak openly about sexuality in the books she assigned, and grade essays with the bluntness of a loved one. In other words, she treated her students as if they were already in college. Although a few hypersensitive kids had filed complaints over the years, none of them dealt Ms. DeGroff a real consequence. Most students, she'd found, *preferred* being treated like adults.

So it was in this state of mind that Ms. DeGroff made what turned out to be—in Kush's mind, at least—her famous remark. In the course of discussing "Bartleby, the Scrivener," in response to a student who deemed the defiant Bartleby a "jerk," Ms. DeGroff told the class that sometimes, the world could use more Bartlebys. "Soon," she said, "some of you will be asked to fight this illegal war, for example." And God, she went on, would she be proud of any of them who said to the administration, "I would prefer not to."

The aside took fewer than twenty seconds of the class. But as soon as Ms. DeGroff said it, Kush and the other students looked around at each other with despair. Ms. DeGroff must have known the trouble she'd just put herself in, because immediately upon saying it, she cleared her throat and changed the topic.

One of the students must have passed the news on to his or her mother; a petition began. Facing the possibility of another visit from Peter Thorpe and his cameraman, the school's principal suspended Ms. DeGroff.

But her removal couldn't erase from Kush's mind the perceived lesson, the idea that pride, in certain cases, wasn't reserved for those who went along with the plan. Kush started checking out certain books at the library and reading political articles on the internet. He attended an empty Sunday morning screening of *Fahrenheit 9/11*. He read as much Orwell as he could get his hands on, searching always for contemporary analogies. He began scoffing internally at the yellow ribbon-shaped magnets adorning every fender in town. Seeing Berkeley come up in so many of the articles, he started to dream of going to school there. He felt as though he'd been born in the wrong era, that he should have been alive in the 1960s and '70s, and listened to nothing but sad music from that time—Simon & Garfunkel, Joni Mitchell, and Jackson Browne. For a kid who wanted to travel back in time, going to Berkeley for college seemed to be the best option. He had some time to apply. Until then, all he had were Karinger and Watts, so he expressed his opinions only in his personal journal, safe for the future, and kept his mouth shut around his friends.

Which is why—even though he'd grown tired of the sport a while ago, he'd begun to see it as a fetishization of war—when Watts asked him for another game of paintball in the desert, Kush agreed. Again they rode their bikes, just the two of them. On the ride out they didn't speak, and the only sounds came from the gravel squirming under their tires. As they approached their spot in the desert, Kush and Watts realized they'd already played their last game.

All around them in the dirt were the chevron tracks of farm equipment. The trenches had been filled. The walls had been leveled. The plaid sofa, the mirror, the piles of tire shreds—all of it had been hauled off. In fact, the only evidence of its being the right place at all was the polychromatic paint freckling some of the Joshua trees. At the side of the road, a newly embedded realty sign swung in the wind.

"Well," said Watts, turning his bike about-face. "Paintball had to end sometime."

It was what had to be said, but Kush hated to hear it. He understood the end of paintball to be the evaporation of the final strings of glue holding him and his friends together. He said, "I have to get out of this place."

Without aiming his gun, he took a quick shot at the realty sign.

Lloyd asked me to swing by the bookstore, said he had a gift. When I arrived, he hugged me and told me to stay put. Then he trotted off to the back of the store, out of sight. When he returned, he was wheeling behind him a purple carry-on bag. "I'm taking you up on your offer," he said, beaming.

"I never offered to travel with you," I said, honestly confused.

Lloyd laughed. "No, stupid. It's my novel. I printed out a copy for you."

"Oh," I said, taking another look at the carry-on. "Oh my."

"Printing it cost me, like, forty-five dollars." Of this he seemed proud.

"Well, thanks," I said, and took hold of the retractable handle. I wondered if he expected me to pay him back.

"Don't worry about line-edits," he said as I was leaving. "Just give me your gut reaction on the big-picture level."

When I got home, I opened the bag and pried apart the manuscript to the last page, to see the page number—1423. I closed the manuscript, zipped the bag, and wheeled the luggage to the corner of my apartment, next to the DustBuster.

Not too long ago, I would've left the damn thing in the corner and rolled my eyes every time I happened to look over at it. In college I'd been surrounded by rich, comfortable kids who called themselves writers, and the prospect of getting into a relationship with the most flamboyant member of that self-assured bunch would've made me puke. But now I looked at that purple carry-on luggage, imagined the box of pages inside, and felt something like admiration. Someone else might've seen a carry-on with torn fabric and muddy wheels. But I looked at that bag in the corner and saw a man's secrets—his ideas, his grievances, his memories, and his fantasies. I looked at that bag and fell a little bit in love.

———

Because of that "substantial pay increase" Karinger kept referring to about the marines, he and Jackie finalized arrangements for a small wedding to be held at the Connolly farm in April of senior year. Kush and Watts shared the title of best men.

Karinger's mother helped with the preparations. In the lawn between the house and barn, she carried two fistfuls of poppies, which she'd picked in the fields northwest of town. "I know, I know—I'm a criminal," she said, placing the orange state flowers here and there around the makeshift altar. The pine panels of the stable—the heads of two horses peering over—provided the backdrop.

A bald priest with an old man's sense of humor had come out to the barn. At one point, he turned to the horses behind him and said, "If you object, say neigh." The children and the parents encouraged him; the wedding parties rolled their eyes.

Beer and champagne were served to the adults—a label extended for the day to include the newlyweds—and soda and juice had been provided for the rest. Kush held a can of Coke at the serving table, and found himself in a conversation with Linda Karinger and the priest. The bride and groom were off chatting with the father of the bride, along with the aunts and uncles. Children alternately chased each other in the grass and petted the noses of the horses. Kush couldn't spot Watts.

The priest asked if Kush aimed to join the marines, too.

"Oh," said Kush, thinking of the antiwar articles he could recite. "No, not me."

"This one is on his way to college," said Linda lovingly.

"A word of advice," said the priest. "Universities are good for the mind, but don't let them train you to neglect God."

Kush put down his Coke and said he had to use the restroom. Could they point him in the right direction?

Kush admired the land and the horses, but the house itself was relatively small and unspectacular. Quickly he found the hallway to the left, following his directions. Counting one, two, three doors on the right, he grabbed the doorknob.

"Occupied," came a voice—the unmistakable, drowsy voice of his friend Watts.

"It is I," Kush said.

Then came a moment of silence.

"Might be in here for a while," Watts said.

"Take your time," Kush said. "I don't really have to use it. I'm just trying to get away from that priest for a bit."

Another pause. This one lasted longer than the first. Kush would have to be the one to break the silence this time. With his fingertips he drummed on the door. "Are you feeling all right?"

"Shit," said Watts, as if he'd just made a decision. "You have to promise me something. You promise?"

"What am I promising?"

"You have to promise not to mention what you're about to see. Ever."

"Did you have an accident?" Kush said, laughing.

"Will you just promise?"

"Sure," Kush said. "I promise, I promise, I promise."

The door shot open, hitting Kush in the shoulder. Out rushed Roxanne Karinger, fixing her dress on her way down the hall. Watts stayed in the bathroom, sitting on the toilet in his suit, buckling his belt. "Promise me again."

Two hundred pages into his novel, I recognized a story I'd told Lloyd at the bar. Three teenaged boys (minor characters all of them, recently added to the book) sit on the hood of a car, talking. They're parked at the beach (not the desert), but the conversation is, more or less, one I'd had with Karinger and Watts almost six years earlier.

The boy heading to the military tells the other two he doesn't want to have a kid until after the wars are over. The boys have just graduated high school, and they're still wearing their caps and gowns. Their thighs are pressed together on the car while they pass around a bottle of whiskey one of them has stolen from his parents' liquor cabinet. The military kid doesn't want to get killed—or worse—thus forcing his child to make up stories about him. He confesses that he himself has been making up stories about his own father—Willem— for years, namely that he saw combat. He hadn't. In fact, Willem had been struck with testicular cancer, and remained Stateside for the entirety of Desert Storm. A few years later, Willem left his wife and kids, and was living, monotesticularly, someplace in Bakersfield.

I called Lloyd and told him to cut the scene. I didn't care if the novel never got published, if I was the only person in the world who'd make it to page 212 to see it. I wanted Karinger's story— and his father's—out of the book.

"I'll cut it, sure," Lloyd said. "But, you know I didn't mean to offend you. This is how the world works. People are just amalgamations of stories. When one person becomes close to another, all those combined stories merge and create new stories. It's not appropriating so much as evolving. Do you see what I mean?"

"Just, cut it. Please."

And he did. But seeing Karinger's story in print—even though the pages were only in a Kinko's box—made falling asleep impossible. I kept rereading Karinger's fear, how he didn't want his kid to grow up without a real story of his dad.

I'd already told Jackie I'd be at the baptism. But I imagined holding that baby, knowing that in my arms I'd be carrying nothing short of the incarnation of my friend's biggest fear.

So I sent the following note:

Dear Jackie,

You know I've always been one dramatic motherfucker. I'm sorry. I just need you to tell me if Karinger would have wanted me there. Please, please be truthful.

Thanks,
Kush

Being the only married couple on campus brought the newlyweds some notoriety. At lunch, girls approached and asked Jackie to show off her ring. One, clearly a freshman, apologized for interrupting, but she had to know, swiping at her black bangs, what did it feel like to be in love?

The new, shared living arrangement, combined with the new-found attention at school, made it difficult for Kush to spend any time alone with Karinger. Karinger didn't even drive his friends to school anymore. Watts started driving his dad's small pickup to school, and Kush started riding with him.

Roxanne Karinger found her own carpool to join, but every now and then, in a moment of crisis, she'd jog up to the truck in the parking lot after school let out and ask Watts for a last-minute lift home. She'd sit between Watts and Kush, keeping her hands between her knees to take up as little room as possible. Kush dreaded these days for the awkward quiet she brought on. Thankfully, graduation was approaching, and the opportunities for this particular brand of discomfort were quickly fading.

On a Friday morning early in May, Watts called Kush to let him know he'd woken up with something nasty—not really, but in case anyone asked—and he'd be staying home. Kush resolved to take his bike like the old days. When school let out, he worked at the lock on his bike near the parking lot. He was adjusting his helmet when he heard Roxanne's voice call his name.

"Where's Watts?" she said.

"Home sick."

"Homesick?"

"Home, sick."

She made the descending hum of disappointment. "I was hoping he'd give me a ride home. My friend bailed on me."

"I can sympathize," Kush said. "Here. Why don't you take my bike? I'll pick it up next week when your brother's around."

"No, it's all right. I'll just walk."

Kush debated saying it, but did: "It's a long walk. I'll go with you."

Roxanne moved her hair from one shoulder to the other. Her brother had been training—lifting weights and running miles every morning—and had bulked up. Roxanne, with her hair pulled to one side, exposing the thin line of her clavicle, looked like a younger, long-lost version of him. "You don't have to," she said.

"A long walk with a friend is better than a short bike ride alone," he said.

"You're strange," she said, not unkindly. She started walking. Kush, bike at his side, jogged a bit to catch up.

Their dynamic changed now that they were alone, now that they were on foot instead of in a car. Talking was easier at this slower pace, in this open environment. Kush guided the bike next to him and thought about how little he knew of Roxanne, despite having watched her, basically, grow up. He told her so.

"I'm a shy person, I guess," she said. "I don't know. I don't like people who talk about themselves."

"Fair enough," said Kush. "Let's talk about other people."

"Ha," she said.

He wanted to ask about Watts, about whether or not their

rendezvous at the wedding was a one-time thing. Instead he asked how she felt about Jackie Connolly.

"Jackie is my sister now," she said. "I love her." After a pause: "I know *you* don't."

Kush offered a self-conscious laugh. "What makes you say that?"

"My brother knows you hate her. You told Watts you hate her. Something about throwing her red headband at her ass?"

Kush felt his grip tighten around the bike handles. "I said 'face,' not 'ass.' Watts was the one talking about her ass. Damnit. He promised he wouldn't tell."

"You should get to know her," Roxanne said. "She's actually pretty amazing. She's teaching me to ride horses this summer."

"I'm not interested in getting to know Jackie better."

"Because you're jealous of her?"

Kush felt his throat and stomach compromise to meet halfway. "Jealous?"

"Look," Roxanne said. "I've known you since I was nine, Daley Kushner. Robert and Dan and Jackie can't say that, can they? In some ways, I know you better than they do."

"I don't know what you're trying to say," Kush said. He could feel tears welling in his throat, and how he was holding them back, he couldn't say.

"Don't worry," Roxanne said. "I'd never tell anyone. Not even if you ratted on Watts and me. But you still shouldn't. Because my brother would kill him. No joke."

Kush wanted to thank Roxanne, but doing so would prove she was right about him. Instead he said, "Why should I care if Karinger kills Watts?"

"Don't be so dramatic," she said, gently kicking the bike's front tire. "You guys can get over a fight. What you can't get over is a death."

And so Kush kept Watts and Roxanne's secret, all the way

through graduation. Karinger, Kush, and Watts donned caps and gowns, walked across a makeshift stage, and shook hands with administrators and teachers they would never see again. Their mothers aimed cameras at them from different angles. In most of the pictures, Jackie (Connolly) Karinger squatted in front of the three boys. Kush, an honor student, was the only one draped in gold. The others wore blue.

Later that night, while most of their peers found their way to house parties across town, and while Jackie went home to the farm, the three boys ransacked their parents' liquor cabinets and headed to the desert.

The winds had eased up and the night air held on to the heat of the day, so the boys tore off their T-shirts and sat on the hood of the Mustang in nothing but shorts, flip-flops, and graduation caps. Karinger sat flanked by his friends. They passed between themselves a glass bottle of whiskey, which threw golden shapes of moonlight over their thighs. The desert appeared orange here and there in the headlights of the car.

"They're going to take this all out one day," Karinger said, drunk. He waved the bottle, motioning toward the undeveloped land surrounding them. "Who's gonna take care of it all?"

"You sound like Kush," Watts said.

Karinger laughed. "I'm serious, though. Who will take care of . . . my car?" He pressed his palm against the royal blue hood between his legs, holding on to the bottle with his other hand. Kush reminded him to pass it over.

"Your sister," said Kush. "It'll be hers soon."

"But who will take care of my sister? Not *you*." Karinger grudgingly handed the bottle to Kush. "You are out of here, Berkeley."

"Don't worry," said Kush. "Ol' Watts here will keep an eye on her." He took a drink. "Won't you, Watts?"

"Give me that," said Watts. He mouthed something to Kush, pleading. Then he said, "Karinger, your sister is my sister."

"Ha," said Kush.

"And you, Watts—who will take care of you?" Karinger patted Watts's floppy curls. "And who will take care of you?" He looked to Kush. "And my mom," he said. "And Jackie?"

"Everyone here is going to be golden," Kush said. "The question is, who will take care of *you*?" He meant it in a funny way, jabbing his finger into Karinger's impressive arm to loosen up the conversation. But Karinger seemed to be mulling the question over with sincerity. They were quiet, all three of them, for a long while.

Karinger pushed himself to his feet. His graduation cap fell to the dirt. Out of Watts's hand he took the bottle. He wound up and threw it with a howl as far as he could into the dark. The sound of the bottle shattering hung between them.

A good amount of time passed. Watts cleared his throat. "That bottle," he said. "It was empty, right?"

The three of them sent their laughter into the world, into and beyond the reach of the Mustang's lights.

———

Dear Kush,

Don't apologize for being dramatic. I don't know how it is for you academic types, but for us regular people, some situations get a pass.

You asked if he would have wanted you here. Let me tell you a story. Not the last time he was home, but the time before that, we got into an argument. It was something stupid—I can't even remember. Maybe it was what to have for dinner? What day to invite my parents over? Anyway, he'd come back this time a little different. He never told me what had changed, but I could tell by the way he talked to me—like he didn't really care either way about anything—that something was off. I brought it up to him that night. I took off his shoes and set them next to his duffel bag, which he'd been looking through, at the side of the bed. Then we were *in bed* in bed—forgive the details, but for some reason I don't care if you know—and again, he didn't respond like he usually did. So I asked him again, what's wrong? Well, you know him. He wouldn't say a thing sober, so I got up and poured him a glass of whiskey, and then another, and another. It was winter, and the whiskey warmed him up. He kept saying so. Finally I asked him one more time, what was wrong? Had anything happened out there that changed him? No, he said, not one thing in particular. That only happened in movies, he said. He put his head down on the pillow and started talking and talking, everything from his dad to the idea of having a baby to what he would do if he wasn't in the marines. You name it, he talked about it. And just when I thought he was about to fall asleep, he said something so sad and sweet I picked up a pen and jotted it down. He said (I'm reading it right off the scrap of paper): "Might not be rooting for me anymore, but I'm still rooting for him."

For some stupid reason I thought he was talking about his dad. He got upset and said I was wrong. Then he wouldn't say anything else, but I always figured it was you he was talking about. Who else could it be?

My point is you're not the only dramatic one. But, yes, to answer your question truthfully. He would have wanted you here—yes, yes, yes.

Best,
Jackie (Connolly) Karinger
☺

From the patio, Linda Karinger called into the house for help. She'd need the outdoor furniture set up before noon, and would someone please get on that while she started the coals going in the grill? She wore a camouflaged apron with white block letters across the front: FREEDOM ISN'T FREE.

Watts, followed by Kush, came outside. Karinger and Jackie would be arriving any minute, followed shortly thereafter by the Connollys. Tomorrow, Karinger would head south to Camp Pendleton to transform into the man he would be for the rest of his life. This was his going-away party.

Again Linda poked her head into the house through the sliding glass door, careful not to let a cat escape: "Roxanne! Get off the dang phone and come help!"

Roxanne put her palm over the mouthpiece and said, "I'm on vacation."

"Not today, you're not. Go help the boys set up the chairs."

As Roxanne came outside, Watts and Kush were fitting their hands underneath the surface of the patio table. They carried it to the center of the backyard's lawn. The day happened to be the hottest of the year—people were calling it 108—and although the furniture was cheap and lightweight, dark circles of sweat pressed through the boys' shirts in the chest and back like giant thumbprints.

The doorbell rang and Roxanne, easing a folded chair onto the grass, went to answer the door. Linda squeezed a bottle of lighter fluid over the coals, and a ball of fire burped out.

Karinger had arrived. There were moments of symbolic importance in life, it seemed to Kush, just as there were moments of symbolic importance in literature. He remembered that day in the desert with Watts, finding their old paintball field dismantled. That was an example of a moment that felt symbolically important to him. But real moments existed, too—moments that didn't represent something, but actually *were* that something. None of these thoughts appeared in Kush's mind that day in sentences—they never did. They were only part of a *feeling* he had—that lame, irrefutable noun—while he watched his friend Karinger on the patio hug the women in his life, one by one: the feeling that this was not symbolically but actually the end of their corresponding lives.

Karinger, adjusting the straps of a backpack, made his way out to the lawn while the girls spoke around the whitening coals. "Thanks for putting this all together," he told Kush and Watts.

"What's with the luggage?" Watts asked.

"I know," Karinger said. "I feel like a freshman again, lugging this thing around. I had some clothes and stuff lying around the farm I wanted to bring over here before I left."

Roxanne came over, dangling a plastic bag of disposable silverware in front of her. "Mom wants you guys to set the table." She ripped open the plastic bag and split the forks, knives, and spoons among the three of them. "Kush, you seem like a spoons kind of guy. My brother's definitely the knives. That leaves Watts with the forks, but I'm not sure what that means." Laughing, she left them to do their job.

By the time the guests arrived, the heat had everyone complaining. Roxanne kept holding her hair up off her neck and saying, "Jesus." She removed her Dodgers cap and placed it underneath the spigot. Once the hat was filled, she twisted it back onto her head, letting the water crash over her face and shoulders. She returned to her seat, encouraging everyone else to follow suit. Kush watched as Watts made a concentrated effort not to stare at her wet shirt.

As flies swarmed the leftover coleslaw and chicken bones on plastic plates, Linda told her son to open his gifts. They were gags, most of them—porno magazines and tiny glass bottles of Jack Daniel's and Smirnoff vodka, none of which Karinger could take with

him to boot camp—but some gifts were given in earnest: a pocket
Bible from his parents-in-law; a single-sheet list of relevant addresses
from his wife; and a few Polaroid pictures of young mom and
kids, in the trailer they lived in before the house, from his mother.
Everyone laughed when they were supposed to laugh, and looked to
Linda—face red with sunburn and emotion—during the sweeter
moments. Gone were the complaints over the heat.

Kush watched the party from a distance, from a canopied patio
swing at the far end of the yard. Initially he'd taken the seat to get
some shade. As the party wound down, however, and as the in-laws
began to say their good-byes, Kush remained there, rocking gently,
alone. Over and over again, he thought about what he wanted to
say to Karinger.

Eventually, it was just the three boys in the driveway. The sky
turned dark, and crickets sang in the hedges. In the white light of the
fixture at the rim of the garage, the three boys drank from the tiny
gift bottles of liquor, smuggled in Karinger's backpack, which he
set down at the driver's side of Watts's truck. "Take these, too," Karinger told them, meaning the porn.

Watts took another bottle from the bag and unloaded the
magazines, stacking them in the cab of his truck. "So," he said, slam-
ming shut the truck's door. "This is it?"

"Those should last you a while," Karinger said.

Watts said he didn't mean the porn; he meant *"this"*—he moved
his hand in a circle between the three of them to elaborate.

"I'll be back for a little after boot camp," Karinger said. "We'll
get together again before I ship out."

Kush said, "I'll probably be up north for orientation, I think."

Karinger nodded. "Well, I guess this *is* it."

"For a while, anyway," said Watts. He finished what was left in
his mini-bottle and tossed it into the bed of the truck, bringing on
the heavy sound of thick glass hitting metal.

"Who knows?" Kush said. "Forever, maybe."

Karinger and Watts laughed. Watts said, "Kush, why do you always have to be such a dramatic motherfucker?"

Near the backpack, Kush took a knee and grabbed the last mini-bottle, which he opened and finished in one swallow. When he stood, he said, "Karinger, you always said I needed to be more decisive, right?"

" 'Indecision is death,' " Karinger said, quoting somebody.

"This isn't me being dramatic."

"Tell me, man. Whatever it is you want to tell me, tell me."

"This war is criminal," Kush said, feeling as though the cold rush of truth came through him.

Karinger turned his face and laughed it off. "Is it, now."

"I mean," said Kush, "you're not dumb enough or sadistic enough to go kill people for money, are you?"

From Watts: "Kush, you drunk asshole. The war is way more complicated than—"

"If you say one more word," Kush said, turning to Watts, "I'll tell him something else I should've told him a long time ago."

"You've got a lot of growing up to do," said Karinger. "A younger me would've knocked you out already."

"You're still a younger you!" Kush said, shouting now. "That's the point! If you die in that war, it's a younger you that'll die, and for what? Absolutely nothing!"

The power Kush felt just a minute ago had already begun to fade. Now he felt something less heroic, but he'd gone too far to pull back. Seeing no other option to try to regain that power, he wound up and threw the empty miniature bottle at Karinger as hard as he could. To his surprise, the bottle hit its target, glancing off Karinger's enormous shoulder and breaking apart against the driveway.

Karinger looked at the bits of glass, which refracted the motion sensor's light here and there against the side of Watts's truck and across his own shadow. He stepped forward and planted his fore-head against Kush's. This was the closest they'd been since their game of chicken in the desert four years earlier. Kush braced for a punch until he heard Karinger laugh.

"Let's not pretend this is political," Karinger said. "I know why you really want me to stay."

He raised his finger to his mouth. "Go ahead, Kush. Kiss me." Karinger closed his eyes. He cartoon-puckered his lips.

And for the first time in a long time, Kush acted without think-ing. He kissed Karinger with his eyes closed. With his mouth he held on to Karinger's fat lower lip as long as he could, and felt the cracks at the center from the dry, searing summer winds. When Karinger seemed to let him have the kiss, every fantasy Kush had tried so diligently to ignore over the years occurred to him at once. The result was a magnificent barrage of embarrassments, sentimental on the one hand, pornographic on the other. Kush never figured out which was more pathetic: the times he'd daydreamed of skip-ping town with Karinger to San Francisco or New York or Paris, or the nights he'd spent alone in his bedroom after a day of paintball, licking from between his fingers his own semen, and imagining the taste—like a desert plant, leafy and hot—was his friend's. Either way, it was in his mouth now, the withered taste of shame itself. It had been rooted in his memory, but now shot from his brain to the wet nib of his tongue, which pressed between the small valleys in Karinger's bottom row of teeth. And before Karinger stepped back and threw his fist so perfectly into Kush's chest that the impact felt to Kush less like a punch than a tree breaking a horrendous fall, Karinger kissed him back. Hadn't he? He seemed to have kissed Kush back, a brief but beautiful hold on Kush's mouth, so forceful and lovely that Kush, after the punch, felt not only the immense pain in his chest but also, in his top lip, a kind of swelling.

Now Kush sat upright in the driveway, one hand pressed against the thudding plate in his chest, the other behind him, for balance, against an oil stain.

Above, Karinger picked up his backpack and, fitting his arms into the straps, said, "Everyone, including you, will be happier once you're in Berkeley. It's where you belong."

Kush, still struggling to take in air, said, more deliberately and honestly than he'd said anything in his life, "Go die for nothing, asshole. I hope you do."

Then Karinger spat on the ground, walked the path to the front door, and disappeared.

"I should have told him about Roxanne," Watts said on the drive home. His hands on the wheel were shaking. "We could've avoided all that back there. I should've been the guy getting punched." Now he was crying, swiping his nose and eyes with the back of his hand. At a red light, he twisted his fists over his eyes, and for the first and only time, Kush felt he wasn't the weakest of the three.

The day before the baptism, Lloyd and I were at a sidewalk café eating crepes with strawberries and Nutella. We'd seen each other every day for six weeks. No one would argue six weeks is a long period of time for a relationship. But look: We were sitting on one side of a small circular table on a sidewalk in Oakland, California, under a cloudless, bright sky. A mother pushing two babies in a double-seat stroller passed us and—when Lloyd licked his thumb and wiped chocolate from my face—smiled a benevolent smile. Six weeks was not separate from ten years, I felt, or any bit of my life. Six weeks, in some ways, was everything.

"So," Lloyd said, "I was thinking. Maybe I can come along with you tomorrow. See your hometown, meet the gang. Maybe even meet that mysterious Armenian mother of yours."

Just then, the blaring sound of sirens wailed by, and I imagined

Watts driving his ambulance around the Antelope Valley. He was
a man now—a man who saved lives, I was proud to say. For whatever reason, though, I couldn't think of Karinger as the husband
and father he turned out to be. I didn't think of him as a man. I
felt awful admitting that. I tried to picture him fighting that war
out there in a climate not unlike what we'd been used to, and all I
could see was the boy in that gas mask, shooting his gun at other
boys, frightened boys crouching behind a sofa. *Hostile, hostile fire,
small-arms fire, Kandahar Province*—I had these bits of information, but none that helped me imagine the scene of his death. So I
thought instead of that silly note I wrote and carried with me for
so long, slipping it into his backpack as I took that last miniature
bottle of liquor in the driveway. I thought of how he must have discovered it at some point, using the same language with his wife later
on, and I tried to imagine what he felt while reading my words. How
close had he come to calling me? What was it he'd said, about my
having to grow up? To have a person so young tell you to grow up . . .

"Well," Lloyd said. "I don't need to come along. But how excited are you to go back home? What do you think it'll be like, seeing everyone again?"

I could imagine. I would head to the church near the old library
a bit early. I'd slip into the back pew and wait for the important
players to assemble at the altar—mother, godfather, baby, priest. I'd
recognize the bald priest, who would joke with the baby: *Come on
in, the water's fine.* The churchgoers, perpetually reminded of the
unspoken sadness of the day, would appreciate the humor. Our
laughter would complement the crying of the baby, who'd be lifted
and dipped, lifted and dipped, lifted and dipped until every last
prayer was heard.

But I was sitting at an outdoor café in a city on the rise with a
man I was beginning to love. I wasn't about to go back.

THE TALLEST TREES IN THE ANTELOPE VALLEY

I. BRIEF OVERVIEW OF AN EVOLVING CULTURE

The town became a city, and so on, but in the transition, there were elements of both, and I happened to be raised there during that period. In fact, depending on who's telling the story, that transition still defines the place.

I'll give you an example of each. On the city end of things, you started seeing department stores, courthouses, various public schools—in short, buildings with elevators and escalators. Our town was literally moving up. Bridges linked stretches of new highway over the anachronistic caterwauls of the railroad. And people were moving in, people from Los Angeles and its boroughs, people who'd been drawn to the cheap, carry-only-what-you-need, fresh-start sort of living the desert represented. People who'd been renting a one-bedroom apartment for the entirety of their financial lives woke up one morning and read the signs that the same amount of dollars and cents got you a modest, one-story home up north. Sure, the desert wasn't L.A. But for the people who headed into my town—and they came then by the thousands—maybe not being L.A. was the most appealing thing about it.

Still, the place remained, and remains, a *town* in certain, immutable ways. To this day, alfalfa plants are farmed on the eastern fringe for cattle to eat, and their shoots come up in local markets for salad ingredients or else midday snacks for children. You'd make a friend in kindergarten and shake his hand at your high school graduation. You felt confident in the possibility that one day his son and your son together would hunt lizards in the heat. In school, they would be, like their fathers were, guided to the military, the police department, the fire department, or the farm. Most girls, as far as you could tell, longed for marriage and motherhood from the start. They taught children or else studied nursing while they waited for the inevitable shift in priority. Of course, these were suggestions, and suggestions only. If you didn't follow the suggestions, there was still a place for you. It just seemed a lot lonelier a place.

Maybe the biggest indicator of its town-ness was the attitude of its citizens. The townspeople looked at the incoming flux of city folk—many of whom happened to be brown—with a slant and baleful eye. They worried about the future of the town, which, as all townspeople understand, depends on the character of its community. They didn't trust people who seemed, in ways both obvious and imaginary, so *different*. It's true that these townspeople were what some might call bigots, or at least a group of people who didn't like seeing things change. But they were also no monolith. Some might say they were persons, not a people.

That's why stories happen. That's why this story happened.

II. ONE WAY TO GET A JOB AT TWELVE

The father of a kid I knew at school: His last name was Reuter—pronounced like the word "writer." On account of divorce, his son didn't share the name, and saw his dad only on occasions like birthdays and lazy weeks during the summer. I saw Mr. Reuter more often. He happened to be my neighbor.

We lived on a block of tract homes. On each block stood an assortment of ten or twelve homes from two or three types. The blueprints had been flipped here and there, and garage doors were painted in different colors to give the illusion of variety. I mowed lawns and pulled weeds for houses that weren't inhabited by children who otherwise would be doing that work themselves.

Mr. Reuter had seen me one weekend in March getting the lines just right on my own front lawn. I should say it took most of my strength to get the job done. Everything about me at that time (and let's be honest: at this time, too) was light. I was a lanky boy with a small head on a thin neck. My heels never touched down when I walked. I used to have to jump and come down on the mower with all my weight to get the front wheels up so I could pivot around the tree in the middle of the yard. Maybe he saw me do it that day. He headed over from his driveway across Comstock Avenue while I heaved the bag of grass over the lip of the compost bin.

"Looks good, smells good," he said. Mr. Reuter must have been around the same age as my dad, but he looked much older. He had a full head of hair, but it was white and thin, and each silky strand of it seemed pluckable without much effort. He wore a pair of glasses with gold frames and these black rubber tips on the ends that hung below his enormous earlobes. He'd lost some weight since I'd last seen him, since before his wife and Drew moved out.

"You want me to do yours?" I asked. Back then I was always looking for business.

"No," he said, drawing it out like we were talking on a porch someplace. "I plan on getting rid of my lawn altogether."

I wasn't surprised. In my limited but obsessive time as a semi-professional landscaper, I'd learned how difficult and expensive it could be to keep a lawn in the Mojave Desert. You didn't have to do yards for a living—you could take a walk through the neighborhood and see how many of the houses had put in limestone or gravel where the grass had been. Some of the newer neighbors from the city chose to neglect their yards altogether, letting the grass turn yellow like giving up, and the dirt that the home had been built on in the first place got to peek its head out again, in some places anyway.

"I've seen others do it," I said. "I guess that means I won't be getting your business, then?"

"Well, that's not entirely true. Not if you want it, that is."

"What's the job?"

"I need a digger, a man to loosen up the soil. I'd do it myself, but I'm a bit past my prime. You're skinny, but I've seen you working the neighborhood. You've got heart."

"Anything more complicated than a shovel?"

"No sir. I figure it'll take the sixty-six pounds of you about six weekends, six hours a day, to make it happen. There's money, of course."

"How much?"

"How much do you get paid to mow?"

"Twenty," I said. The truth was I got paid five dollars a mow. I added: "Plus tips."

"Well, how about that," he said. "By any chance, are you hiring?"

I wanted to laugh, but I figured he'd know I was lying if I did.

"Look," he said, "I've got trees coming in, is the thing. Big trees that'll take up the whole yard. Half the cost is those guys coming in and prepping the land. I'm leaning on you for a discount. How's fifty dollars for the project?"

Fifty dollars to a kid lands in that perfect range of inordinate yet fathomable, and has a lot of sway to make him do something without thinking too hard about it. I'd planned on continuing my negotiations, but the words "fifty dollars" spun me off my game. Immediately I agreed.

Mr. Reuter said his thanks and turned homeward. I finished unloading the mower's bag, holding my breath as the loose dust and grass billowed out of the bin upon landing. I hooked the bag, infinitely lighter now, onto the mower again. From across the street, Mr. Reuter waved and smiled. Then he pulled on the red rope above his white head, lowering his garage door until it was shut.

Work hadn't started. I hadn't yet been paid a nickel. But already I felt it. That was the first time I sensed I owed him something.

III. SOME NOTES ON MY UNDERSTANDING OF ADULTS

Some children transcend their age with patience and understanding—an understanding that you have to go through this thing called childhood before anyone takes you seriously, before you're empowered to drive change. I wasn't one of those children. I was a child in every sense of the word, but mostly I was a child in that I felt nothing like a child.

At twelve, I felt both prepared for the simplicity of the average adulthood and eager to sense the nuances of a more complicated version, one I'd have much preferred to live. Already I'd divided those older than me into these two camps: Pester and Foster. These were actual lists I kept as a kid, written with red ink ("Pester") and blue ("Foster"). And like all camps, they had their leaders.

Unfortunately for my parents, I'd placed them at the head of the Pester camp. Mom and Dad—full-time salespeople of clothing and furniture, respectively—would come home from work, make dinner, and speak exclusively in questions. They'd ask my sister and me about our days at school, what we had learned. Whenever we asked about their days at work, they'd say, "Work isn't worth talking about." I expected as much from Mom—like many immigrant mothers, she considered education and God the only worthwhile topics of conversation—but I kept hoping my dad would break. Once, when I said as much to him, he offered me a piece of advice. He said, "The greatest quality a person can have is to be a deep, genuine listener."

I argued that if he never said anything about himself, I'd never have a chance to listen.

"Without even knowing it, you're learning how to listen right now," he said mystifyingly.

Eventually I gathered that he meant to compliment himself, that by speaking to my sister and me mostly in questions, by hardly ever telling us anything, he was showing us what a good listener looked like.

That's when I put him at the top of my "Pester" list.

I should add that the "Pester"/"Foster" lists were always changing. Coach Vierra, my gym class teacher, fell from the good side to the bad after he issued me a demerit for spitting on the blacktop. (The sizzling effect was something to see.) My sister, Jean—sixteen and impossible, most days, to locate—found herself on different sides of the list all the time, depending on whether or not I saw her that week.

This is a long way of saying Mr. Reuter was different. After hearing my mother's opinions of him (she'd spent some time reaching out to the former Mrs. Reuter, and had come back, like a journalist, with a version of the story), I'd put Mr. Reuter down in red ink, too. According to my mother's vague commentary, after all, this was a selfish bully of a man we were talking about, "the king of cutting corners." But then he hired me for that job. Aside from Jean—who, because she was my sister, hardly counted—Mr. Reuter was the only person who'd ever made the transition from Pester to Foster on that list of mine. I made it out to be—someone breaking a pattern like that—a big deal.

IV. INSTRUCTIONS & INSIGHTS FROM MR. REUTER

In the driveway, Mr. Reuter held out a shovel. He had one hand on it, arm outstretched toward me. His other arm rested akimbo on his waist. I took the shovel with both hands and let the metal hit the cement.

"Hey," he said, "don't let the spade touch anything it can't dig out. That means anything but grass, dirt, and shit. Got it?"

I lifted the shovel and held it horizontal. "Got it," I said.

He went over the plan. The house, like every grass-having house on our block, had two front lawns: a bigger one separated from a smaller one by a driveway. The bigger side was three times the size of the smaller one, about 170 square feet. What he wanted was for the entire smaller side to be dug out and turned. He was going to fill that small side with cement, to extend the width of his driveway by five or so feet. That would take me a day or two, tops, he said, and we'd start there. The next step in the plan was to dig out a circle—ten feet in diameter—from the bigger side of the lawn. To the best of my ability, I was supposed to center the circle in the yard. I'd have to measure it and mark it off somehow. Then I'd get to digging.

The job seemed more complicated than what I'd signed up for, what with all the calculations. I told him so.

He scoffed. "You think I was going to give you fifty bucks to turn grass into mud? The money is for the precision."

"I don't know," I said. Fifty dollars wasn't as much as people made it out to be.

"The problem here," Mr. Reuter said, looking me in the eye, "is that you're not used to being entrusted with things you could easily mess up. Is that true?"

It sounded true. I didn't think too deeply about it, and said yes.

"It's a shame. It's the death of a young man, not being given the opportunity to earn trust. The *opportunity*, you know? Just that. It's bigger than anything. Oh, you'll find ways to make fifty bucks here and there. That's not really what you want out of this. I can tell. It's not every day you get the chance to point at something you've done and say, 'I could have ruined the shit out of this, but I pulled it off.' You don't think I could've—if I really wanted to—done this myself? Hell, it would've saved me a lot of time, not to mention the fifty. But I see you mowing lawns around the neighborhood, itching to make your mark on something. Grass, though, it grows back quickly, doesn't it? Not even a couple days later, all your work is invisible. It's gone. You're trying, and I give you credit for that. But this—" He grabbed the shovel's handle between my hands. "—this is permanent. You'll see."

I asked if I could say something.

"Sure," he said.

"I'll do it for seventy-five."

V. SOME REALITIES OF MY FIRST DAYS DIGGING

It took two full days of digging to finish the smaller side of the lawn. I didn't really have a strategy. Starting in the middle, I stepped the shovel into the ground as far as I could (about two inches) and pulled. In layers, I moved back until I reached the perimeter.

Mr. Reuter spent most of the time inside the house. At the beginning of each day, he placed a full pitcher of water and a cup on an oil stain in the driveway. The first day, I drank all the water in a couple of hours. When I got thirsty again, I went to the front door and knocked. Mr. Reuter answered, holding the telephone to his ear with his shoulder, carrying the holder and its wires around with him. With a look of disappointment—his glasses seemed to sink lower the unhappier he got—he took the pitcher from me and said he'd bring more water out in a bit. I went back to work. He never showed up with more water. Some time later I took a break, crossed the street, and drank as much water as I could from home. In a strange way, I came back with a feeling that I'd failed. I hadn't made that pitcher last, and had to run home for help. The next morning, when I saw that a full pitcher of water had once again been placed on the driveway, I made a point to drink nothing more.

As I worked, so did the heat. In the desert, the idea of spring was a myth from another culture. It went from winter to summer like flipping a coin, and it seemed as though I'd lost the toss. The heat turned the saliva in your mouth and throat to mush. Your skin turned white until the burn settled in, some hours later. You'd go home after work and cling your lips to the mouth of the tap the way two animals might kiss, chugging water until your stomach ached with it. Still somehow you'd piss only once a day, this orange urine that came out smelling like the heat itself, liquefied.

The clouds came and went in clumps, leaving spots of shade here and there on the pavement. From time to time, the garage door opened upward like a salute, and Mr. Reuter would walk out, barefoot, careful not to stand on a sunny spot of the driveway. He'd say something like, "Progress," or else, "You're getting it." Then he'd hop from spot of shade to spot of shade until he was back inside the garage, pulling closed the door. These tiny moments of encouragement had an enormous effect on me. More than once I thought the heat was too much, or the work was too much, or else the money was too little, and then Mr. Reuter would say his little something, and I'd go right back to work, doubtless in my efforts.

I distinctly remember thinking, going into the job, that my mind would be free to wander while I worked, and that I might imagine some extraordinary thoughts to express to those adults on my "Pester" list—thoughts that would create in them a doubt in their belief that I was unable to change things without their help. But the truth was that nothing, not a single memorable moment of reflection or imagination, sprouted from or arrived at my head during my hours digging up that lawn. In every rare moment I caught myself thinking, the thought happened to be about the work in front of me. When I told Mr. Reuter about my surprise, he said, "That's called pride, and that's a great thing." He taught me to laugh in the face of anyone who called physical labor "mindless" work.

A part of me already knew that. My father spent his entire life working, after all, and I'd never considered him a mindless man. But I wondered why he refused to talk about work. Boredom, maybe, but a lot of people say "boredom" when what they really mean is shame.

VI. MR. REUTER ASKS A FAVOR

When I finished turning up the dirt on the smaller side of the lawn, I allowed myself a minute to admire my work. There had been spots in the middle (my first attempts) that looked uneven, and I'd gone back to make them flush with the pavement. Since the lawn and driveway were at an angle from the house down toward the sidewalk, it was tricky to get the leveling just right. But I'd done it.

After a few knocks on the front door, Mr. Reuter emerged from the house. He saw the work I'd done, and put out his hand for a shake. I took it, the first earnest handshake of my life.

"You're exceeding expectations," he said.

My fingers twitched at the praise. That would have been enough to keep me working with pride, but he went one step further.

"In fact," he said, "I think you've earned yourself a raise. One hundred dollars seems more fair for this kind of work, wouldn't you say?"

I tried to keep the face of someone who'd earned something and knew it. But I must have said thank you for every extra dollar he'd just offered me.

"You just keep it up now, all right?"

"Yes sir," I said. "I'll do even better."

"I'm sure you will," he said.

"See you on Saturday," I said. "And thanks again."

"Saturday, yes," he said.

I started back across the street. He called after me.

"One more thing," he said. He tugged at the black rubber tips of his glasses, moving the frames up and down until they sat on his nose just right. "You still see Drew from time to time at school?"

His son was a seventh grader—a year ahead of me. I'd seen him at lunch from a distance, but we hadn't spoken since he moved. We knew each other only from having lived across the street—we used to play with his wrestling action figures. Once he moved, our friendship changed. That's how kids have relationships with people sometimes—they're based on situations. Sometimes that's how adults have relationships, too, but that's a different story.

"Yeah," I said. "I see him."

"Oh, good. I've got a favor to ask of you."

Still in the mode of praises and raises, I was in no spot to decline.

"Ask him to come help out with the digging. Your money won't get divided, I promise. I'd ask him myself, but his mother won't let me speak to him without her on the line, and she'd put a stop to it before he'd even get the chance. You see what I'm saying?"

"Got it," I said.

"Great," he said. "That'd be great."

"Saturday, then," I said.

"Saturday. With Drew, maybe?"

"Maybe," I said.

VII. THE WATCHER, WATCHED

Memory is more a play than a book, a play in which the character of you is one of many. You piece together the furniture and the school halls and the people using details (some true, some unwittingly borrowed from other moments in your life, or the lives of others) and your imagination. Then you get to watch. You *watch* your memories, don't you?

And the watcher knows—especially if the watcher happens to be a townie—that he is not the only one doing the watching. His stories, then, involve a great deal of the looming anxieties stemming from that quintessential doom-knowledge found in towns: That always you are being seen, that always you are being judged. Not by some force above the clouds, but by other people. And unlike in a city, where a person knows he may be seen by any number of people at any point in the day, this is a different sort of doom-knowledge. It's the knowing that those who see and judge you are inevitably people who, in some way, *matter.* They're people who know you or your family, or else the person with whom you're interacting. They're people you've let down in the past. They're people who may have gone *out of their way* to watch you mess up.

I was aware that my involvement in Mr. Reuter's plans hadn't gone unnoticed. I'd looked up from my shovel's blade from time to time as a car rode past. Every once in a while, I'd catch the eyes of the driver, or else the passenger. Sometimes there'd be that millisecond of recognition, and maybe even a reflexive wave from inside the car. One of those drivers or passengers must have been curious about my working on this particular man's lawn. (My mother wasn't the only one talking about him.) One of them must have seen the two of us talking near the mound of dirt I'd assembled near the green compost bin. One of them must have said something to a person who mattered to the story, because when I went to school after that conversation with his father, Drew Zelinski (formerly Drew Reuter) cornered me in the hallway.

VIII. THE CLOSEST I'D EVER BEEN TO A FISTFIGHT

I was small, I think I've mentioned. Drew happened not to be. His shoulders had spread away from his center like the geological birth of a valley. Only it happened overnight. Not two years before, when we sat on his front lawn screaming the names of wrestlers, we were about the same size. Something had changed for him, and before I remembered how this newfound strength might be used against me, I admit that it gave me great hope for my own physical potential to burgeon. (I'll point out again that it would never happen for me.) He slid his thumbs behind the straps of his backpack and jutted out his elbows. With my backpack against the wall, I asked as casually as possible, "Are you about to hit me?"

"Are you going to keep being friends with my dad?"

"No," I said. "I'm just working on his yard. For money."

"He's a piece of crap," Drew said. "He's a liar. Don't fall for it."

"I'm almost done with the job," I said. "He said he's getting some trees."

"It's all a lie," Drew said. "He makes things up. He's full of shit."

The urge to defend Mr. Reuter came unexpectedly. I disassembled it, thinking of my vulnerable position.

"Look," I said, "I'm almost done with the job."

"Go ahead and finish it," he said. "You don't know him like I do. He only hired you because he thought we were still friends. He thought I'd come over to hang out with you. Trust me. Those trees aren't on their way. That money isn't on its way. He makes every-fucking-thing up."

A moment passed where neither of us said anything. Kids walked by in groups of two and three. He backed up.

For some stupid reason, I said, "Thank you."

IX. ADDING THE FORMER MRS. REUTER TO THE "PESTER" LIST

I added her in red because I assumed that Drew's negative portrayal of his father stemmed from her own broken and cyclically reassessed misunderstanding of their relationship.

Let him make up his own mind, I scribbled next to her entry.

X. BACK TO WORK: A GUIDE

That Saturday I headed across the street early in the morning. The sun had been up for less than an hour, but the heat started climbing without much of a wait. I held on to a yardstick I'd sneaked home from school, and took a look at the bigger side of the lawn to survey the extent of work that loomed ahead of me. Mr. Reuter had stopped caring for the grass weeks ago. By now, shaggy but burnt, the lawn looked like a field of wheat you might find behind a base-ball fence someplace in the middle of the country. I could have turned and looked at the face of my house, but standing there in that yellow plot, holding this basic tool that was supposed to help me make some sort of difference, I felt suddenly that I was as far from home as I'd ever been.

The garage door opened. Inside, Mr. Reuter held on to its red rope above his head. He said, "You're early."

"I thought I could beat the heat," I said.

"Ah," he said. "I remember when I first learned how impossible that is out here." He looked around, past me. "You alone?"

"I am," I said. "Drew couldn't make it."

"Is that so?"

"Well," I said, "he said he's busy."

"Is that so?" he said again. He batted the red rope for some time. "His mother," he managed to get out.

"Yeah," I said. "That's my guess, too. Anyway, I'm about to measure the lawn."

"What a thing to say," he said wistfully, as in a daydream. I thought he was upset with me for mentioning his ex-wife. But he was talking about something else entirely.

"You expect the word 'mow' there, don't you?" he said. "And your word—what was it, 'measure'?—your word just takes its place so sneakily. 'I'm about to measure the lawn,' you said. What a thing to say."

"That is funny," I said, not knowing how to respond. What was funnier, I thought, was that I was using a yardstick to measure the yard. I kept the joke to myself.

"About Drew," Mr. Reuter said, "you're sure he's not coming? Today, I mean."

"Mr. Reuter," I said, leveling with him the way a man should level with another man. "Drew doesn't trust you. He's never coming back here, I think you should know."

"Well," he said. He cracked his knuckles and let all the air out of his nose. "You've got a lot of work to do." He pulled down on the rope until he disappeared.

That last thing he said was true: In order to measure and carve out a near-perfect circle in a front lawn with the equipment afforded to me, you need patience. First you have to lay the yardstick along the border of the grass and the sidewalk. From the smaller side of the lawn, composed now just of dirt, collect a handful of small rocks, most of which will crumble in your hand if you make a fist over them. As you pivot the yardstick along the length of each side of the big lawn, place one of those soft rocks at every point for measuring purposes. Then do the math to figure that the yard spreads out just over fourteen feet wide and about twelve feet up to the house from the sidewalk. The paved walkway up to the front door changes the shape of the lawn to something a bit more geometrically complicated. Basically, though, you're off to a good start. The next step would be to find the center of the lawn. There, step on your shovel a couple of times to mark an X. Use the yardstick again from the center to a number of equidistant points in different directions. Leave enough room to make arcs between those points to complete the circle. Keep using those soft rocks to mark your points. Gather more if you have to.

Take a break for water. Drink just a little from the pitcher; leave plenty for later. Sing a dumb song you've made up: *Thirsty from the sun, and work's just begun.*

Now you're ready to dig.

XI. ON THE ACT OF FINISHING

I can't remember the last plunge I took with the shovel on that lawn. What I can remember is the first time I saw the end closing in on me. I laughed out loud. Nothing maniacal, just a single bark of joy escaped. I startled myself with it. You can blame the heat or the overinflated importance of completion to a twelve-year-old kid with low self-esteem. Either way, I laughed, and kept digging until the digging was done.

I went to the front door to bring Mr. Reuter outside. I knocked and waited. I rang the doorbell, looking over my shoulder at the circle of dirt I'd created. The circle wasn't perfect from an aerial view, but its mistakes were subtle, and its positioning was centered well. Corners of yellow grass still hung around the circle's edges. That was an easy fix, I figured, once the trees and their protective shade came into place.

Beyond the yard I saw my own house. Its grass had become overgrown in my time across the street.

My knocking turned violent. In the window, I could see Mr. Reuter's shadow pacing back and forth. I yelled his name. I said, "I know you're in there!"—which, because I'd heard it so many times in movies and TV shows, came out flawlessly. Finally I moved around to the driveway, where the pitcher, now empty, sat on its oil stain. I waited for some time, a good amount of time. I kicked the garage door. A car passed while I did it.

XII. THE CLOSEST I'D EVER BEEN TO A FISTFIGHT (UPDATED)

I saw Drew at school the next week. I went over to him at lunch and said, in front of all his friends, "You were right. Your dad *is* an asshole."

He punched me in the eye.

XIII. THE FLOTILLA LANDS ON COMSTOCK AVENUE

Before giving up, I tried Mr. Reuter a few more times with no success. Some weeks passed. In that time, I'd explained the black eye to my parents by saying a girl at school had accidentally opened a door in my face. Even my mother, the amateur journalist, was too embarrassed for me to ask any follow-up questions.

Then came the trucks. They rolled in on a windy Saturday morning. There were three of them, white dump trucks with blue block letters: WATTS LANDSCAPING. Each had been loaded with sod and landscaping accessories, including a number of boulders and bags of what I found out later were decorative wood chips. A group of Mexican men, five in all, parked the trucks at sharp angles at Mr. Reuter's house. They worked in an assembly-line sort of way between the trucks and the front lawn. Cars took care to move slowly past the equipment, which created a sort of barricade around the driveway and into the street. Some of the drivers even pulled over to investigate further the work that was being done.

The curiosity spread. As the hours passed, a fleet of neighbors emerged from their homes to witness the transformation of Mr. Reuter's yard. My own parents, if they hadn't been working, would have been among them. I imagine that some of the witnesses must have worried that the Mexicans, yelling their Spanish at each other between heaves, were moving in.

As for me, I chose to watch from my living room, parting the blinds with my fingers.

The next day, my parents left again for work, and—wouldn't you know it?—the trees arrived. Three huge supplanted palm trees rolled in on the towed trailers of a new armada of white trucks followed by green-and-yellow John Deere machinery. This time, the news spread even more quickly, and neighbors and passersby came together in the street. Even I had to go outside to watch. People who had heard about the activity the day before also came, anticipating more action today. What you had then was a group of people from all over town, the largest assembly I'd seen of them, and yet the only sounds came from the machinery.

A John Deere drilled a hole within my circle for each tree. Another, with an extended mechanical arm, plucked one of the palms from its trailer bed and hinged it toward the hole. The machine tilted its pull on the tree until, slowly, accompanied by the eerie creaks of the pulley, the palm stood upright in the air. It hung there for a moment like a specter, swinging perilously in the wind, and the people beneath it had no choice but to fear and worship. Carefully, the machine lowered the bulbous root of the tree beneath the ground. This process was repeated twice more, and each time it happened, the crowd held its breath as the tree, like some monster, stood unaided for the first time. We half expected a roar from the trees, and when—as the workers began to hose down the bark—no roar came, we ourselves supplied it.

XIV. THE TALLEST TREES IN THE ANTELOPE VALLEY

They still own the record. The tallest of the three clocks in at over fifty feet. You can see them from the 14, if you're riding through the high desert: Three pineapple tops watching over everyone on the east side of town.

I ended up telling my dad one night about my involvement in their planting. He came to me after I'd snapped at my mother, and asked very seriously why we weren't so close as we'd been when I was younger. The question was a simple one, and he said it with this grainy, soft voice like I'd never heard. We were in my bedroom. I sat on my bed, and he'd chosen to sit on the carpet. It's amazing how powerful that memory is for me, a grown man sitting on the floor, asking for something he felt was important. He wanted to understand why things had changed. I didn't have my complicated Pester/Foster analyses at hand, so I just said, "I don't know." Then I felt as though I owed him something more, so I told him the story.

"Don't worry," he said. "We'll get you your money."

But he wasn't listening. It wasn't about the money.

XV. THE LAST TIME I SAW MR. REUTER

He'd lost his hair. I hardly recognized him. I saw him only for a moment—I was coming into the house late one night, much later than my curfew. I was expecting a fight when I got home. And before I turned from the sidewalk toward my door, a light came on across the street. Mr. Reuter stood on a short stepladder, arms shaking above his bald, bespectacled head, installing what I found out later to be a motion-sensor light on the rim of his garage. I'd been under the impression, like others, that maybe he'd moved away. It was a shock to see him bald—it was a shock to see *him*.

This was a couple of years after the trees had been planted. In that time, rumors had spread that Mr. Reuter was ill and had spent the last of his money creating a living barrier between his house and the rest of the town in an attempt to die in peace.

I crossed Comstock Avenue that night. It must have been January because you could see ice gathering over the windshields of parked cars. He stood on that stepladder and I didn't want to startle him. From a short distance, standing barely in the driveway, I asked if he needed help.

MY UNCLE'S TENANT

My mother's brother Gaspar owned a scattering of apartments and trailer parks in Los Angeles County. His drinking—vodka, mostly, from a bottle with an Armenian label I should've learned to read by now—brought out the gossip in him. At my sister's engagement party, before she and Patrick called off the wedding, Uncle Gaspar cornered me and shared a story that took place at one of his trailer parks, the one in my hometown. "My tenant," he said, "a long time back. More of an employee, actually. Name was Phil. Told me *ev-uh-ree-thing*."

"I know Phil," I said cheerfully. I was putting on that exaggerated enthusiasm you put on when someone you care about has had too much to drink and wants your attention for an unspecified amount of time. I said I knew Phil, but what I meant was this: When I was thirteen, this gangly white man who could pass for anything between twenty and forty occasionally accompanied Gaspar to my house. My uncle, who lived with all the other Armenians an hour away in Glendale, every now and then spent a weekend in the desert to check on his properties. Sundays he'd swing by our house on the way back to the city, and a few times—maybe a total of four or five Sunday evenings—he'd bring along this kid, this man, whose name I'd forgotten until my uncle breathed it, vodka-drenched, back into my life.

I began to remember how my uncle would sit on the floral sofa alongside my mother, and how Phil would settle into my father's favorite red chair. As far as I can remember, my father and my sister were never home during one of these visits. It was always just the four of us, Phil and Gaspar and Mom and I, and all we did was talk and eat, eat and talk. One topic of discussion I remember was the unresolved election between Bush and Gore—Phil wanted to leave the country if one, I can't remember which, came out the victor—which is how I knew these visits occurred when I was thirteen.

Phil's baggy clothing underlined the gaunt, ghostly look he already had. He would shovel my mother's cooking so belligerently into his bony face that he reminded me of a character in one of the novels I was reading at the time, a man who had been rescued many days after a shipwreck. As for me, my job was to get a fire going in the fireplace, and I'd kneel on the bricks, stuffing swaths of paper towels or newspaper or catalog pages into the nooks and crags of the logs. I'd strike a few matches until the fire finally caught and the smell of woodsmoke filled the house. I'd brush the soot from my pants and wash my hands. Then I'd collect my payment, a small dish of desserts my mother had baked and arranged for our guests—one or two honey-dripping pieces of rolled baklava, maybe, or a few powdered khurabia cookies—and sit on the hardwood floor, devouring the sweets and watching the fire I'd made consume everything and anything I allowed it to.

That Uncle Gaspar had forgotten I'd met Phil—on numerous occasions—didn't surprise me. Those visits happened, after all, a long time ago. Plus, Gaspar had just tried to light the filtered end of his cigarette. I knew then he would tell me the truth. This far down the bottle, he couldn't invent a story to save his life.

Not often, my uncle said, but sometimes, a person would ask Phil what it was that he did. And by that they usually meant, how do you make your money, how is it that you *earn a living*. His response wouldn't exactly fill him with pride: hired help, here and there, painting houses or else moving lumber with Jim, most of the time out of work. "You're only twenty-one," Jim reminded him. In fact, Jim had been reminding Phil of his age with the word "only" in front of it for years—only seventeen, only eighteen, and so on. Phil wondered how much longer the word "only" would apply. But for now, he supposed it was true. He was only twenty-one. So despite the fact he hadn't offered as *meaningful* an answer as he'd have liked, the question—what do you do?—didn't tug at him too bad.

What helped was that he had something in the works—a project, a big one. He was collecting old VW buses. So far he had six, all of them incapable of running, all of them rotting with thirty years' worth of rust and dust and backseat lust. That line—that was Jim's.

Phil found the first bus abandoned in the desert, out on the northeast edge of the Antelope Valley. From time to time, Jim took him out there, far enough from law enforcement to shoot the rifles and pistols he collected. Jim Durant, a hardworking but carefree man double the twenty-one-year-old's size, was someone Phil felt lucky to have on his side. It was Jim who'd let Phil tag along on jobs, and it was Jim, too, who had talked the trailer park manager—Uncle Gaspar—into letting Phil shack up there when he needed the help. Jim might have been "only" a decade older than Phil, but these acts of kindness and the faint, final wisps of hair that clung to the top of the big man's scalp seemed to give him a type of paternal authority Phil hadn't sensed from anyone. Sometimes Phil saw him like an old Southern politician, wagging a finger at bureaucracy, making sure of certain things, like, no one takes care of your business but you. Like, being given a hand up from a friend is different than getting a handout from a program.

So they'd go out to the nearby desert and shoot together. But this one time, Jim loaded his favorite rifle, a .44 magnum Marlin 1894SS, into the covered bed of his Chevy pickup. The gun shot at about 165 decibels—too loud even for their regular shooting grounds. So they went out farther into the desert. Jim drove—careful, once they'd left the road, to avoid the softer sand that collected in patches around that time of year, in May.

And the long and short of it is, there was this old VW bus, dull green, fossilizing out there beneath a Joshua tree, as if someone had searched long and hard for a parking spot with shade. The two men got out of the truck. They considered the bus. Phil said, "Hey, someone might be living out of this thing." Jim unlocked the hatch on his pickup and found a handgun. He checked the magazine to make sure it was loaded, and told Phil to stay put. Then he traveled the fifty feet or so till he reached the bus.

The way he held the gun up near his chest, the way he put his back against the bus before peeking over his shoulder into its window—it all seemed, to Phil, so *televised*. Still, he watched his old friend and mentor pull the VW's door handle and climb into the thing with a level of anxiety he hadn't felt in some time, as if this were the first moment in a long while that felt even a little monumental.

Not much time passed before Jim returned, rattling a set of keys attached to a blue tether. "Looks like the sons of bitches left it for us," he said.

"Engine work?"

"Don't look like it."

Then they talked about how to rig up the bus to the back of the Chevy, how to tow the big green monster back through the desert. Wasn't too tough, really, once they got the momentum.

That was the first one. The other buses, the newer five, didn't have the same accidental backstories. These were simply purchased here and there through classified ads Phil and Jim started keeping their eyes on. Always fixer-projects, never running. Dirt-cheap, each of them. In fact, one of the orange ones was given away for free. All the buses, one after the other, towed into the unused gravel lot adjacent to one of the trailer parks over on Avenue I, where they both lived rent-free. Jim had convinced my uncle to shave off the rent and fence in the lot, all in exchange for working odd jobs around the place, including their big-duty, park security during the nights: Jim on Mondays, Wednesdays, Fridays, and Sundays; Phil on the in-betweens.

In this way, the two men started working every day, as much as they could, on the VW buses, gutting them and sweating over their motors, eventually looking to give them all new paint jobs, trying to hawk them to young kids who seemed to find the old things hip. That was the plan. That's what Phil had in mind.

The girls came to the fence on a Saturday afternoon sometime in November. Despite what the calendar said, the summer hadn't really ended, not in the daytime anyway, and the girls wore outfits to prove it. There were two of them, a brown-haired white girl and a light-skinned black girl, both of them in short cutoff jeans, both of them in tank tops and flip-flops. They each looked around the same age, maybe fourteen or fifteen. They were just walking along the fence, on their way to wherever they were headed, when Jim mentioned them to Phil, who happened to have his head under the hood of the green bus, the first one.

"Look at these," said Jim.

Phil turned to see what it was he'd pointed out. "Not bad, not bad," Phil said. "At all," he added, and went back to work.

Jim was the first to speak to the girls. Phil didn't hear what it was but looked back to see their reaction. They giggled, and the white girl said something in the ear of the black girl. They kept walking, only now they were checking out the buses.

"They aren't pieces of meat," Jim said to the girls, motioning to the cars. "You can't just stare at them without introducing your-selves."

Now the girls stopped at the fence and leaned into it, hanging their fingers onto the chain-link holes there.

"The gate's unlocked," Jim said, pointing to the girls' left. "En-ter, if you dare."

At this point, Phil said, "You're going to get me into trouble, Durant."

The white girl said, and you could hear the laughter in her voice when she said it, "Why don't you come over here?" Then she turned to the other girl, who, once she caught her breath from laughing, called out to Jim, "And bring your friend!"

"You hear that?" Jim asked Phil. Then, to the girls: "We don't have egos, girls. We don't mind heading over to you. We don't . . . play games."

He took his time on his way to the fence. He pulled a pack of cigarettes out of his back pocket and beat his left palm with the pack as he moved. Phil walked a step behind.

"Where you girls off to?" Jim asked once he got close enough. The girls, still on the other side of the fence, never stopped smiling.

"The movies," the white girl said.

"The movies? How about that! My buddy Phil here, he was just talking about heading to the movies."

Phil laughed a little and crossed his arms, unsure what to do with them.

Jim slipped a cigarette between his lips and put the pack away. "Oh," he said, retrieving the pack from behind his back. "How rude of me. Didn't even offer. You girls want one?"

They both said no. They said thank you. They were very polite.

"Smart girls," said Jim. "Bad habit. What movie you girls going to? Maybe we're heading to the same one."

The white girl began to say the name of the movie, but her friend interrupted her. "You first," the black girl asked.

"You know, we're torn," said Jim. "Torn between that new action movie with the different cities getting blown up, and that romance with the young girl and the older guy falling in love." He paused. "You girls know about love?"

The girls, still seemingly enjoying the flirtation, let go of the fence. They started walking again, not in a rush, and the white girl looked over her shoulder at the men. "We're fast learners," she said. "Maybe next time you could teach us."

Jim loved it. He said, "Next time it is," and then asked for their names.

"Allie," the white girl said after a laugh, clearly lying. "I'm Allie, and this is Caitlyn." And when they were gone, Jim looked as though they hadn't left at all. He said, "Are you kidding me?" over and over, socking Phil's arm. He said, "Which one you like best? I don't discriminate." They worked on the buses some more that day, with Jim talking about the girls and Phil talking about the girls, too, both of them wondering aloud what it was they'd do the next time those girls walked along that fence.

That night was Phil's turn to patrol the park. He was alone, and the heat of the day had become a frigid, windless cold. He was supposed to walk the paved paths between the trailers from ten o'clock till sunrise. For the job, my uncle had provided Phil and Jim each a flashlight and a two-way radio (one to share between the two of them; the other stayed with Gaspar). Phil knew that Jim, on his nights, would bring along some extra equipment—a gun, namely—but Phil carried only what he'd been given. He knew that most of the criminals in the Antelope Valley were kids, as he'd been, scared off easily enough by a bright light and a holler.

At some time past midnight, he decided to head over to the lot to check up on the buses. Eventually, the space would be used for more trailers. But for now, the new fence was all that separated the place from the park on one side and the uncultivated desert on the other. It used to be that kids would set up a basketball hoop out there. Phil had known the family that owned the hoop, and they'd left a few years back, taking the thing with them. In the time between the basketball and the VWs, the only objects that ended up on the gravel were either dumped and abandoned, or led there by the wind. My uncle didn't tell Jim and Phil outright, but he was glad to have the VW buses; he liked the idea of the lot being put to some good use.

The buses, all six of them, were parked in a single row. From where he stood, Phil could see the front ends, those big, bubbled headlights, the VW insignias between them. To save the flashlight's battery, Phil kept the thing off unless he needed it, which meant that the only light on the gravel lot now came from the orange-bulbed arc lamps that lined Avenue I. In that strange, muted glow, the buses looked new. The spots where oxidation had done its job on the paint hid in it, reflecting and absorbing the hazy light just as the more polished areas did. The headlights, all twelve of them, crystallized the light back at Phil in a way that reminded him of the twinkling eyes of cartoon children.

He moved on, working the perimeter of the place, and then inward toward my uncle's office at the center, and then back outward again. In this way, in layers, he worked the remainder of his shift.

Sunday, at about the same time as the day before, the girls returned. Phil hadn't expected them to come back at all, and even Jim was surprised to see them again so soon. He thought, at the very earliest, they'd come back the next Saturday. He said to Phil, "How bad can a girl want it?"

This time, Allie asked the men if she and Caitlyn could get a closer look at what she called the "hippie cars." Jim let them in through the gate, telling them they could sit behind the wheel of one, if that was something they'd like to try. It turned out that, yes, that's exactly what they had in mind.

So in went Allie, into the driver's seat of the yellow one. "Yellow's my favorite color," she said more than once. Jim closed the door behind her, and she rolled down the window. With one hand gripping the top of the wheel, she waved her fingers down at Caitlyn, who stood flanked on either side by the owners of the bus. "How do I look?" Allie asked the three of them. Great, they said. They all agreed that the girl looked great.

"Take a picture of me," Allie said, and Caitlyn slid from her back pocket a thin red camera. Allie posed in various ways. She made certain faces, many of which featured sticking out her tongue. From several angles, Caitlyn snapped pictures. Then she climbed up to the passenger seat and handed the camera, along with instructions, to Phil.

"You girls know how to drive one of these things?" asked Jim.

"Caitlyn can't drive a bicycle," Allie said. Her friend disagreed, loudly. The girls found this funny. "But I," Allie continued, "have my driver's license."

"Driver's *permit*," Caitlyn corrected.

"No difference there," said Jim. "But do you know how to drive a manual transmission? A stick shift?"

"Not really," Allie said. "Learned on the other kind."

"Not surprising," said Jim. He made a joke about putting the "man" in "manual."

Allie pivoted her body in the driver's seat to face the men, letting both her arms fall from the open window. With her palms she drummed a soft beat against the door. Phil snapped a picture of her this way. "Teach us," she said.

Phil slipped the camera into his shirt pocket for safekeeping. He said, "Don't you girls have fathers for that?"

"Quiet all along and the first thing he says is negative," Jim said. "Don't mind him, girls. Of *course* we could show you what you need to know. Only problem is: None of these dinosaurs are in what we call 'running condition.' Good news is, I've got a manual transmission in my own vehicle, a working truck, just over there." He threw his thumb over his shoulder in the direction of the trailer park. "What do you say?"

Allie looked to her friend. "Can't," she said, turning back to Jim. "Caitlyn has to be home before her mom gets there."

"And that's soon?"

"Real soon."

"Sorry," Caitlyn said genuinely, as if she'd forgotten Jim's birthday. As if she'd broken his heart.

And with that one word—"sorry"—the fourteen or fifteen years Phil had pegged for the girl suddenly seemed exceedingly generous. Now that he looked at their faces in the enormousness of the windshield, now that he focused on Allie's miniature fingers tapping against the side paneling, he was struck by the fact that these girls were children.

Jim didn't seem to share the epiphany. "Tell you what," he said. "What are you ladies up to later tonight?"

They drew up a plan for the girls to sneak out of their homes after midnight and come back to the trailer park, where Jim would be the only security guard on duty. Phil said, yeah, maybe he'd show up, that his being there that night was a possibility. In all likelihood, Jim knew Phil wouldn't join in on the fun, but that didn't seem to bother him too much. He might've looked forward to the time alone with, what were their names? Allie, yeah, and Caitlyn.

The first thing Phil did when he got home that night was he poured himself a glass of water from the tap. From the freezer he grabbed the only ice tray he owned, which he discovered hadn't been refilled before being put away. He spilled the water from his glass into the slots of the ice tray and placed that in the freezer. Then he refilled his glass and swallowed the water warm.

What he did next was he ate in front of the small, wood-paneled TV, getting up once in a while to tinker with the antenna. He focused on nothing for too long, though he did pay some attention to a show about saving money at the grocery store. Their big idea was websites with printable coupons, but Phil didn't have a computer or a printer, let alone access to the web. What good was saving money, Phil thought, when you didn't have any money in the first place?

While undressing, he realized he still had the girl's camera. He removed it from the pocket of his shirt, turning the thing in his hands like a puzzle cube. He pressed the power button at its top and switched a small dial from the icon of a camera to the icon of a Play button, the way Caitlyn had shown him, so he could look through the pictures the girls had taken earlier and the ones he had taken, as well. He searched through them backwards, clicking the left arrow button. There they were, the girls, smiling from the yellow van, making faces, alternately flipping the camera the bird or the peace sign. Then, further back in the camera's history, he found the photos Caitlyn had taken of Allie alone up there, pretending to look out onto an open highway. At the edge of the picture Phil noticed himself and Jim. Just standing there, squinting in the harsh light of the sun. Phil's arms crossed and Jim's akimbo, hands at his hips, both men looking in Allie's direction, mouths open as if they were laughing. Phil thumbed the circular button with the icon of a trash bin, and the image was gone.

But he kept going. The photographs were innocuous, childish things, pictures of four pairs of feet in a circle, toe to toe, or else the bottom-up image of a Joshua tree against the clouds. Phil didn't know what he was looking for—naked pictures, or what?—but he didn't find it. He guessed he just wanted to be surprised. Find something in there he wasn't expecting. So, to give the girls what he'd been hoping for himself, he flipped the dial back to the camera icon, aimed the lens at his face, and pressed the shutter.

He'd been in bed for an hour when the knock came at the door.

"Phil," a voice said from outside. "It's me."

Phil caught the accent. He opened the door to let Gaspar inside.

"Where is he?" my uncle wanted to know.

He asked as though a reward had been posted for Jim's scalp, a tone that made Phil question if this was the same Gaspar Lusparyan he'd come to know. On the weekends he was around, Gaspar had always treated Phil with dignity, is all, and Phil had never pictured him as a man with a temper. He'd even asked Phil over for dinner from time to time, citing his sister's culinary skills. And that part turned out true enough—my mother would serve Phil whatever it was she'd cooked, exotic foods with names Phil couldn't pronounce at the time or remember later, always at the tip of his tongue. All of it Phil had never seen before, most of it some of the best food he'd ever tasted. Now Gaspar, larger than usual in an oversized white jacket, puffy in the chest and arms, seemed more like an enraged father than a dinner host.

"Jim, I think, is patrolling," said Phil.

"That's where he should be," my uncle said. "Isn't, though, as far as I can tell. Noise complaint from woman in number four-oh-three. Sarah. Says she thinks someone is messing around in the lot back there, with your buses. So I call Jim on the two-way, get nothing. Know what I do next?"

"No."

"I get up. Out of bed. Tomorrow already, when I should be on my way home to Glendale, but how could anybody tell? Exactly why I let you keep buses out there, so I can sleep these hours and not be forced awake by noise in the lot. So I head out there to check it out, what do I see? Nothing. Nobody lurking—and no Jim Durant, that's for sure. So I'm thinking, where the fuck is this guy? I spend twenty, twenty-five minutes driving around the park to find this man, the one I am letting live here for free, keep shit here for free. For the work he is not doing."

"It's not right," Phil said. "What he's done isn't right, and for that I'm sorry."

"You know I'm a good man," Gaspar said. "I don't give people shit for things. I let people be happy so long they're not making me, my family, unhappy. Sometimes I have too much to drink, and for that I'm working on it. But I'm a fair, good man. I know that about myself, so I can get pissed off once in a while."

"No, you are, I agree. Let me cover his shift tonight and we'll figure out why he dropped the ball tomorrow morning. How about that?"

My uncle considered it. He removed the big white jacket and placed it on some newspapers spread over the kitchen table. "Wear it when you go out," he said, heading to the door. "I saw you on patrol last night, no jacket. You'll get sick."

Secretly Phil had a better answer to the question, What is it that you do? He imagined telling it to people who had asked him before, and hoped to tell a person who'd ask him in the future. He'd say: I do what we all do, which is we gain or we lose momentum. He'd say, We've only got the verb "to do" because we've got the verb "to become." The question, What do you do? inherently looked to the future: What will you become? What will become of you? As soon as the question was asked in the past tense, however, the meaning became, suddenly, an accusation: What did you do? What have you done?

A lot of what Phil had done in his life he did without knowing why, or caring, until after. Sometimes the answer was simple and easier to know beforehand. For instance: why Phil took the camera with him when he left the trailer was an easy one to understand, if not an easy one to explain later. It was as simple as this: He wanted to get rid of the camera. Holding a child's camera made him sick. Before leaving, he deleted the picture he'd taken of himself, wishing he could erase more than just a photograph.

Aside from his clothes, all Phil took with him were the camera and the flashlight. And he wore Gaspar's puffy white jacket. Didn't even bother to lock his trailer or bring the key. That's all he had on him: the camera, the light, and the jacket. None of them actually his, a thought that did more than cross his mind.

Nothing moved, nothing sounded. Phil passed the cars lining the pathways of the trailer park. Fog, inside, and frost on the outside clouded their windows. He half expected a kid to finger-draw a happy face in the fog from inside one of the cars. In front of Jim's place, an empty space where his Chevy should have been. Phil skipped the layers he usually worked through to get to the park's perimeter and headed straight to the gravel lot, figuring that Jim would be there, and the girls, too, if they'd made it out that night.

But when Phil arrived, he didn't see anybody. The six buses glowed in that orange light, and that was about all there was to find. Jim kept the keys to the gate on his patrol nights, so Phil could only peer at the buses through the locked fence. He stood on the sidewalk along Avenue I, just before Twentieth Street East, exactly where the girls had stopped that first time. He took out the red camera and placed it in the gutter along the curb there. He debated leaving it. Maybe he'd keep it until the next time the girls stopped by. Maybe he could keep it for himself, but what pictures did he have to take, and what good is a digital camera without a computer? The thought of selling it crossed his mind, but not seriously. The truth was that it didn't matter what he did with the camera, because before he could make up his mind, a gunshot went off somewhere to the east, away from town, out in the desert. And another.

Phil didn't run away. Later he explained that he felt as though he were literally stuck in place. All he could do was remove the flashlight from his pocket, let it hang at his side toward the gutter, and flip the switch. On and off, on and off. A spot of light on the cement, unsteady, and then gone, and then there again. He had on his mind at that moment two things: first, a number, and then a name. The number 165—decibels—occurred and reoccured to him. Then came the name: "dolma"—he'd remembered the name of the food Gaspar's sister made for him when he'd first moved into the park as a teenager, alone at seventeen. She removed the stems from grape leaves, and then boiled the leaves and rice separately. In a large bowl, she used her hands to mix the rice and the tomatoes and the lemon juice she squeezed in there, careful to pluck out any seeds that might have crept in. She said that in Armenia, she had her own grapevines and her own lemon tree, and the taste—you couldn't imagine the taste of a real grape leaf, the strange sweetness of an Armenian lemon. Then she filled the grape leaves, spread across a cutting board now, with the stuffing she'd created in the bowl—you can use meat, she said while she did it, you can use lamb or you can use beef, but why not spare a life? She poured salt into the center of her palm and spread it over the rice on the leaves just before rolling them perfectly into little green tubes. You could see her fingers shine there with the juices and the oils of the dolmas, but it didn't seem to bother her. She was a beautiful woman. Once, she'd been—plucking lemons from a branch—a beautiful girl, and Phil felt for her and for all of them.

Since that first time I heard the story, I knew what my curious but informal research would later prove to be true, which was that the gunshots meant the end of the two girls. For months afterwards, however, when I retold the story to people I wanted to count as friends, people I thought I could impress with a certain proximity to tragedy (here I'm not proud of myself), I was shocked to find that most felt unsatisfied by story's end. The sound of two gunshots, apparently, couldn't convince anyone that the two girls were killed. People wanted a clearer picture of the scene. They wanted to see the girls struggling to survive, fighting over the Marlin rifle in the cramped cab of the truck, which must have felt—someone once told me in a kind of prodding voice—"like a kind of coffin, no?" People expressed cautious, politically ambiguous doubt regarding two girls willing to leave home at midnight to meet a strange man. They would never blame the victims, they were quick to point out, but wouldn't it also be likely that girls like these seemed willing— eager, even—to have sex? What else had they gone that night to find? Which precise sequence of events, these people wanted to know, had the power to transform Jim Durant—a creep, to be sure—into a killer?

These cravings for gruesome variations on a story surprised and saddened me, and then stopped surprising me and only saddened me, at which point, I stopped telling the story altogether.

The truth was I, too, felt unsatisfied—a horribly callous word to use in situations like these—but not because I missed out on the full experience regarding the rifle, or the imprisoned fate of the murderer. I wish I could say my lingering curiosity had to do with the two victims, whose real names were Sabrina Muller (Allie) and Ashley Simms (Caitlyn). They were only thirteen, and deserve to be understood in more context than the roles they played in this particular story. But this particular story, being the story I was trying to understand, had me returning again and again to the question of Phil.

After a confession from Jim Durant and a testimony from my uncle, Phil was not indicted. He was free to go. But until I did the math, I didn't know where, exactly, he went. I looked at the date of the crime, November 1999, and realized that Phil's visits to my house came after, not before, the events of the story. My mother and uncle had put me in harm's way. When it came to the matter of Phil's innocence, I did not agree with the law. Toward my family I felt a kind of retroactive indignation. "You did *what*?" I shouted at my mother. "You invited a man like Phil into your home when your children were roughly the same age as his victims?"

"You're just like your father," she said, waving me away. "He always took Jean out of the house when we had that poor boy over, as if Phil were a hungry wolf. I love your father, but he's a real

American, isn't he? They love to talk about second chances, but only Armenians—the first Christians—understand that the only way you can change people is through forgiveness. Not prison bars, not shunning."

I asked what it was, exactly, she'd been trying to change about our man Phil. "His stupidity, or his indifference?"

"He was a young man with nothing," she said. "He had no family. No home. No place he wanted to be. This can fill a person with shame. He was choosing, God bless him, whether or not to die. My brother? Me? All we were doing was trying to convince him to live."

That's when I asked if they'd been successful.

Under her breath, my mom cursed her brother for getting me involved. Then she said, "I want to tell you a story, too, one where he fixes one of his Volkswagens and drives to a place where he can feel at home, where he can live."

"But?"

"For some, there is no such place. Not in this world, anyway."

NOTES FOR A SPOTLIGHT ON A FUTURE PRESIDENT

———— ✤ ————

THE INCIDENT

The mascot—a cartoonlike Confederate soldier known affectionately on campus as Rebby the Blue—had been defiled. Unfortunately, the African American sophomore commissioned to wear the costume at the spring pep rally didn't notice the freshly painted Hitler mustache until it was too late. Joshua Stilt fist-pumped his way onto the gymnasium floor, where he expected to be swathed in the intoxicating energy of school spirit. Instead, he was met with a wild mixture of laughter and hissing from the overwhelmingly white audience of five hundred. Afterwards, the local news sent a camera crew and a reporter to interview Joshua Stilt and the high school's white principal about what was already being described in the Antelope Valley as the third or fourth greatest controversy of the year.

"To equate a Rebel soldier with Nazis is ridiculous," said the principal in his prerecorded interview. "Rebels fought for freedom, you see, and Hitler fought for power. Anyone who knows history understands states' rights and dictatorships are like Chinese food and cheese—totally incompatible."

Peter Thorpe, the local reporter—having already heard the joke over Panda Express takeout at the principal's house two nights earlier—decided against challenging his old friend's logic. They had graduated as Rebels fewer than thirty years ago.

Quickly the conversation turned to identifying the culprit. For his part, Joshua Stilt—whose last name provoked jokes about his five-foot-nothing frame—became the first suspect. "If I'd wanted to make a political statement," he told the reporter when he began to feel accused, "I'd have come up with something more intelligent."

The story might have ended there had the local news segment not been seen by a famous film director, who happened to be this far north of Los Angeles to shoot an explosion scene in the desert. The director, a woman whose own fight for legitimacy in the male-dominated field of Hollywood action films had nurtured in her a sensitivity to the just indignations of others, sent a brief but excoriating email to the chiefs of major news organizations across California. Word spread. Soon, reporters at every major television network wanted a sit-down with Joshua Stilt. The *local* interest—who sullied Rebby the Blue?—was replaced by a *national* interest: What young black kid in twenty-first-century California would willingly don the uniform—cartoonlike or not—of a Confederate soldier?

Interview after interview produced the same response from Joshua Stilt: "I really enjoyed being the mascot, and I couldn't change what the mascot was." But what Joshua Stilt felt he could not do, national media attention proved able to. Shortly after the story broke, petitions, rallies, and lawsuits were organized to replace Rebby the Blue with a less political mascot for Antelope Valley High. After consulting his conscience, his Bible, his school district, and an online national poll, the suddenly apologetic principal revealed the new mascot at an assembly on the football field. An actual desert tortoise had been borrowed for the event from the conservatory, and, released from its cage, began eating blades of grass that had been painted white with the high school's logo, a Stars and Bars flag that had not yet been replaced.

THE MEETING

A decade later, I planned to meet Joshua Stilt at a Mission District café in San Francisco, but saw him almost an hour early, standing at the yellow edge of the Rockridge BART platform in Oakland. The weather—warm and overcast—lent a cinematic, quiet texture to the whole scene, as if we were waiting for a steam engine and not a commuter train. For a moment I considered avoiding him until our planned meeting. Checking the overhead electronic platform scrolls, however, I saw that our train had been delayed due to a post-Occupy, largely impromptu protest a station ahead. Fearing Joshua Stilt might catch me avoiding him in that time, I went over to introduce myself.

He was donning those large white plastic headphones everyone our age seemed to be wearing in transit, and I had to reach out and touch him on the shoulder to get his attention. When he slid the headphones down around his neck, I said, "I'm Daley Kushner, the guy who's writing about you."

He'd grown up to become a stylish, handsome young man. He'd sprouted a good eight inches not including his early-'90s-style flat-top fade (an additional two inches), complete with lines shaved into the sides of his head that reminded me, for whatever reason, of the wingtips on classic American cars. He wore large-framed black glasses and, despite the warm weather, a slim-fitting suede blazer that, only when the clouds passed temporarily, proved to be navy blue. We talked about the chance of rain and the clearer skies we could already make out across the bay until our train arrived, at which point, we found two empty seats and began to talk more comfortably.

"I won't turn this on," I said, showing him my digital recorder, "until we get to the café. Too much noise on these rails."

"Very strange to see another AV kid outside the desert," he said. "I guess you and I are special."

"Ha," I said—actually saying the word. I wondered (a) if he remembered me from high school (probably not) and (b) if I—far less stylish as an acne-scarred, uncombed, short-but-lanky white dude in a polo shirt—had made a good first impression. I resisted the urge to ask, and told him that once the recorder came on, the conversation would be about the ways he—and only he—was special. "Trust me," I said. "My editor has no interest in getting to know me better."

"You'll seep through anyway," Joshua said, not unkindly. His music was still on, and I could make out the snare hits through the headphones around his neck. "As soon as you choose what to say or write," he said, "you start seeping through. And it only gets messier the more you say."

THE ASSIGNMENT

My class—Antelope Valley High, 2005—was the first to graduate not as Rebels, but as Desert Tortoises. Joshua's was the next. After earning his bachelor's degree in Political Science and Philosophy at Stanford, he became, at the age of twenty-three, the seventh-youngest city council member in Oakland's history. Now, at twenty-five, he was mulling his first mayoral run. It was too early in the campaign for him to be followed around by reporters, but his name had been floated as a possible candidate, and early polls were lending credence to some—if not all—of his confidence. My assignment was to:

1. Conduct, over lunch in San Francisco (where he'd scheduled a cross-Bay photo-op), an interview with Stilt.
2. Return to Stilt's Oakland apartment for a prearranged photoshoot with his friend, a photographer named Jenna King.
3. Attend, in the evening, a "green jobs" event at which Stilt was scheduled to speak.
4. Write the spotlight, tentatively titled, "The President of the Future Presidents Club."

The publication for which I was writing—a Los Angeles–based, century-old magazine turned website—wasn't the first to speculate on Joshua Stilt's bright future in politics, but it was the first to acquire an exclusive feature with him (citing his L.A. County birthplace). Stilt and I had never been friends, but I'd been thinking a lot lately about what motivates a person from our hometown to leave, and whether there was some essential difference between people like us and those who chose to stay. In fact, that's how I'd pitched the article in the first place—from the point of view of someone who went to high school with Joshua Stilt—but my editor advised me to keep the focus on the subject at hand. "Do whatever you need to do," she added at the end of our conversation, "as long as you don't turn this into a story about you."

And so I'd kept certain facts of my life—some more important than others—from Joshua Stilt. I hadn't told him, for instance, that for the previous two weeks I'd had a dull but constant headache, the result of getting so little sleep. I'd been living with my partner,

Lloyd, for nearly a year in San Francisco, but a recent series of disagreements (he wanted to meet my mother) had me sleeping on the stiff corduroy couch of a friend on the south side of Berkeley.

I'd stayed up the night before searching the internet for old interview clips with Joshua Stilt regarding the Hitler-mustache controversy. Some of the footage showed panning shots of the high school during lunch, and when I started looking for myself among the crowd—going so far as to pause the video—I knew it was time to shut off the laptop and try, again, to sleep.

THE TRANSCRIPT, 1/3

JS: You can probably tell your readers more about the Antelope Valley than I can, Daley. I'd rather talk about Oakland.

DK: We'll get there, but I'd like your thoughts on growing up in the AV. Like, how did growing up there affect your worldview, et cetera.

JS: On the record or off? [*Laughter.*]

DK: Whichever, just let me know which is which.

JS: Okay. On the record: The AV's an interesting place. Edge of the Mojave Desert, so, hot and isolated. Not a lot to do. I ended up spending a lot of time in my own head. I thought the Joshua trees were named after me, for example, and then I thought I was named after them. [*Sounds from the espresso machine.*] I couldn't face the fact that we had absolutely nothing to do with one another, other than accidentally being in the same place. Mostly I thought about leaving, and what I was going to do after I left. I wanted to live in a place where I wasn't the only one trying to change things, you know? When you're basically the only one of your kind in a town, whether it's an activist, or if it's the only black kid in class, or the only gay kid, or both, like—

DK: James Baldwin?

JS: I was going to say Frank Ocean—[*laughter*]—but sure. There are specific challenges for each minority—black and gay aren't the same, obviously—but the common link if you're the only one of your kind is that it's tough to get taken seriously by the majority. People hear you complain and say, "If you don't like it here, then leave." If you don't complain, you start feeling complicit. I just had to learn to ignore everyone, even myself, wait it out, and save my energy for a more worthwhile [*inaudible*]. Turned out to be a good place for me to grow up, actually, because good politicians aren't only adept at being frustrated, but also at knowing what to do with that frustration.

DK: I'm afraid to ask about your off-the-record response.

JS: Off the record? It's where I'm from, but it's not what I'm about. I've been able to move, the fuck, on. [*Laughter*.]

THE PLAZA

Some notes on the city at Sixteenth and Mission: In the corner are the steps leading down to the BART platforms, to the trains, all trains this way, this way all trains. Between you and those steps lives a micro-city; women selling homemade tamales; women nursing babies; pigeons loitering near the bus stops. There are the homeless and cheery—the jokesters, the peddlers, the I NEED MONEY FOR WEED sign-holding, missing-tooth-grinning, dog-owning variety; and there are the homeless and despondent—asleep, you hope, bundled up on the concrete in eighty-four-degree, windblown weather, nearly indistinguishable from the trash bags tethered to their ankles with yellow, flapping drawstrings. Their pockets are full of fifteen-cent, shoeprint-stomped BART cards they've peeled from the ground in their travels through the macro-city, travels that must occur in the night, though you can't imagine them getting up off the checkered floor. Note the checkered floor. Black-and-white diamonds on the plaza, and you think: Makes sense. Chess is a game, checkers is a game, but chess and checkers have nothing on this. This—surviving a place—is *the* game. The hiss-stop, gun-shot blare of a bus shakes everyone but the permanent inhabit-ants of the micro-city, and a heat wave from the bus's exhaust turns the whole scene into a watery mirage you can't wait to get close enough to dispel. You arrive at the steps and turn the corner, careful not to touch the handrail, and a black man in a battered three-piece suit is selling flowers on the stairwell. Just in the seven seconds it takes to cross the plaza to the steps, you've grown so used to ignoring these people that you've already made it to the bottom of the steps before realizing the person you've been walk-ing with is still at the top, backlit by the day above him, fishing through his navy blue suede jacket for cash as the man in the suit bundles together the stems of four or five flowers with twine. The stench of urine—faintly at the back of your throat since arriving in the Mission—is faint no more. The stairwell, ground zero for the smell, is no place to linger. Your train is coming—you can hear it and feel the molecules in the air come to life, a savior—and you call out to the person at the top of the stairs: Our train is coming. The two of you jump on just before the sliding doors close, and take the two green, carpeted seats beneath the royal blue RESERVED FOR PERSONS WITH DISABILITIES sticker. No one will call you out on sitting here, but a small-town kid like you cares about rules. You practice your response just in case: *As soon as someone needs this seat, I'll be happy to move.* In your mind, the response comes off as less forthcoming and more self-righteous, so you practice until you achieve the desired tone. Beside you, the subject of your assignment—the future president—cradles a newspaper-wrapped cluster of yellow-and-orange violets and acacias, water seeping through last week's top stories. You live in this world, it occurs to you. You've lived in the Bay Area for years, but you never felt comfortable calling it home. For the moment, you've been considering yourself a visitor *on assignment,* and you've enjoyed the label, the justification for being here, but there is no such thing as a visitor, and you know it. Maybe there is only one city, micro or macro, and you happen to be a citizen. A woman approaches. Your heart jumps.

THE CONSTITUENT

A white woman in her fifties, wearing a purple sweatsuit and an enormous camouflaged backpack, asked Joshua, in a voice chipped away at for decades by the fiberglass in her filters, if she could have his seat. She pointed to the disability sticker, and, although she seemed perfectly capable of standing and showed no signs of physical impairment whatever, Joshua stood and said, "Of course." This forced me—though I knew I'd be giving up my seat to a piece of luggage—to follow suit. Once Joshua and I grabbed ahold of the rail above our heads, the woman, by way of thanking us, shimmied out of the straps of her backpack, molting from the thing like a cicada from its exoskeleton, shouldered it onto the seat next to hers, and coughed out the following: "If all fags was nice as the two of you."

I felt a shame so immediate and physical that I had to grip with both hands the bag of leftovers from the café so as not to slap her.

But there was something comforting, too, to be thought of as part of a duo for the first time since Lloyd asked me to leave. All this, combined with my lack of sleep, prompted me to do what I'd avoided most of my life. I spoke up.

"First of all," I said, "only one of us is gay. And even if we both were, what would happen?"

"What would happen if you two was gay?" she wanted to know.

"No," I said, reminding her impatiently: "You said, if all fags were as nice as us . . . and then you stopped. Well? Go on. Finish the sentence."

The woman stared up at me and scrunched her face in that curious way my mother always did when she'd forgotten why she came into the room. Joshua put his hand on the small of my back, and it took me a moment to realize this wasn't the touch of a lover, but the touch of a wrestler tagging in.

The train had reached the tunnel beneath the bay, and the sheer volume of the electricity and the steel and the aluminum put our conversation on pause.

By the time we emerged from the tunnel and reached the quiet, outdoor stop at West Oakland, bracing from the sun coming greenly through the tinted BART windows, I'd moved on from the incident with the woman and prepared a question for Joshua regarding the evening's event promoting job creation in the clean energy market. I was surprised, then, to see Joshua kneel on the train's green carpet, face the woman in the purple sweatsuit with hardly two feet between their noses, and ask, in a calm and beguilingly respectful tone, if the woman happened to be a resident of Oakland's third district.

"Currently I live off Telegraph and Twenty-third," she said. "I don't know what the hell district that is."

"That's it," Joshua said, letting his legs slide under him, now that the doors had closed and the train was about to move again. What his smile couldn't do, I didn't know. His smile seemed capable of the vital but inglorious work of removing simple obstacles from otherwise happy days—it could jump-start a car, probably, or un-clog a toilet. With this smile he introduced himself as the woman's representative.

The woman coughed a laugh. "You're a child."

"The seventh-youngest city council member ever," I offered.

"What's your name?" Joshua asked.

"Shelly."

"Nice to meet you, Shelly. You have a job?"

"I'm between things," said Shelly. Suddenly her tone changed, which I attributed solely to Joshua Stilt's charisma. Her skepticism had been replaced by a revelatory joy, as if she'd trained for this con-versation her entire life and now had to try desperately not to vocalize or repeat the phrase, "This is not a test."

"I'm a certified bus driver," she said, "but for the furloughs. And we went on strike and nothing never came from it. And in the meantime, all the banks get free money, and there was protesters living on the streets a year ago, making the news every day, but they went and shut them up, too. My son Elijah—he's sixteen—he gets a citation, but the banks, they get away scot-free. . . ."

And the conversation went on in this way back and forth for a few minutes, with Joshua expressing his sympathies and his plans, and Shelly expressing her doubts. When her stop arrived, Joshua thanked her for the talk and promised to bring up her concerns at the next city council meeting. He invited her to that night's green jobs event. She heaved her backpack over each shoulder, stood framed in the doorway, and said, "You seem like a good enough young man, but there's a lot, a lot, a lot of angry people in this city, people you can't just sit down on the train with and talk civilized to. Know that."

Later, on our walk to his apartment, I could hear Joshua

muttering to himself: "Shelly Retivat, bus furlough, Twenty-third and Telegraph."

"You memorize all your constituents?" I asked.

He looked back at me. "Only the angry ones," he said. "So, yeah. All of them."

THE TRANSCRIPT, 2/3

DK: Tell me about the incident with the Confederate mascot.

JS: I'd rather talk about my plans for the City of Oakland. Can we—?

DK: Really quick, I want to get your take on what some people see as the reason you're in politics in the first place.

JS: Well, that's not entirely true. I was always the kid who participated. I ran cross-country in elementary school, did every geography and spelling bee in middle school, and did the whole pep rally, spirit thing in high school. It wasn't until I got to Stanford that the urge to engage just sort of arrived in the form of politics. But, sure. We can talk about the mascot, briefly. Being the mascot was a mistake—I'm reminded every day by black voters who've seen those pictures of me. But I was a kid—and a lonely one, at that. I was fourteen, fifteen, and my main focus was just getting through my time in the AV. I was my mother's son back then more than I am now, and I wanted to be as undisruptive as possible. Even though I knew what the Civil War was all about, obviously, I'd internalized the idea that the Confederate flag had become a postracial symbol of independence, nothing more. Remember, there weren't many black kids in our high school, and the others didn't seem to want anything to do with me because I was on the pep squad with all these white kids, and [*sounds of the espresso machine*]. So, I understand why Hollywood stars and progressive talking heads were furious on my behalf—a Confederate mascot in California in the twenty-first century simply shocked people who don't know how *un-California* most of California is—and I appreciated their concern. But the truth is: I was the one who had to keep going to that high school once the mascot was changed. And most of the students and teachers and parents— many of whom had gone to Antelope Valley High themselves—hated me for messing up a tradition they'd come to love. The parents were the worst. They saw it as the triumph of political correctness, or else feared the mascot-change represented some larger change they weren't ready for. I don't know. A lot of racists can co-exist with black folks just fine as long as you don't ask them to change anything. The way they saw it, you've got how many hundreds and hundreds of students, and you have to change the mascot on account of hurting a few black kids' feelings? I had a mother leave a message on my home answering machine, politely informing me that if I wanted to be more comfortable, Compton was only an hour away. I got threatening letters from self-proclaimed skinheads and Nazis. I looked around and couldn't spot any of the people who'd had my back before the mascot changed—not a single movie star, director, talking head, or politician. They'd all gone back to their lives of making money, and I was left to defend this political stand I'd never had any intention of taking in the first place.

DK: So, the media attention during that time shaped your career, inadvertently, in a productive way?

JS: Let's just say I learned how to pick a fight—I'll never pick one I don't intend to fight forever. And now, that fight is for Oakland, so can we talk about that?

THE SHOOT

When we arrived at Joshua's apartment, the photographer was already there, dragging a reclining chair from one side of the room to the other.

"You're going to sit here," she told Joshua, "and you get to choose six books to stack on this radiator next to you. Not five, not seven. Six."

Jenna King was an old friend of Joshua's from his days in the Black Student Union at Stanford. Some of the curls in her short hair were painted blue, and a yellow ring hung from her right nostril. When I asked if she'd been given a spare key to Joshua's apartment, she said, "Man, Josh has a spare key to *my* apartment." I figured out the two of them lived there together. Nina Simone's *Black Gold* was spinning on an actual record player while Jenna set up the lights and probes. To get out of the way, I stayed in the kitchenette overlooking the living room and—"Is it cool if I . . . ?"—brewed some coffee. Jenna King and Joshua Stilt danced lightly near the bookshelves, deciding which six books to include in the photograph.

"I love Nina," I said.

"Who's Nina?" Jenna asked.

"Nina Simone," I said, pointing to the record player.

"Oh, okay. Just wanted to make sure you called her by her first name like you knew her." She laughed, and Joshua laughed, too.

At one point while Joshua browsed the spines along his shelves, Jenna came over to pour herself a cup of coffee. Without saying anything, she reached around me to grab the pot. I moved and said, "Sorry. I know my one job here is to stay out of the way, and I've failed." I was hoping she'd laugh, but when it became clear she wasn't going to, I started toward Joshua to see which books he'd selected to be photographed with.

"Why couldn't you get an Oakland writer to do this," Jenna asked Joshua. "I don't know. Maybe a black writer, even."

"We go back," Joshua said. "He's from my hometown."

"Oh, good," Jenna said. "So his article that's supposed to be about you and the City of Oakland is actually going to be about him and Nazi Valley." She looked at me. "You seem uncomfortable."

I was. My discomfort was the result, I think, of simultaneously wanting (a) to engage in the discourse on race and the unavoidable white frame of my article, and (b) to pretend that because I had acknowledged said frame, I'd earned the right to ignore it altogether. The fact was, Jenna was right: I was finding myself less interested in Joshua's political career, and increasingly drawn to the ways in which our histories had collided, the odd angles at which they'd spun out after the collision.

"You know we need all kinds of folks behind us," Joshua said.

"Folks," Jenna laughed.

"The truth is," I said, "I'm not putting anything about myself in the story. My editor won't let it happen, and I'm boring anyway."

She studied the tiny alligator on my polo shirt, the pleats in my skinny-legged khakis. "You don't say." Then: "Why do you need to be here—Daley, right? I mean, *here* here. In this room. Do you want to be in the picture, too?"

"I'm doing a day-in-the-life kind of thing—"

"Jenna," Joshua said. "Come take my picture."

"Look," she said. "I'm not mad. But hear me out. I'm *from*

Oakland. I think you'd be a great mayor, Josh, because you're my friend, and you're brilliant, and I know you've got your heart in the right place. But you should've got a local writer to do this story! Dude, he's from your hometown. I get that. But if you want this kid around your campaign, maybe you should go run for mayor out there." She let out a harsh laugh and turned her attention to me. "Shit, you guys should go run together in the city. It's a long, vibrant tradition in San Francisco for white people to take credit for everything good Oakland's ever done."

For a minute no one said anything. Joshua flipped open one of the books he'd chosen and leafed through it. "Jenna's not entirely right," he said into the pages, "but I would appreciate it, Daley, if you stopped asking me about the mascot thing, or the Antelope Valley in general." He looked up from the book, first at Jenna and then at me. "Let's focus on Oakland, and we should all be good to go. Yes?"

Jenna took another mug from the cupboard, filled it with coffee, and handed it to me. "That mascot shit means a lot of things to a lot of people," she said, "so I understand why you're interested in it. But for me, the mascot means someone else told him their version of his own story, and he bought it. He dressed up in their version of his story. You know? The difference between having the power to tell your own story and allowing other people that power is the difference between scuba diving and having your head held under water. Put *that* in your notes."

"I will," I said.

"And don't use me as some vehicle for a different point of view. If I show up in your piece, remember that I'm a whole thing. That most of my time is spent with my camera weighing me down, looking for an interesting shot. That I care enough to pay attention and love this man over here, who isn't just a representative, you know, and neither am I."

THE EVENT

A stage had been set up in a park at the western edge of Lake Merritt, and the three of us made our way through the swelling crowd and dozens of organizers' booths to a man who pinned a microphone on the lapel of Joshua's suede jacket. Jenna, camera at her eye, stayed busy recording every detail. I remembered this was my job, too, to record, so I began to pay more attention.

Joshua couldn't take five steps without an attendee at the event approaching him to shake his hand. I took note of his remarkable ability to remember names, faces, occupations, and situations specific to each voter. At one point, he asked an older black woman in a wheelchair how her granddaughter was adjusting to college life at Mills, and even this woman seemed stunned by Stilt's memory. I looked to Jenna, who didn't miss shooting a single embrace, to see if she was as impressed as everyone else seemed to be, but she only pulled her camera down from her face long enough to check the lighting in the previous photograph.

I had fifteen minutes before Joshua Stilt was scheduled to speak, so I took a walk around the park. Lining the perimeter were tables manned by volunteers of various city organizations and businesses. Food and beverage booths, including a vegetarian soul food restaurant called Souley Vegan, sent into the world the thick smells of fried polenta, tempeh burgers, and Ethiopian coffee. Every plate, cup, and utensil used for the event was compostable, and marked green bins had been arranged in neat rows throughout the park for that purpose. I bought an ear of barbecued corn, still in its husk, and found an open seat on one of the park's benches. The whole setup reminded me of a more sophisticated version of a vaguely political rally I'd attended in my hometown, years ago. This was why my article wasn't going to work, I thought. My central question—how had Joshua transitioned so seamlessly and successfully to life outside the Antelope Valley?—interested neither Joshua nor my editor. I realized this was why I'd never been interested in politics: I wanted to understand the past while everyone else wanted to talk about the future. I felt tired. Nearby, children tossed bread crumbs to the geese at the edge of the lake, and, behind them, a white kid—a high schooler probably—pulled up, one by one, his baggy pant legs.

I watched him wade into the lake, one long, splashless stride at a time. I had no idea what this boy was doing. I was confused and my headache was flaring up—otherwise, I might've shouted, *Someone's getting into the lake!* When he was knee-deep in the water, he hunched over and covered his ears.

Then the ground shook, and I dropped my corn.

THE TRANSCRIPT, 3/3

DK: What do you believe in?

JS: I believe in Oakland's next beginning. I spent a lot of time reading Zen philosophy in high school: D. T. Suzuki, mostly, despite his charmless nationalism. I still believe in some of that, the illusory nature of beginnings and endings. I believe in working to make beginnings breed off each other. I believe everyone can contribute their own beginnings to the city—whether it's business or art or an idea for the classroom—if they have the time and energy and luck and support to find out what it is. I believe in celebrating differences instead of pretending we're all the same. What else do I believe in? I believe in Beyoncé. [*Laughter.*]

DK: Are you dating anyone?

JS: You're never going to ask about my plans as mayor, are you?

DK: I just want to paint a more complete picture of your life than your career.

JS: She's a photographer and a sound artist I met in college, believe it or not.

DK: A sound artist?

JS: Yeah. She makes noises on her computer, and then syncs them up with symphonies in Japan. I don't really get it, either, but it's what she does, and she keeps winning prizes and everything, so I just trust, at this point, that she's a genius.

DK: Is she Japanese?

JS: No, she's a black girl from Oakland. She'll be photographing me when we get back. Speaking of Oakland—

DK: One last question about the Antelope Valley. I promise it'll be the last.

JS: [*Sounds of the espresso machine.*]

DK: Did you ever find out who painted the mustache on the mascot?

JS: No. I couldn't imagine anyone at that school making a political statement like that. Nobody I knew thought the mascot was in bad taste, but the Hitler mustache seemed to suggest, albeit crudely, that *someone* did. Did you? I mean, did you find out who did it?

DK: I'm trying to find out. I'm interviewing people. Unless you think I should let it go?

JS: Hey, if we're not going to talk about my plans for Oakland, we should get going. We've got to wade through the micro-city at Sixteenth and Mission to get back to the train.

DK: I like that, "micro-city."

JS: It feels that way sometimes. Like we live in a Russian doll made up of one community on top of another.

DK: I know we've been off the record for a while now, but can I use that for the article?

JS: No, it's dumb. It doesn't make any sense. [*Laughter.*] Let me think of something better.

THE CALL

After the park was evacuated, we worshipped our phones. We knew when and where, so we searched the internet for information regarding the other three Ws: What, Why, and Who. I was on the corner of Grand and Perkins, aiming my phone's video recorder at the emergency crews. I thought we'd had an earthquake, but then I checked Twitter. According to @Markus_2987, two homemade pipe bombs had been set off at the stage. According to @EllaElla11, however, only one bomb went off, from a compost bin at the center of the park. The low-pitched swell of the blast was still vibrating in my stomach, and I felt queasy. I couldn't find Joshua or Jenna. I knew I may have seen a suspect in the lake, but I couldn't remember anything about him other than his race. The name Elijah Retivat—Shelly's son—entered my mind, but what were the chances that he and the bomber were the same person? I checked my notes, but nothing was there. So I sat, legs out, on the sidewalk, and called Lloyd.

We knew my mom wouldn't survive through the fall. I kept pushing off introducing her to Lloyd until it was too late. He hadn't forgiven me, and I was beginning to think he never would.

"Babe," I said, still shaking, and as soon as he said a word—his first to me in two weeks—I started to cry.

THE BEGINNING

In the beginning, a gay sixteen-year-old boy, desperate to convince himself of the falseness of that first adjective, tried to get a sixteen-year-old girl to show him her braces.

When Kate Schaffer used to laugh, she flashed her wild teeth like the triangles of a sliced orange. Now with her braces she giggled like an aristocrat, lips closed behind a chubby white hand. Obviously I used the word "love" without meaning it just yet, but I wanted to grow into that word with her, and the only way I figured I could was to make her laugh again the way she used to laugh. This—a straight boy might've concocted a more sexually explicit plan—should have been my first clue that the whole experiment was a waste of time.

However. On the day of the pep rally, Kate Schaffer and I ditched our history class to—to do what? I don't remember. She was everyone's crush in middle school, but now she'd put on some weight and had been relegated to kissing a boy she must have known was gay. She kissed shyly; my bottom lip, for the most part, rested gently between hers. I remember liking the fact that she was bigger than me, and remember uttering the phrase, "Kiss me, Kate": if there had been any doubt to my sexuality, these should have been strikes two and three.

The gym's back door opened from the inside, and we stopped kissing to duck behind an air-conditioning unit. I peeked over to see a janitor prop open the door with a large trash bin and walk off some fifty feet for a smoke. He kept his back to the open door, and I grabbed Kate's hand and ran into the equipment room.

"What are you doing?" she asked.

"I'm going to kiss you in every room on campus," I said, and kissed her on the mouth. I could feel the metal behind her lips. "This was a tough one, but, equipment room: check."

"Let's go to the next one before we get locked in here," Kate said, happy to play along.

Plopped in the corner near the basketballs and volleyball nets was the cloth head of Rebby the Blue, his blank, meshed eyes staring blandly ahead. Above him, a dry-erase board, its black tray stocked with four fat markers of blue, black, green, and red.

"One minute," I said. I grabbed the black marker, uncapped it, and aimed it at the mascot's face.

At the rally, when the mascot came out onto the gym's floor, and everyone around us jumped from the bleachers and hollered and laughed, I watched Kate Schaffer laughing wildly, and saw those braces. God, I was proud—I thought, stupidly, that being able to fix the way Kate Schaffer laughed meant I'd be able to fix myself.

"Was that the last girl you ever kissed?" Lloyd asked me once, years later. We were in bed in the Noe Valley apartment we shared with two other couples, alone for the first time in a long time on a lazy weekend afternoon. The sun through the windows turned the sheets on our stomachs an impossible white.

"The one and only," I said.

"I know it's ridiculous, but I hate to think of you kissing someone else, even if it's a girl. Even if it's ten years ago."

Our faces were so close, it didn't take much work for me to kiss him.

"There," I said. "Now you're the last person I've kissed, no question about it."

"Take me home," he said. "Let me meet your mom and dad."

"I will," I said. "I promise I will."

THE END

The police arrested two nineteen-year-old boys (neither named Retivat) whose four homemade bombs—of which only two were set off—proved less effective than they'd planned. Now those boys were adults, forced to reconcile the perfection of what they'd imagined with the defectiveness of what they'd actually done. No one was killed, thankfully, though among the seventeen injured were Joshua Stilt and Jenna King. Both had checked out of the hospital with various degrees of burns and lacerations. I met with them at their apartment that night, just before heading back to BART.

"Well," Jenna said. Her right arm was bandaged from the elbow to the wrist, and her nose ring had been—by choice or not, I didn't ask—removed. To my surprise, she hugged me with her good arm. "At least this'll give your article some pizazz. You might even win an award."

The flowers Joshua had brought home from the man at the Mission Street BART station stood in a colorful Tiffany-style vase on the radiator. The day-old newspaper they'd come wrapped in had been thrown out, apparently, and now there was no way to tell the flowers apart from those purchased at an expensive boutique.

"I'm not sure I'm going to write the article after all," I told them. Instead, my plan was to stop thinking so much about the past, to bring Lloyd home with me to the Antelope Valley. I wanted him to meet my father. I wanted to start our future. But that was another story.

If Joshua was disappointed by the news, he didn't let on. He was sitting in the chair he'd been photographed in earlier that day, holding a plastic blue ice pack against his knee. He said, "What are you going to do with all your notes?"

"They're yours," I said, presenting my notebook. "If you want them."

Joshua Stilt narrowed his eyes. He was in pain. "If I read them," he asked, "will I find what I think I'll find?"

I nodded.

Then he smiled—that smile—and told me exactly what I could do with these notes.

YOU'RE ALWAYS A CHILD
WHEN PEOPLE TALK ABOUT
YOUR FUTURE

———— ✣ ————

We didn't love the circumstances, but for the first time in years, my sister and I were home at the same time. Dad took a nap on the brown leather couch in front of the TV, and Jean and I tiptoed past him on our way to the kitchen like kids. We weren't kids. In a month, Jean would be twenty-nine. She was an attorney but worked, in addition, for free. Pro bono. My dad, if awake, would have made his favorite joke on the subject: He'd always been, himself, pro-Cher.

At twenty-five, I wasn't a kid either, but compared to the Mother Teresa persona Jean had wrapped around herself, I didn't feel much like a contributing adult. A day earlier I'd called her that—Mother Teresa—when she'd told me about a community center she was planning for low-income survivors of domestic abuse. I said, "Damn. Mother Teresa over here." She told me never to call her by that charlatan's name again, and recommended the book by Hitchens.

My mom was in the kitchen, making coffee the Armenian way. When I'd left home for college, I discovered most people knew it as "Turkish" coffee, but in my house we knew the truth. The Turks had taken enough from us already. We drew the line at espresso.

Jean and I took seats at the kitchen table, an oak-top rectangle with white, ornate legs like a piano's. Jean saw me noticing the legs of the table and mentioned how Victorian they were. I corrected her. "Victorians would have sawed these off," I said. "Too lurid. Too ribald."

My mom rubbed her head and made a joke about herself being too bald. The treatment had taken her hair and weight, but not her jokes.

That's when we asked her to tell us a story.

Jean and I both knew Mom was getting impatient with us about starting families of our own. She was particularly frustrated with Jean, who had just ended her engagement to a physicist at Cornell. Mom hadn't heard of Cornell before meeting Patrick, but after the breakup, she couldn't help bringing up the school every time she heard something intelligent. As for me, I had time. An Armenian man—even a halfie like me—could claim his mother as his girl for as long as he wanted.

"Tell us a story," my sister and I said, afraid silence would lead into another eulogy of Patrick.

"First, put on socks," said my mom, turning from the counter-top with two miniature cups of coffee. "On this cold floor? Go put on socks."

When we got back to the kitchen, my mom had our coffee cups on the table. She said she didn't have any stories to tell. "Ask Daley," she said, gesturing to me. "He's the writer."

"I'm a blogger," I said. Then, to improve my self-esteem: "And a freelance journalist."

Jean said, "Emphasis on 'free.'"

"Story," my mom muttered to herself, fetching her own cup

of coffee. "Story." Then she took a seat at the table and started talking.

When my mom was a girl in Armenia, she'd eat apples until she grew sick. She and her older brother Gaspar practically lived in the apple tree outside their farmhouse in Kirovakan. The other brothers and sisters would leave them up there all day, until Raffy, the eldest, went out after sunset to talk them down. My mom blamed all her current dental trouble on those early days eating apple after apple after apple in the twilight.

She moved to New York at twenty-three, the first of her immediate family to emigrate. Nights she took English courses in Brooklyn. She feared the people in the subway, clutching the railings like weapons, until one day she didn't. Nothing happened to signify the change—only time. Time replaced her fear with an immense loneliness. She missed her family and her country. In the Big Apple she missed her apple tree, and on the subway she cried and cried.

Eventually the rest of her family came to America, and she moved with them to Glendale, California. She worked in retail at the local mall. The mall security guard, a Midwestern transplant hoping to break into the movies, asked her to meet him for coffee. Jean and I knew this part of the story well. Our dad—the security guard with a head shot folded up in his back pocket.

While my mom and dad started dating, there was another man involved. An Armenian, a friend of Uncle Gaspar's, named Armen. This was the first time Jean and I had heard about this other man. My mom said Armen definitely sold and probably used inordinate amounts of drugs. "Which drugs?" we asked. "Just drugs," she said. "The bad kind."

In any case, Armen—even though he'd never spoken to her, had seen her on only a handful of occasions—kept telling my uncle Gaspar how badly he wanted to marry my mom, how it was destined, how he'd do anything, anything, anything for her. My uncle, being of a certain generation of Armenian men, obliged. He told my mom to stop dating the white security guard so he could introduce her to his friend. It's destined, he said, and it's better that he's one of us.

A few years earlier, my mom would have buckled. But remember: she'd lived in New York for two years by herself. She was not the same person she'd been before she left home. She wasn't the girl her brother remembered, lounging in the limbs of an apple tree.

No, she said. I love Ed—my dad's name—and I don't want to meet anyone else.

My uncle must have hated her for making him return to his friend, tail between his legs, with a no. What kind of man lets his younger sister tell him what's what? But they were in America now. The rules were different. What could he do?

On that topic, Armen—dealer of unspecified drugs—had an idea. Late one night, he drove to the apartment my mom shared with her parents. He brought a shotgun. Probably it rode in the empty passenger seat like a child. He was so high, it was a wonder he'd driven the whole way, but when he arrived, he removed the gun from the car and walked along the gravel parking lot to my mom's first-floor apartment window.

My sister and I had a hard time swallowing the next part of the story. According to my mom, two angels appeared in her dream and told her to leave her bedroom—which faced the parking lot—and head into her parents' bedroom, where she'd be safe. So she did. Less than a minute later, the blasts from the shotgun shattered her bedroom window, glass and buckshot splattering the walls like water from a shook, wet hand.

The next day, my uncle made an anonymous phone call to the LAPD, and his friend Armen was arrested for possession with intent to sell. He was deported to the Soviet Union, and even after that log of a country broke into its splintered parts, my mom never heard from him again.

We drank the last of our coffee. My mom kept saying, "Are you sure I haven't told you this before? I'm sure I've told you this before."

"We're sure," Jean said, and I agreed. "We'd remember the time you were visited by angels and almost murdered."

"Oh, well," my mom said. "That's it, really. Not a story. Not really. More like an anecdote. Nothing changed because of it. I would have married your dad even if this crazy man never existed."

We all fell quiet. We had nothing to say about her story. I was amazed at learning something new about her, amazed at the fact of a person's unknowability, but this was a feeling more than a statement to proclaim. Eventually the silence was broken when Jean asked Mom to read our fortunes in our coffee grounds.

As millions of Armenian women had done before her, my mom set each cup upside down over its saucer with care and with grace. Then she crossed herself. For Mom, the possible contradictions between a soothsaying tradition and a devout faith in the Bible were nonexistent. I'd heard her say many times that Armenians were the first Christians. "For us," she would explain, "there is no difference between religion and culture." I'd argued with her on that point in the past, but now was different. Now I just stared at the gold-rimmed bottom of my overturned cup, half-seriously willing my future to read a certain way. I felt nervous, to be honest, and restless. I was sweating.

"Patience is the biggest thing," she said, noticing. She reminded us not to peek until the sludge had dried on the inside of the cup. A few minutes passed, and we were all so curious as to our futures that no one dared start a conversation. At one point, Jean giggled, and I laughed at her for enjoying this so childishly. My mom said there was nothing wrong with enjoying this like a child, because no matter how old you were, you were always a child when people talked about your future.

Jean said, "Please don't say anything about Patrick. Promise?"

"I can't promise anything," my mom said. "His face might appear in the coffee, and I'm supposed to ignore that?"

She turned over my sister's cup first. Jean and I were rationalists. We knew how silly we were being, how superstitious. Still, we also knew this might be the last time, so we studied our mother's face as she inspected the patterns against the porcelain walls of the cup. As she read the lines and waves and peaks and dips of the coffee grounds, we read the crannies along her forehead and the cracks in her painted lips, the bluing, beautiful pouches beneath her eyes, flanking the bridge of her long, arched nose.

"Interesting," my mom said, and Jean couldn't help scooting forward on her seat. "Very interesting."

"What does it say?"

"Do you see these?" My mom tipped the cup toward Jean to point out a number of circular blots near the lip. "These are very rare."

"What do they mean?"

"Children," my mom said. "One, two, three, four—four children in your future."

"Oh, come on," Jean said.

"I'm only the messenger," my mom said.

"What else?" Jean said. "Tell me there's something besides kids."

"Let me see," my mom said. "Daley, go get my magnifying glass out of the computer room."

I found it easily in a drawer. The handle was white porcelain like our cups, painted blue in a paisley pattern. The circle of glass was the size of our saucers.

"Okay," my mom said, taking the magnifying glass. "Let me see." She adjusted the distance between the glass and the cup like a trombone player in a game of charades.

"Well?"

"Well," my mom said. "This is amazing." Again she tipped the cup so that Jean could see her future. "You see these ripples, how they start far apart from each other and then get close together? That means you will be rewarded for your good work. It will take time, but your good work will be widely recognized."

Jean liked this, but I pointed out how arbitrary it was to read the ripples as getting closer together. "Why isn't it the other way around?" I asked. "Why don't you say they start close together and drift apart?"

"How many years have I been doing this," my mom said. "I know a start from a finish, okay?"

"My turn," I said, preferring to be a nonbelieving participant over an enlightened spectator.

"Okay," my mom said, and began to read my grounds. Jean turned her own cup over in her hands as if she could check her results for errors.

"Look at this splash mark," my mom said, holding my cup. "This is your first book! It will be a big splash."

"Yeah, the splash thing," I said. "I get it. But, Mom, I write for the internet."

"Shut up," Jean said. "At least it's not children."

My mom ignored this and kept reading my fortune. "First book," she said again, "and what's this?" She reached for the magnifying glass on the table and took a closer look. "It's like a little star you see in books," she said. "What do you call it?"

"An asterisk," I said, and the tiny mark on the cup did, surprisingly, look just like an asterisk. "What does it mean?"

For a minute, I thought my mom had finally been stumped. She'd never seen this particular accident, and she was taking a long time to come up with some wishful thinking to pass off as a fortune.

"Well?"

My mom looked at me. For the first time in a long time, we met eyes without saying anything.

"Well?" I said again. And then I was struck with fear, convinced she could see it—my life in San Francisco with Lloyd.

"You're going to live a very long life," my mom said, looking back into the cup. "One hundred, one hundred ten years."

"That's not what it says." I could tell by her hesitation that something rotten lay in my future.

The sound of bare feet kissing the hardwood floor came from the hallway, followed by the unmistakable drawl of my dad's yawn.

"Hey," he said, meeting us in the kitchen. "What are you guys up to?"

"Reading fortunes," Jean said, lifting her cup.

"Anything good?"

"Yeah," Jean said, "if you like children, old age, and successful careers."

"Children, check. Old age, check. Two out of three ain't bad," said my dad.

"And what about you?" he asked my mom, hands on her shoulders from behind her chair. He kissed the top of her bald head.

"We haven't done hers yet," Jean said. "Mom, let's make Dad his own cup so we can do his, too."

"Nah," my dad said. "I just want regular coffee. Our fortunes are tied together anyway. Read your mom's, and you'll read mine, too."

"Daley," Jean said. "Help me out." I scooted my chair over to my sister and leaned into her. She flipped my mom's cup, and we began our inspection.

I could hear my dad at the counter, running water for his Folgers.

My sister and I conferred. A black wiggle draped one side of the cup. Two smudges intertwined near the lip. I pointed to this and told Jean I saw an infinity sign. She saw it, too.

"We've got it," I said. "Mom, Dad: you'll both live forever. You are the first people in the world who will never die."

My mother slapped the table, startling everyone to silence. "You're not taking it seriously," she said, as angry as I'd ever seen her. After a minute, she reached across the table to touch my wrist with her fingers. They were cold. They had thinned so much that she couldn't wear a ring. "You'll never have a child," she said. "That's what I saw. I'll put it that way, Daley, that you'll never have a child."

"He can have one of mine," Jean said, and this got everyone, even Mom, to laugh a bit.

"God knows what I'm trying to say," Mom said, letting go of my wrist with a little pat.

God's not the only one, I wanted to tell her; Jean and Dad knew what she was trying to say, too, and had for years. But God would have known more, wouldn't he? He would have known how much I loved my mother and how much I resented her, how desperately I needed her and how urgently I needed to rid myself of her, how impossible it was for me to imagine my life after her death and how many times I already had. Among a million things, her death meant that I would never have to introduce her to the man I loved. In equal parts, this liberated and devastated me.

"At least," my mom said, "read my fortune seriously. At least you could do that."

And to some extent, I could. What I knew about her future was this: that she would not sprout wings and ascend to heaven, that she would not, in a time of danger or despair, come to my aid. But the more closely I examined her cup—the coffee grounds, yes, but also the cracked, orange prints of her lipstick at the rim, the ghosts of her—the more I couldn't be sure.

THE STARS ARE FAGGOTS, AND OTHER REASONS TO LEAVE

——————— ⚜ ———————

1. No word, in the desert's language, for "moderate." For months, the heat clocked in at three digits until, for months more, the temperature dropped below freezing. The surrounding San Gabriel and Tehachapi Mountains acted as perfect curtains behind which we could either hide or misbehave. Most preferred the latter. In the Antelope Valley, even the plants—Joshua trees and cacti—were ugly and mean, and the Santa Ana winds conspired with the tumbleweeds, compelling them to dart through traffic like suicide bombers. From the Bic'd and Doc Marten'd skinheads to the howling and hungry coyotes, from the braided, defensive leaves of the California juniper to the resentful and resented black and brown teenagers dragged there from Los Angeles—in a place where toughness and tribalism permeated everything living and everything dead, it was not the best thing to be a sentimental, thin-skinned fag like me.

2. You wouldn't know by looking at me, but my mother was raised in another country and spoke with an accent. One effect of the

accent was that she pronounced *p*'s as *b*'s. When I was a child, this
seemed inconsequential to me—my sister and I heard the correct
pronunciations from our dad, and were rarely thrown by Mom
ordering *bineabble* on the pizza, or asking if we'd prefer black, green,
or *bebbermint* tea.

But one day my third-grade class had, for some reason, a
sleepover party. The party wasn't actually held overnight; the kids
were simply supposed to wear pajamas, bring toys, and pretend.

As far as I can remember, my father had never said the word
"pajamas." I'd only heard my mom say it, usually after coming home
from work, when she'd tell my sister and me to join her in getting
comfortable.

At one point during the pretend sleepover, I made all the boys
laugh by asking which of the girls had the best *BJ's*. I didn't understand why they were laughing, but I enjoyed the boys' attention.
When one of the girls told the teacher, no matter how much I cried
and argued my innocence, Mrs. Chance issued me a demerit for using foul language. She said, "You're lucky I'm not calling your parents," but that's what I wanted most in the world: for my mother to
exonerate me, for my father, the Midwestern all-American, to tell
me what I had done wrong.

3. Drew Reuter, the boy across the street, was obsessed with professional wrestling. His favorite wrestler was a face-painted, arm-
tasseled bodybuilder named Ultimate Warrior. Drew owned all the
action figures, and let me play with every one of them except for
the Warrior. We played in his front lawn, where the toys stood as
tall as the wildest tufts of crabgrass. I was eleven years old and he
was twelve when he asked if I wanted to play with Warrior. I said,
"Heck yeah." He pulled his penis from his shorts and said he'd let
me play with Warrior if I licked him. Some other boy might've

called him queer or punched him, but I felt my own erection forming. I remember thinking the penis and the stomach must be connected, because as my erection grew, my stomach shrank, turned hollow as the plastic muscles of the action figures. Now and then a car passed, and I timed my lick perfectly between them. Drew wanted more than the one lick, and I obliged. Soon he moved to his mother's house, and we never played together again.

4. Otherwise, I had exactly zero sex in the Antelope Valley.

5. When my sister was a sophomore in high school, and I was in the sixth grade, she waited until my parents were at work to bring home a boy named March. He was pale as a used golf ball and had recently shaved his head with a Bic razor. I could make out two fresh, bloody nicks at the back of his skull. When I caught him and my sister kissing on the patio swing in the backyard, Jean yelled at me to mind my own business. March told her I hadn't done anything wrong. This—a boy standing up for me—made me like him. When Jean went to the bathroom, he pulled me aside and said, "One day, you'll be a dude trying to get some pussy, and some little brother's going to get in your way." He laughed. Then he asked, "Want to see my tattoos?" He lifted his shirt, and I saw a purple bigwheeler along his smooth white rib cage, a pair of crossed pool cues over a flaming eight ball, and a set of initials that read NLR. I asked what these stood for. "My crew," said March. "My motherfucking crew, man."

6. The Nazi Low Riders tried to indoctrinate my sister. This is cheating—I didn't know this until after I left. March tried to tattoo Jean with a homemade needle, and my sister, from his couch, kicked him in the teeth and ran away.

7. When I was ten, the only objects that really belonged to me were a few books and magazines, some video games, and a baseball signed by two famous and rich Dodgers. My dad had taken me to a convention center to get the ball signed, and when one of the famous and rich Dodgers asked what position I'd go on to play in the big leagues, I told him, "Home," which made everyone laugh. My dad explained how we were just getting me started in the game, and that although I had a lot to learn, I seemed to love it and that's all that matters, isn't it?

The famous and rich Dodgers agreed. Love of the game was the difference between the good and the great. They didn't mention what kind of person was indicated by pleasant, yielding ambivalence.

One night—not much later, but long enough afterwards so that my father and I had stopped pretending I cared about sports—I decided to get rid of the signed ball. Maybe the baseball was a reminder of the heteronormative boyhood my father pined after for me, but the truth is I simply thought the baseball ugly. The sloppy, illegible signatures were scrawled in a hideous green ink, and the spherical shape of the thing itself didn't seem to belong with the rectangular shapes of my books, magazines, and video game cartridges. Even the furniture in my room was boxy and sharp, and the ball—a lone, edgeless blob—bothered me. I needed to get rid of it, and fast.

During my period of baseball-inculcation, I had seen the movie *The Sandlot,* and I planned an almost precisely opposite plot. I waited until my parents and sister had fallen asleep, opened my bedroom window as quietly as I could, and chucked the ball over the neighbor's wall. His yard was full of towering, wispy grass I'd always mistaken for wheat. My hope was that the ball would nestle at the bottom of that tall grass, and be lost forever.

And for a brief time, it was. I explained to my parents, tears in my eyes, how I'd taken the baseball to school. To show off. Some-how, on the walk home I guessed, the ball had fallen out of my bag. "Stupid!" I said, palming my forehead. My mom absolved me us-ing the loving, passive voice: Accidents happen. A mistake was made. A lesson has been learned.

My father—who had probably taken the day off from work to take me to that Dodgers convention, probably spent more money on admission and gasoline for the drive than he'd spent on himself over the course of the month—only said, "That's too bad."

Eventually—weeks later? a year?—the neighbor knocked at our door while I was at school. Having cleaned up his backyard, he dis-covered a baseball he assumed was ours. When I came home, my father was sitting on my bed, cradling the ball in his hand, careful not to touch the signatures.

"What's so bad about owning a baseball?" he asked. "What's so wrong with keeping a gift? And why would you lie? Who taught you to lie?"

I didn't know which question to start with. My answers—nothing, nothing, self-protection, innate ability—wouldn't have done much good anyway.

My dad stood and placed the ball back where it had been on my desk, alongside my books. He said, "You know I'm an excellent listener. Why won't you talk to me?"

8. The Antelope Valley is not the California most people imagine. This could be a good thing, but almost never is. Instead, it's a point of pride, which is almost always claimed by people who are proud of the wrong things.

9. Members of NLR, including March, were indicted for the mur-ders of three black teenagers in East Palmdale. March is currently serving a life sentence in the California State Prison, Los Angeles

County—fifteen miles from where he stabbed to death a fourteen-year-old black boy named Curtis Allen, a member of a rival gang called SHARP: Skinheads Against Racial Prejudice.

Redlining—discriminatory zoning restrictions I didn't understand until my late teens—effectively segregated town: east for minorities and the working class, west for the well-off whites. The Sharps seemed like the only people willing to change the place. That skinheads could even *be* black seemed to break down, for me, the central tenet of segregation: that certain people behaved in certain ways, and thus belonged together.

As a teenager, I considered joining the Sharps, but I was too small and too weak and too afraid to declare sides, let alone join a gang. Another way of saying this is I wanted everyone to like me.

10. My friends and I dug trenches in the desert, shot each other with paintball and airsoft guns, built fires and jumped the flames on our bikes, forced each other to eat dirt and cactus and snake meat, rode our bikes to the aqueduct, ignored the signs warning of drowning, put our feet in the water, stripped off our clothes, sunburned on the cement slope, downloaded songs whose lyrics were growled, burned CDs, and, while collecting dented beer cans and abandoned bullet casings deep in the desert, listened through a boom box, growling along.

11. My mother served me breakfast in bed every Sunday until I was fourteen years old. "For my *pashas*," she said, calling me her prince.

12. Everyone started driving pickup trucks and SUVs and taking up two parking spots apiece. Once I saw a black F450 diagonally block four spaces outside Wal-Mart. Dangling from the back of the truck, as if the symbolism weren't clear enough, was a giant set of chrome testicles.

13. In the fall of 2001, Mom was working in Men's Suits at Dillard's. At least three times a week, she said, she helped a customer who, hearing her accent, asked to be helped by someone else. "They say they want a man's help." She was wearing her pajamas as she told us this, but she was still the daughter of a tailor. "I've been altering suits for how long?" she asked no one in particular. "The reason is *me*. They hear my accent, think I'm Muslim. These *beeble* are idiots," she said. "Don't they know what Muslims did to Armenians a hundred years ago?"

My dad laughed. "These people don't know what an Armenian *is*," he said. "Honey, these people don't know there's such a *thing* as a hundred years ago."

14. My best friend, Robert Karinger, shot me with an airsoft gun on the left half of my upper lip, which swelled nearly to the size of my thumb. We were out in the middle of nowhere and all I wanted was ice. Karinger and Dan Watts both called me a faggot until I got tears in my eyes, which is when Karinger spat on the ground and turned away to shoot cans. Watts, feeling bad maybe, started to compliment the way the fat lip made me look. "Like a badass," he said. "Like a boss."

15. People told me I didn't have a violent bone in my body, but they didn't know my bones vibrated to notes of violence like tuning forks.

16. The word "faggot" became so ubiquitous among my friends that sometimes, when I'd slink off to the desert to lie alone in the dirt and let the universe rocket through me for a change, I'd whisper, "The stars are faggots, the moon's a faggot, the Milky Way's a faggot, but I'm no faggot."

17. Though we lived on the east side of town, my sister and I tested well enough to surpass the zoning restrictions and attend a better-funded west-side high school. Our mascot was a Confederate soldier.

18. After being shot, I wanted to see my dad—or, I wanted him to see me. My lip was still fat and sore and, from what I could see in my bike's chrome frame, turning a shade of plum. I rode out to the furniture store where he worked, and tethered my bike to a lamp-post whose bulb, despite the hour or so left of daylight, sputtered on just as I disarranged the combination on my lock. Inside, my dad and two other salesman played cards at an overpriced oak kitchen table.

Dad introduced me to his coworkers, who looked up briefly from their cards to say hello.

"Slow day, huh?" I asked.

My dad said, "Just died down soon as you got here. Busy, busy beforehand." I looked to his coworkers for confirmation, but they kept their eyes on their cards.

I lifted my chin, trying to catch the light on my fat, purple upper lip.

"Notice anything different?" I asked.

My dad took his time to study my face, raising an eyebrow when he gave up.

"I should get back," he said. "See you for dinner?"

I asked if I could use the bathroom before heading out. He pointed me past the poker game into the back of the store. In the bathroom, I looked into the mirror and found that the swelling in my lip had gone down to about normal. The healthy pink color had returned. On my way out, my dad shouted a friendly, "See ya, son!" As I unlocked my bike, I checked my reflection again in the chrome. The plum color had moved to my forehead. I realized the color was on the bike, an old splatter from a paintball.

19. My sister, visiting from college, told me my acne—spreading from my forehead to my throat, purple cysts studding my back, chest, and shoulders—wasn't "normal." Jean said, "Everyone gets pimples, but your pimples are getting *you*."

20. I'd seen queer men on TV, and I made it a point not to let my wrists go limp, not to speak my *s*'s like a cartoon snake. But one day, Roxanne Karinger told me I walked "different." Recently I'd been fantasizing about her brother, and I was afraid she'd caught on.

"Different how?" I asked.

"I don't know," Roxanne said. She was two years my junior, but her girlhood made me admire her and even want, at times, to be her. "Like, more of a bounce? Your heels never touch down."

After that I walked in small, lazy steps. I leaned back and kept my weight on my heels. Took twice as long to get anywhere.

21. My mom took me to a dermatologist and, after listening to his suggestions for medication, said, "He used to have the cleanest skin." She hadn't said "smoothest," she hadn't said "clearest." She'd said, as if I'd neglected to bathe, as if my acne were the manifestation of a deep filth within me, "He used to have the cleanest skin."

22. Every fender in town carried a magnet in the shape of a ribbon to support the troops in Iraq and Afghanistan. Once, in the Best Buy parking lot, forty-three magnetic ribbons adorned the bumpers and front grille of a yellow Hummer. By the time I walked past, the count had been reduced to forty-two.

I'd stolen the stupid magnet as a joke to myself, as a kind of silly protest, but when the Hummer's owner yelled at me from across the parking lot, I started to run. The owner caught me, tackled me to the curb along a parking-lot island filled with coconut-sized rocks and miniature cacti. I lay on my back, and the man stood, shoving his foot against my chest like a pro wrestler. In size and looks, he bore a striking resemblance to Danny DeVito, but he was strong, giving me just enough air to breathe. He plucked the magnet from me and said, "What the hell is wrong with you?"

I said, "It was a joke." Blood trickled down my arm—I'd been scratched by one of the cacti—but I was too afraid to feel any physical pain. My qualm with the magnets—why wouldn't these flag-wavers *actually* support the troops, by demanding the end of the war?—gave way to a stuttering desperation to escape unscathed. "I'm sorry," I said, nearly crying. "I didn't think you'd miss one of your five hundred magnets."

That's when he told me he had forty-three: one for every AV kid hurt or killed over there. Before letting me go, he said, "You may have taken my son, you little fuck."

23. My parents went into debt so I could take a drug called isotretinoin, which dried my skin to flakes. For six months I couldn't be touched. My mom would blow me a kiss from across the living room, and if I blew a kiss back, the powder of my skin would blossom from my palm like chalk. At school I stayed in classrooms at lunch to avoid the sun, and when I got up to leave at the end of the day, I had to brush off my seat and desk. Everywhere I went, I left pieces of myself.

24. Once my skin cleared up, Jean took me to one of the four new Starbucks in town and bought me a caramel frappé. I asked about life at UCLA, but she kept batting away my questions. "The real question is," she said, "when are you going to come out already?"

According to Jean, Dad had asked her if she thought I might be gay. "You should ask *him*," she'd said, "but what if he were?" My dad said all he knew was that Mom couldn't find out. "It would kill her," he said. "Being from another culture, it would kill her."

25. In the months before *Brokeback Mountain* opened—my final months in town—Christian protesters outside the theater carried signs complaining of obscenity. In the parking lot, I counted three pairs of chrome testicles and a set of mud flaps bearing naked cartoon women.

26. Condescension didn't necessarily make you wrong, but in the Antelope Valley, it seemed to help convince people you were right. For all I knew, Dad *was* right about Mom. Maybe finding out I was queer would have killed her. Still, his using her as an excuse to avoid talking to me was a kind of cowardice that, because I recognized it as a trait I'd inherited myself, broke my heart.

27. Jean and I had to pay for our SATs and college applications ourselves, so we got jobs every summer. I'd worked as a neighborhood landscaper, an ice cream parlor boy, and a driving range ball-retriever. The summer before moving away to college, my dad set me up to deliver furniture. The store had a yellow Penske truck with its name plastered on the side—MAVEN's. I lugged mattresses and box springs and entertainment hutches and curio cabinets from the store's loading zone—a curb painted green in the small lot—to the houses of people who, seeing me struggle so thoroughly, either offered a tip or offered to help. No one did both.

One week in, I quit. I told my dad I'd tweaked a shoulder, but the truth was I'd nearly tipped the truck over and died on Avenue N. I was driving past an open stretch of desert—one of the last this deep into town—and a tumbleweed the size of a bear bounded into my lane. Thinking it was an animal, I jacked the steering wheel, and the whole truck—freshly unpacked and flimsy—wobbled behind me. The right-side wheels lifted off the pavement, hollowing my chest. By the time the wheels landed, I'd taken the truck into a trench along the side of the road.

While I waited for AAA to free the truck, I watched other tumbleweeds scamper across the road like the severed heads of Gorgons. The screaming wind slapped ropes of sand against my face. I thought, *This place hates me just as much as I hate it.*

28. The faces of missing girls appeared in the newspaper only to show up again six months later, when their bodies had been found in the desert. Violence, the threat of it, was the desert's language, and like a student in Spanish unable to roll his *r*'s, I felt unequipped to join the conversation. But, God, I wanted to. I scanned the inky faces of the raped and murdered girls and was filled with an enormous, unforgivable envy.

29. The day my acceptance letter to Berkeley arrived, Robert Karinger enlisted in the marines. Dad said both were noble endeavors. "He can fight the current threat, and you can help prevent the next one." But no one could agree on which threats were current, and which were still to come.

30. Just as the war was beginning to lose national support, and as I was packing to move, the local newspaper ran a front-page story under the headline, 31 REASONS WE SHOULD BE IN IRAQ. I remember thinking that if you needed thirty-one reasons to defend a position, you were probably wrong.

HABIBI

The day was warm and tedious, as it usually is when the weather's gray and dull, when clouds have been hanging overhead for a long time, and you're waiting for the rain that doesn't come. My sister and I were already tired of walking, and Brooklyn seemed endless. Across the East River peered the Midtown skyline, chalky and plain under the gray sky. On our side of the river lay an empty stretch of unmown grass that—on sunnier days, according to Jean—served as a place for people to read books or to picnic. At one point, Jean said she could imagine a version of her life in which this day were set on repeat, with me in from California and nature still and pensive. In the past, I'd have made fun of her for a sentence like that, but this was the first time I'd visited since Mom died, so I nodded along in agreement.

Jean wiped her nose with the long bone of her thumb and cleared her throat into her thin orange scarf. Then it started to rain. And a minute later there was a downpour, and we couldn't tell when it would be over. The two of us hopped from puddle to muddy puddle, amazed and then laughing at the sheer volume of rainwater coming down on us. We ducked into a small corner restaurant whose windows advertised falafel and yogurt sandwiches.

Other shelter seekers, a dozen of us, gathered in the little place. Most stayed at the windows, keeping an eye on the weather, waiting to push back out into the world. But Jean and I took stools at the counter and picked up menus.

The restaurant was called Habibi. At every wedding reception or party on our Armenian side of the family, a song by that name was played toward the end of the night, when the only people around to hear it were too drunk or happy or both to take offense at the word "Allah." *Habibi* means "beloved."

As Jean was talking, a disheveled man in his forties with graying shoulder-length hair and thick black eyebrows came out from the kitchen.

He had heard us, and now was looking us over: Jean, dark haired, tan skinned, large nosed like Mom; me, pale and blond, like Dad, with pink, chapped nostrils from an ongoing bout with a cold. The man wore a small gold crucifix that fell gently against his white polo. At his throat, three tattooed bars: red, blue, and orange, the Armenian flag.

His name was Simon. He told us that the owner—"a Turk, but a good one"—had the day off, leaving him in charge. Simon took our order, suggesting items along the way. "You don't eat meat?" he asked Jean when she'd turned down three of his suggestions. Then, to me: "She doesn't eat meat."

He lopped generous scoops of hummus into a Styrofoam container and included two extra grape-leaf dolmas at no cost.

The storm outside began to look staged; rain and wind beat furiously against the windows. Through the steam in the glass you couldn't see the rain, exactly, but you got an impression of it, its wild gray intensity. That blurring reminded me of Whistler's painting *Sea and Rain*. Jean let me say this and, with the same leniency I'd given her earlier, didn't call me pretentious.

Simon returned with two large folded white towels, one in each hand. He offered them to Jean and me. "Never eat wet," he said. We rubbed the towels over our heads.

And when the lights flickered and the backup generator kicked in with a whir, and when the line cooks, bored, emerged from the kitchen and leaned against the counter facing the front windows, and when Simon took our towels and flung them to dry over two cheap stained-glass chandeliers—that's when Jean began her story, and it was as if not only Simon and I were listening but also the line cooks and the shelter seekers who, even as they ignored us, looked back every now and again to distract themselves from the rain.

Since she was five years old, my sister said, she had a best friend named Emily Goodson. I knew Emily, but I didn't know her well, so this would mostly be news to me.

After high school, when Jean left for college at UCLA, Emily stayed on in the Antelope Valley. UCLA was only an hour away, so Jean would come home some weekends, and she spent a lot of her summers back in the AV with Emily. They'd get into their bikinis and splay out in Emily's backyard and act as if nothing were different from when they'd been bored teenagers so desperate for change that even a tan line made them feel like they had control, at least, over *something*. Only, things *were* different, of course, namely that Jean was only playacting as though she was happy to be home, and Emily wasn't. For Emily, life in the Antelope Valley wasn't something to escape. She was serving tables at Chili's and taking classes here and there at the community college. With tips and a promotion, Emily was making decent money for a single woman in town, and the way she saw it, with Jean's student loans piling up, she'd made the better choice by skipping university and staying home with her mother.

Our mother, who continued her whole life to exchange lipstick-kissed letters with her best friend in Armenia, must have seen herself in Jean and Emily's friendship. This is the only reason we can come up with to explain why she made Emily the one exception to her rule that Jean couldn't spend the night at anyone else's house. Mom had no idea, of course, that Emily's dad was addicted to methamphetamine. She would've died even earlier had she found out. Jean put two and two together only because Emily's house always smelled like cleaning products but never looked clean. The Goodsons owned a pet iguana, and Jean used to pluck out the cigarette butts Emily's dad tossed into the terrarium. Emily's parents fought constantly—screaming at each other for hours into the night—and Jean rarely got any sleep. In the mornings, Emily wouldn't look Jean in the face during breakfast, and then she'd apologize. But Jean always told her she never heard the fighting, told her she slept like a rock.

When Emily's parents divorced, she moved in with her mom, a cake decorator at Albertsons. The two of them supported each other, and Jean couldn't exactly blame Emily for staying in the Antelope Valley after high school. Still, Jean felt sorry for Emily. She even began to feel, secretly, superior.

Which was a first. All their lives, Emily had been better at everything. She was blond and big breasted, for one, in a town that seemed to appreciate that kind of thing. Jean, on the other hand, had always described herself as a hairy-armed, bespectacled, dark-skinned dork. (The most serious boyfriend she'd had, for God's sake, turned out to be a skinhead.) Together Jean and Emily spent most of their adolescence at the mall, scouting for cute boys with skateboards, and Emily always ended up making out with someone in the photo booth at the arcade while his invariably nerdy friend killed time with Jean, aiming for 100s on the Skee-Ball ramp. On top of this, Jean wasn't even the better nerd between them—Emily scored higher on every test and appeared in more club photos in the yearbook. She even started an animal rights group her junior year, leading protests at KFC, which, partly due to Emily's looks, Jean suspected, were broadcast on local television. All of which is to say, Jean looked up to her friend, and sometimes, years later, when people asked about her early political life, Jean fibbed and used parts of Emily's story as her own.

And so she was disappointed with Emily for doing what most girls in the Antelope Valley did: for staying in the desert, for not getting an education, for not using her intelligence and her passion and—yeah, sure—her good looks to make some major changes in the world. Emily would have been a better activist than Jean, probably. But there was Emily's mother, newly single, and for that reason, Jean kept her disappointment to herself.

But then Emily's mother remarried, purchased a cute and memorable domain name for her cake decorating service, and was getting along better than she ever had, and yet Emily still stayed. She got a new boyfriend, a twice-her-age engineer named—Jean couldn't believe it—Gunnar. Gunnar set Emily up with an office job at Lockheed Martin or Northrop or Boeing—Jean could never remember which. The pay was three times what Emily was making at Chili's, and when she moved into Gunnar's brand-new, three-thousand-square-foot tract home, the first thing she did was she called Jean. Jean told her over the phone how great Emily's new life was, how exciting, all while stifling the various moral questions being raised in her mind. Namely: (a) Emily's contributions to suburban sprawl, (b) her work—even as a secretary—in the military–industrial complex, and (c) her decision to share her life with a man named Gunnar.

And then, just a few months ago, Emily called again to say she was engaged. Gunnar had taken her out to the desert on his four-wheeler, proposed to her from his dusty knee while she sat on the ATV. How *romantic*—imagine how Jean must have sounded on the phone, trying to congratulate her. Emily—still not dumb—could sense Jean's condescension, and so my sister started to feel like a jerk. She loved Emily, after all—she really did. So she said, You know what? If you'll have me, it'd be great to visit, to meet your fiancé, and to say congratulations in person.

And so Jean took two days off from work, bought a plane ticket, and stayed with our parents the night before she planned to meet up with Emily.

The next afternoon, Emily came by to pick her up. My parents hadn't seen Emily in years, and Mom tried her best to bridge the awkward gaps in her knowledge of Emily's new life. Eventually Mom—she was feeling pretty good that day, Jean thought—resorted to the past. They spoke of sleepovers and grade school teachers and the time Jean, chasing an eight-year-old me through the house, cut open her head against the corner of our kitchen cabinet. Before taking Jean in for stitches, Mom had come home from work to find Emily rinsing Jean's scalp with the garden hose out front.

Even after they said good-bye to my parents and left for Emily's house, in the car on the ride over, Jean and Emily slid back into their old roles with one another—Emily the star and the storyteller, Jean the supportive listener—using a kind of muscle memory learned only in friendships developed before puberty. In fact, in those fifteen minutes before they pulled into the four-car-wide driveway of *chez Gunnar,* Jean laughed at a joke Emily made, looked out at the blue mountains surrounding the desert, and felt, for the first time since she'd left for college, happy to be home.

The house, though, was an underfurnished monster. Everywhere Jean looked, she saw spiral banisters, hardwood floors, and mirrors.

Dozens of mirrors, not a single wall spared. A couch sat in the middle of one room, facing an enormous flat-screen TV. As far as home furnishings went, that was all Jean could find.

Unless you count Gunnar, which Jean was prepared to do, just from what she knew of him already: right-wing, war-profiting, typical AV white guy that he was. But when he shook her hand—"The famous Jean!"—and pulled her in for an impromptu hug, she had to admit she liked him. He was long-haired and handsome, wearing a sports coat and brown saddleback shoes—she'd imagined him in fatigues, for some reason. He smelled like a green tea latte. He feigned embarrassment about the size of his house and the proposal on his ATV, mocking himself, calling the four-wheeler "the adult skateboard." This, of course, reminded Jean of their predilection as kids for boys on skateboards, a reminder she found sort of endearing. Not to mention he was kind to her, and curious about her work, and asked follow-up questions even Emily had neglected to ask. If he thought something wicked about Jean helping undocumented LGBT immigrants seek asylum in the United States, he didn't let on. They all three stood in the kitchen around a rectangular marble-topped island, drinking red wine. At one point, Emily said, "Isn't my life pretty great?" And Jean said—without having to lie even a little—that, yes, it was.

Then Emily went to the fridge and pulled out a large dish covered with aluminum foil. When Emily uncovered the dish, Jean saw eight bloody strips of steak. "Marinated London broil," said Gunnar, "once I get it marinated, broiled, and London-fied."

Emily knew Jean had been a vegetarian since high school. She knew because she'd been the one to convince her, way back in her animal rights days. Apparently, Emily had given up vegetarianism herself in the years since, but Jean couldn't figure out why Emily would invite her over for lunch without having anything she could eat. Jean took it personally, as if Emily were making a point. On what, she couldn't say. She just knew that the point felt directed at her—chicken in the salad, bacon in the macaroni and cheese—and she considered faking a stomachache and calling home.

Instead, Jean said she wasn't hungry—large breakfast, you know—but they should go on and cook, obviously, and she'll fill up on wine, ha, ha.

This last joke turned out to be truer than she'd meant. Every time the three of them finished a bottle, Emily found another to open. Jean became drunk—so drunk, she couldn't tell if Emily was even drinking with her any longer or just pouring. Soon the meat was done, sizzling on a porcelain platter on the kitchen island between them, and Gunnar and Emily were digging in—except for the occasional swipe of a lemon-scented wet wipe—like hyenas.

Which is when Jean saw, in one of the kitchen mirrors, the old terrarium, iguana and all. She went over to look, drunk enough to confuse mirrors with hallways. When she found the terrarium, she reached into the tank and stroked the iguana's back. Gently she pinched the tail and turned the loose skin this way and that around the solid flesh, as if twirling a flower by its stem. The feel of the tail between her thumb and fingers made her laugh, and she leaned against the wall until Emily came over to insist she eat something.

"Oh," Emily said, "I know what you can eat. It's not much, but . . ." Off to the fridge she went, and when she came back, she was holding a tiny circular cake. It might've been four inches in diameter and two inches tall, and was covered in a dark chocolate ganache topped with an elaborate series of miniature roses—red, yellow, and white. Jean knew right away that Emily's mother had made the cake, and for some reason—the wine, maybe—Jean started to cry.

The wine wasn't entirely to blame. Jean cried because she understood for the first time that everything she had accomplished, everything she had become, was what she'd once had in mind for Emily, and now, because Emily had a mother and Jean soon *wouldn't* have a mother, none of Jean's accomplishments—not one—mattered.

Emily went over to hug her, and she was crying, too, Jean realized, and soon they were both laughing, embarrassed. Gunnar fetched them two forks, and together, Emily and Jean ate the small cake. Gunnar threw his arms around them both and asked Jean, "Are you sure you don't want a bite of steak?"

And before Emily brought Jean home and said good-bye, before Jean kissed Mom on the way to the airport and told her how much better she was looking every day, Jean took Gunnar up on the offer. For one bite, she pretended to be someone else, someone who had stayed in that place and never wanted to leave. Her only bite of meat in over a decade—though it wasn't her bite, really, but someone else's—and the meat was *good*. A shred of the steak stuck between her teeth, and the person who was not Jean tongued at it all night, even in the morning. She never got sick, and she never felt guilty.

The rain had steadied, light enough now for some of Habibi's shelter seekers to pull their outer layers up over their heads and walk out into it. The line cooks seemed no less bored for having heard Jean's story, if they'd heard the story at all. Maybe, what with the steam in the windows, they'd kept their ears perked for a sexy moment that never came. One by one, they fell back into the kitchen. Simon lifted his hands to the chandeliers to inspect the towels. Still wet. By the time Jean and I finished eating, we were ready to brave the weather. Simon tossed us the wet towels, told us to keep them.

He mimed the act of stretching one over his head in a storm. New customers came in, putting him to work. We gathered our belongings and tossed out our trash to the sound of the rain dulling itself against the windows. As we were about to leave, Jean turned to the counter and asked in our mother's language—which I understood but never learned to speak—for dessert.

THE IMMIGRANTS

———————◆◇◆———————

D anny Watts" always sounded to me more like the name of
an old peasant song, belted out by Irish scallywags lining the
fogged windows of a pub, than the name of the half-white, half-
Mexican boy I'd later call my friend. But there he was, Dan Watts,
unpacking his cafeteria-issued burrito with the air of an archeolo-
gist, complaining to his lunch partners about the inauthenticity
of the tortilla.

"You can tell whether or not the dough was kneaded by hand,"
he said. "My mom always does this thing where, after she rolls out
the dough, she slaps it between her palms, back and forth, back and
forth, for no reason at all other than to get her skin on it."

"Gross," I said, though my mother made her Armenian recipes
the same way, and though having another son of an immigrant in
the group seemed to me a perfectly symmetrical and therefore agree-
able thing to have: Robert Karinger, so fully white that his buzz
cut appeared gray under most light, flanked like a kind of chess
piece by two loyal but divergent halfies. I'd spent every day of the
summer with Karinger, hoarding the treasures we'd scraped from

the desert in his bedroom, and I thought I knew him well enough—
eighth-graders as we were—to anticipate his saying, starting in a
mock-parental tone only to devolve into vulgarity, "Daley Kushner is not often right, but when he is, he's fucking *really* right. That
skin-on-tortilla shit is *gross.*"

But he didn't. Instead, he pulled apart his own burrito, inspected
it, and said, as if he'd just realized the all-too-simple purpose of an
alien instrument, "Huh."

Which is when I knew Dan Watts had officially joined the
group.

As I said, I was happy to have Watts around to buttress the
clear leader of our gang. On the other hand, I was also disinclined
to share the only friend I'd ever been able to make, and feared
constantly—at lunch and on the weekends, in class or in the desert, jumping tumbleweeds on our bikes—that the two of them
would ditch me. A bigger fear than being left entirely alone was to
be left and then watched, in my aloneness, by the two boys some
short distance away, hidden in a trench in the dirt except for their
heartbreaking and eerily natural laughter.

Because of this conflicted take on the new kid, my kinship with
Watts would for a long time be reliant on Karinger's presence. Years
would pass before Watts and I spent any significant time together,
just the two of us, and even then our conversations inevitably returned to Karinger. In other words, our friendship was more of an
alliance, and the fact that I now—as an adult—speak more to Watts
than I did to Karinger before he left to fight in the war, is a surprise my younger self would never have believed.

In college I'd picked up an internship at the *Oakland Tribune,* where
I spent most of my time fetching frozen yogurt for the perpetually shrinking paid staff and peering, a safe distance from the wall-

to-wall windows on the twenty-first floor of the sky-rise, out onto
Lake Merritt, waiting for the next bit of instruction from my boss.
I'd told my parents the newspaper needed me back as soon as possible, and that my visit home that summer after my freshman year
could only last a weekend. The truth was my boss had encouraged
me to take the entire summer off, and even hinted that my return
next fall was less than necessary. But I wanted to be back in the
office as soon as I could. I craved the light-headed kind of vertigo
brought on by standing near the windows, looking from a building literally ten times the height of any I'd grown up around, out
onto the lake, which—even though it wasn't a lake, but a tidal
lagoon—made the desert back home feel lifeless and beige in com-
parison. So I booked the short flights to and from home—an hour
each way—four days apart and packed a tiny gym bag that read,
along one side, ESSENTIALS.

The cheapest tickets had me landing at LAX at two in the afternoon on a Thursday, when neither of my parents could leave work
to pick me up. I looked through my phone for other options: My
sister was a law student living in New York; Karinger was in the
midst of his first tour of duty, and we hadn't spoken in a year anyway.
I resorted to calling Watts, whom I knew to be taking courses at the
local community college, training to become a paramedic. Two days
before the flight, I went to a poetry reading on Berkeley's campus,
not for the poetry—though Robert Hass read beautifully from work
that would go on to win a Pulitzer—but to stock up on wine, which
I couldn't yet legally buy. I stole a bottle of red from Wheeler Hall
and drank three-quarters of it in my off-campus bed before having
the courage to call someone I'd known, more or less, for six years.

"Kush?" said Watts, sounding genuinely surprised to hear from
me. After my fight with Karinger a year earlier, Watts and I had
seen each other exactly once, at Christmas, and spoken over text
only a handful of times. But when he answered the phone using

my nickname, and when I responded with his last name, a kind of fold in the fabric of time occurred. Our conversation was as comfortable and easy as though Karinger, silently, were on a third line somewhere, and we were all fourteen again.

The drive from Los Angeles to the Antelope Valley normally took about as long as the flight in from Oakland, but the traffic, even after leaving the city, was denser than usual, so Watts and I had a couple of hours to catch up. He was driving what used to be his father's pickup truck, and the confined space of the cab along with the fact that we'd shared this exact seat many times in the past, prompted me to think in terms of contrast. The truck hadn't changed, as far as I could remember, except for the addition of a rosary hung from the rearview mirror. I'd always vaguely known Watts was Catholic, but the beads surprised me. Watts himself looked more or less like he always had, his signature brown curls coiling to his shoulders. Whereas I—fair and wispy—looked like a scrawny version of my dad, Watts had always been his mother's son, dark skinned and a bit pudgy. He'd been training for the physical portion of his EMT courses, and he looked as fit as I'd ever seen him. His forearms—one of which flexed every time he adjusted the steering wheel—were full of thick, rootlike veins. During my fight with Karinger a year earlier, Watts discovered I was the kind of man who fell in love with other men. Looking at him so intently now, I didn't want him to mistake my intentions. I started to explain.

"Kush," he said on a particularly bogged-down stretch of the 14, "I get it. No need to explain anything to me." And, as if to prove how seamlessly he'd reconciled the laws of his religion with his friend's queerness, he asked in his most comfortably warm and scratchy voice if I'd met anyone, you know, *special*.

I said I hadn't, not in that way, and turned the question on him. "Any women in the AV you want to tell me about?"

"Just the one," he said.

I knew he meant Karinger's younger sister, Roxanne, who was about to become a high school senior. She and Watts had been seeing each other, secretly, for a couple of years. The only reason I knew was because I'd once discovered them half-dressed in a bathroom, and had been asking for periodic updates from Watts in the time since. Last I'd heard, they were still sneaking around together, waiting until she graduated before coming clean. I asked how she was doing.

"That's the thing," he said. "I don't know. We haven't talked in a while."

"What happened?"

Watts adjusted his rearview mirror, causing the rosary to sway even more violently than it had over the bumps in the freeway.

"I really have no clue," Watts said. "She just stopped answering the phone. Won't text me back. It's been, like, a month."

"You guys didn't have a fight? You didn't say anything to piss her off?"

"No, man. It's a serious mystery."

I told him Roxanne's issue was probably more about her than about him. "She's closing in on eighteen," I said. "She's probably freaking out about what's in store for the rest of her life. She just needs space, is my guess."

"Yeah," he said. "Maybe it's not about me." He passed the speed limit for the first time since I'd come on board. And that was the last we talked about Roxanne.

Then we were at my house, and before I left the truck, he asked if he'd see me again before I left town. I told him the truth, which is that I'd promised my mom I'd spend the whole weekend with her. "It's the only way she let me come home for such a short amount of time," I said. I thanked him again for the ride and offered him gas money, which he refused.

"Keep your cash," he said. "But maybe I'll call in a favor one of these days."

"Please do," I said. I laughed because I thought he was joking. By the time I'd reached the front door, he'd already sped off.

I found the key under the doormat. By the time my parents came home from work, separately but only fifteen minutes apart, I'd been in the backyard pool for almost two hours. The three of us stayed outside talking until sunset, which didn't happen until nine. My dad complained about the recent surge in traffic— "Remember when ours could be the only car on the road?"—while my mom, every now and then, brought me feta-sprinkled cubes of fresh-cut watermelon, or reapplied sunscreen to the acne-scarred terrain of my back.

"Are you sure they won't let you stay longer?" she asked more than once. And although a part of me envisioned a full three months of the kind of pampering given by an Armenian mother to her only son—the kind she'd argue was selfish because of how much she enjoyed it—I swallowed the cold bit of melon I'd plucked from the tray she set at poolside and said, "I'm sure." It sounded, from what Dad was saying about the traffic, that the last thing the Antelope Valley needed was another long-term resident.

Friday morning I woke remembering a dream in which I was an indignant, nameless worker in a chemical factory, a dream I attributed to the smell of chlorine I'd brought with me to the sheets. My mom entered my bedroom bearing breakfast. She set the French toast and milk in my lap and perched at the foot of my bed to watch me eat. She'd already called her manager at the department store, she explained, to say she was sick and unable to make it to work. Without pausing to signify a change of topic, she asked how the food tasted— "Great," I got out—and then asked how I wanted to spend the day.

My mother didn't know I was queer—at least, we'd never spoken about it—and until I met someone worth bringing home,

I didn't see a need to tell her. But I suspected she could feel I was hiding something from her, and began seeing her adoration as a means of getting me to talk. If I turned down her pampering, I'd be giving credence to her suspicion that I had something to hide. So I wiped the syrup and powdered sugar from my lips and said, "I want to do whatever you want to do, Mom."

What she wanted to do was this: First, she wanted to go to Starbucks, the one by the Target, and then take our coffees to Payless ShoeSource, where she wanted to buy me a pair of flip-flops. ("It's too hot for socks," she'd told me the night before, "but it's not good to go around barefoot.") Next, she wanted us to meet Dad on his lunch break, somewhere near his furniture store so he didn't have to waste time in transit. (Here, she reminded me of the traffic.) How did Primo Burgers sound? I hadn't become a vegetarian like my sister, had I? Lastly, she thought the two of us could spend the rest of the day at home. She had to wash the car in the driveway—I could spend some time reading then; she knew I probably wanted some time alone to read—and then she could make tea and *hatz banir bamidor* (bread, feta, tomatoes, and salted cucumbers), and we could sit in the backyard and eat and talk and drink tea and relax.

I found the plan exhausting. Intuiting this, my mom gathered my dishes and said, "There's no rush. You're on vacation. But for your dad's lunch break, you know, we have to time it right."

So I showered and dressed—without my mother's help, I'm proud to say—and joined her in the driveway.

We waited for twenty minutes in a long line of cars inching to the intersection at Sierra Highway and K, expecting to find an accident or construction at the light. But when we finally passed through, I couldn't spot signs of either. Outside the Starbucks, the drive-through line looped around the building, all the way out into the parking lot designated for Target garden center customers. Inside, however, the coffee shop was empty. "Don't they know it takes longer in the drive-through?" my mom said once we'd gone back outside, triumphantly sipping caramel Frappuccinos and peering at the line of drivers waiting beside us. "Nobody wants to leave the car anymore," she said, "not even for a minute."

In an act of defiance, we decided to walk the three-quarters of a mile across the enormous parking lot separating us from our next destination, the shoe store. The weather reports might've called the temperature in the low 90s, but between the unobstructed sun and the asphalt, surrounded by the gleaming bodies of minivans and SUVs, and equipped with nothing but a melting milk shake to press against our foreheads, the heat was unbearable. We got maybe a fifth of the way to Payless before my mom stopped, shielded her eyes with a flattened hand, and asked if we could go back to get the car.

I was trying on my third pair of flip-flops when a woman who wasn't my mother called my name. I recognized the accent, but didn't realize who she was until she brought me in for a hug. Mrs. Watts— née Teresa Estrada—moved her long braid from one shoulder to the other and stood back to see me in full.

"Your skin looks good," she said. "You look younger now than you did in high school."

"Thanks," I said, feeling a zit form on my nose. We talked about college and how I was enjoying the Bay Area, where she had some family, actually, in Richmond.

"How's business?" my mom asked, a clumsy attempt to join the conversation. The extent of their relationship was that they'd met a handful of times over the years. They were both immigrants, loved their God and their families, and were notoriously good cooks. But these not-insubstantial overlaps hadn't been able to spark a friendship, for whatever reason. I doubted Teresa would've approached my mother if I hadn't been there.

"Business is wonderful," Teresa said, though the way she stuffed her hands into the front pockets of her jeans hinted that she'd rather not talk about work. She and her husband ran a landscaping company, whose blue-and-white trucks I'd seen around town since before I knew Watts. "I'm on my way out," she said, citing the curled receipt drooping from the plastic bag at her feet, "but I wanted to say hello."

"Well," my mom said. "Hello."

"Hey," Teresa said, "I want to have you over for dinner. The whole family."

"Oh," my mom said, putting on a ridiculous performance of gratitude. "I wanted to have *your* family over for dinner!"

"No, no—I offered first!"

"Well, Daley's only here a couple more days," my mom said, "so maybe the next time he's home—"

"Hey, this is actually perfect," Teresa said. "Daley and Daniel probably want to spend some time together this trip, right? This way they can do that without you having to sacrifice any time with your son, no?"

I couldn't pin down why Teresa was being so pushy. Did she want to have dinner with us, or was she simply competing in a mom-off, where the object of the game was to embarrass the other mother with sweet, undying insistence? Had Watts put her up to this?

"Oh," Teresa went on, affecting a pained sympathy. "Tomorrow night's probably too short notice for you."

"You know," my mom said, planting her feet. "Tomorrow night should be perfect."

"Okay, great," Teresa said. "I'll make sure my son will be available. He's in school, too, I'm sure you know. Summer school, even, for the emergency medical training."

"That's right," my mom said, seeing an opening. "And I'm sure he's saving a lot of money by staying home and going to the junior college."

"He is," Teresa said. She widened her stance and shifted her braid to the other side. "It's a good thing he doesn't have to take out all those loans you see in the news, crippling loans students can never pay back."

"I look at it this way," my mom said. "A loan is just a bet we place on ourselves."

"True," said Teresa, "but gambling can be a vice."

The conversation went on this way for a few minutes, during which I found a suitable pair of flip-flops. After Teresa left, my mom pretended to look at the small selection of jewelry at the front counter, giving her enough time so that we didn't run into Teresa again in the parking lot. When the coast was clear, we got back in the car.

At lunch, my dad had some bad news for my mom, who was in the middle of an enthusiastic pitch for the next night's dinner plans: He wouldn't be able to make it. "Tomorrow," he said, "there's supposed to be some kind of rally on the Boulevard. Apparently, tons of people are going to be in town all weekend, so we're being asked to work late. I guess my boss thinks the protesters will finish marching, turn to each other, and in one passionate voice declare, 'Now let's buy some furniture!'"

My mom didn't laugh or even seem to hear him, clearly plotting what she was going to say to Teresa about her missing husband. Would appearing without him prove that she was somehow an inferior wife? Could she tactfully back out of the plans?

While my mom's machinery was at work, I asked my dad about the rally on the Boulevard.

"I heard it has something to do with zoning issues," he said, his confidence waning with every word, "or a new business park development? The environment? I don't really know, to be frank." He resumed chewing the last of his burger. As a kid in Michigan, he'd been hit by a car while riding his bike, and had to have his jaw reset. Now every time he bit down, I could hear a snap. After the last snap, we got up and said good-bye.

My mom and I were stuck at another achingly long red light on the drive home. As casually as I could, I asked why she didn't seem to like Teresa Watts.

"What?" She turned in the driver's seat to face me, genuinely wounded. "I have nothing but respect for Teresa."

I said I didn't mean any harm. From the outside, I explained, the two of them seemed to give off a kind of competitive, unfriendly vibe.

"We're mothers," she said. "We believe our sons are the best. And we know there can only be one best." After we traveled a few feet closer to the stalled intersection, she put the car in park—good for the brakes, she claimed—and pulled her short legs beneath her on the seat. "Stop acting like your father," she said. "All these questions. You're integrating me."

"I don't mean to *interrogate* you," I said.

At home, I changed into my trunks and glided splashlessly back into the pool. I could hear my mother in the driveway out front, hosing down the car. Not just the desert, but all of California was in a severe drought, and as I lay floating on my back, I felt immensely guilty, remembering an old teacher of mine, a farmer, who'd once made us draw bar codes on our faucets to remember that water wasn't free. But the guilt, as always, passed. I hoped tomorrow's rally was in the spirit of environmentalism, but soon the hope passed, too, and I simply floated, focusing on nothing at all but my own breathing.

Saturday. In the kitchen, my mother grated cheese for a stuffed pastry called, depending on the dialect your kind of Armenian speaks, *boreg* or *borek*. My mom pronounced it with a hard *g*—so I did, too, and it was one of the twenty or thirty words in the language

I spoke with any confidence. I used the word now as a replacement for hello.

"Good morning," my mom said, taking a break to kiss me and then returning to her work. "I called in sick again so we could be together."

"You weren't supposed to make anything for tonight," I said, stealing a pinch of shredded cheese from a growing mountain of the stuff. "It's Teresa's dinner party."

"Just something small," she said. She moved to the oven to check the bulb labeled PREHEATED. "Most of this is for us, but we'll take a few over. Those Mexicans love anything with a lot of cheese, I think."

"Mom," I said, reflexively offended. But she hadn't said anything foul, really, except for the unnecessary inclusion of the word "those," so I left it at that.

"You're already dressed," she noticed. "You have plans?"

The answer was yes. I'd decided to go to the rally on the Boulevard as soon as my dad mentioned it. I couldn't imagine what a political rally would look like in a place where everybody's politics aligned. I had to see for myself.

"You have to stay and be my taste tester," my mom said.

"I'm sure they'll be as delicious as they always are," I said, which was true. "But my boss at the newspaper emailed me." A lie. "He said I should go to that rally on the Boulevard and take notes for a feature. I'm heading out now, actually."

"You're going by yourself?" The way she spoke—accusatory and bewildered all at once—made going to the rally alone seem like the most ridiculous thing in the world. And so, for the second time in as many responses, I lied.

"An old friend is one of the organizers."

"A girl or a boy?"

"A girl," I said, knowing she'd prefer it that way.

"Why doesn't she just come here after the event? I can make tea, and you two can sit by the pool. I won't bother you."

"Well, we're *doing* something," I said. "We're not just sitting around, talking."

"Talking is doing," she said. Then—"Ugh"—she nicked the top of her thumb against the grater, sucked the shallow wound, and, leaving her fist against her mouth, grumbled, "What is this rally, anyway?"

I went to the drawer where we kept the Band-Aids and peeled one from its packaging. "Immigration reform," I guessed, taking her cut hand in mine.

"Not too tight," she said. I kept my attention on her thumb, but I could feel her looking at my face. All my life she'd paid a comical amount of attention to me, but this trip was the first time I felt as though she were studying me, analyzing my every move, for . . . for what? I couldn't say. I finished applying the Band-Aid without looking her in the face.

"What immigration?" she said.

I went to the trash can under the sink to throw away the wrapper. But the trash can had moved since the last time I was home. Now it stood near the sliding glass doors that opened out onto the backyard. "Oh, you know," I said, strangely disoriented. "The rights of immigrants, I'm assuming. The stuff you hear about in the news every other year."

"Maybe I should come," she said. "You did promise you'd spend the whole weekend with me. Plus, I know a thing or two about immigration."

"I don't think it's a forum," I said.

"A what?"

"Like, I don't think we're going to talk. I think we're marching."

"That's the first mistake. Nobody talks anymore."

"I thought you were upset that nobody gets out of the car

anymore. At least we're doing that. And anyway, the march is supposed to spark a conversation. I think the conversation that follows the march is the point."

"So I can't come?"

Now she was cutting filo dough into little triangles, hands white with flour. I wanted to say that her kind of immigration—from Soviet Armenia through New York and Los Angeles, thirty years ago—was different from this kind, across the border with Mexico. This kind was more deeply entwined in contexts of racism, for one thing. Plus, I wanted to say, we had a two-party political system that, encountered with a phrase like "the largest growing demographic," preferred to accomplish nothing, knowing that actual solutions would only hamper xenophobia and large anonymous political donations. In fact, I wanted to say to my mother, talk was the problem. All anyone did was talk.

Then I remembered I'd entirely made up immigration reform as the cause for the rally. As far as I knew, people were marching for creationism in the classroom.

I asked if the Band-Aid felt okay.

"You think your mother is weak," she said. "But I've survived more than a cut."

"I'm sure you have," I sighed. I grabbed her keys from the nearby rack and jingled them to let her know I was borrowing the car. "I'll be back before you're done with the *boreg*," I said on the way out. "So this isn't me breaking my promise."

Now, at least, the traffic was no mystery. Thousands lined the sidewalks and spilled out onto the Boulevard, a recently renovated stretch of small businesses and venues in the heart of town. Mostly those rallying were white men and women, and many wore camouflage in one form or another, which quickly snuffed out any hope I had that the event would save the environment. Some people carried seated children around their necks like airplane pillows. Invariably the children waved miniature American flags, and most of their parents carried homemade signs declaring their right to free assembly, signs I found eerie in their redundancy. I pulled off on a side street and had to drive a few blocks before finding a parking space. Then I trekked back to the Boulevard and joined the flow of the crowd.

Although I'd lied about my boss at the *Tribune* sending me to the rally, I did bring a notepad, and more or less pretended to be a reporter. I asked some of the protesters why, exactly, they were out today. Every response was a variation on some vague patriot-babble: "Because I'm an American, and that's what we Americans do," or, "I just want to be out here to show support." When I followed up by asking what it was, specifically, they were supporting, my interviewees responded with some version of, "I'm supporting freedom and democracy," and the question returned to why that support was necessary today, and I found myself in an endless feedback loop of nationalistic vapidity. I kept checking the homemade signs, hoping to find a clear cause, but the signs were just as nebulous as the people who'd made them.

My last attempt to understand the event came when I approached a middle-aged white man pointing a handheld, battery-operated fan at his face. I said, "What do you think is at stake today for your town?"

"I hate to break it to you," he said, "but this ain't a town." He threw his arms out, enveloping the Antelope Valley as thoroughly as the San Gabriel and Tehachapi Mountains, and in so doing dropped his fan. Bending to pick it up, he said, "Look around. This is a city now."

"Well," I started, but decided not to press the point. How do you explain what makes a city? Not the number of people or the sluggishness of traffic, but what? What I'd had in mind was something like my daily commute to the office at Lake Merritt, where I would stand in the aisle of the crowded 88 bus and listen to secrets traded and affirmed in the boundless languages of the world, where I'd hold on to the chrome bars so tightly that when my stop finally came, my hands smelled strikingly and perfectly of blood. A city got its smell on you, the smell of life itself, and no matter how inflated its population had grown, the Antelope Valley was no city.

I thanked the man and went on my way. The day was hot and dry as usual, but a thin cloud cover kept everyone marching in relative comfort. Along the grass meridian bisecting the Boulevard, beach umbrellas and foldout tables had been set up, and opportunistic capitalists were selling bottled water and snacks. Although I was enjoying the reporter character I'd invented for myself, I suddenly began to feel sick. I'd always imagined that I was born in the wrong place, that I was a metropolitan kid playacting the small-town boy. But now the truth set in: I was a small-town kid pretending to be a big-city reporter, and the inversion of my mask, along with the heat, had me dizzy. I went to buy a bottle of water.

At one of the umbrella-covered kiosks, I found a stack of flyers for the day's event, held down against the wind by a rock. DON'T BELIEVE PHONY POLL NUMBERS, said the headline, beneath which came a few hundred words debunking the media's declaration of the war's growing unpopularity. The protest was a general assembly of the new, so-called American Popularity Party. Just as I was beginning to understand the day's event, I spotted Roxanne Karinger. Although she looked not unlike a hundred other girls at the rally—blond, self-tanned, and pretty—I knew it was Roxanne. She stood the same way Karinger did, perfect posture except for the toes pointed inward. If she'd been alone, I might've gone to her and started the long work of mending my friendship with her brother. But she was with her mother, a woman who had been, until the fight, something of a second mom to me, not that I needed one, and suddenly I felt so absolutely silly for carrying a notepad and a pen that I dropped them where I stood and walked back to the car, ignoring the voice yelling after me, "Sir! Hey! You're littering! You can't just litter!"

Again we were in the car, but this time I was behind the wheel. Half past seven and the sun was still up. Dinner started thirty minutes ago, but the traffic and the daylight made it impossible for me to feel rushed. My mom didn't seem to share the sentiment. She bounced in the passenger seat, rattling the lid of the porcelain dish in her lap, telling me to cut the line.

"There's nowhere to go," I said.

"Well, if you hadn't gone to that rally, we would've left on time."

That I'd returned from the Boulevard hours earlier, that I'd spent the entire afternoon listening to her assessment of my sister's chances of finding a husband in law school, didn't seem to matter. I had left her, briefly, and now our whole weekend was thrown.

"What time is your flight tomorrow to San Francisco?"

She always treated Berkeley and Oakland as neighborhoods in San Francisco, and I'd stopped correcting her a long time ago.

"Not until noon," I said. "But I should get there by ten, so, leave here at nine?"

"Why did you make it so early? Couldn't you have spent the day here, one more day?"

"I just bought the cheapest flight," I said.

"Twenty dollars cheaper," she scoffed, almost to herself. "It's not the money, and you know it. Don't lie to me. You just don't want to be here with us. You'd rather be in San Francisco."

This wasn't untrue. But she was implying I didn't love her enough, or something more insidious. Maybe she could sense I wasn't my real self around her, whatever that is, and that I could fake it for only so long without bursting at the seams. I decided to say nothing.

"When I visited home a few years after I'd moved here," she said, "everybody told me I changed. I was talking different, they said, walking different, taking my coffee different. I didn't think so, but that's what everybody back home told me."

I said, "The traffic's starting to move, so that's good."

"I've been watching the way you are," she continued. "Now I understand what they meant. They meant I had become an American. And now I can say you've changed, too. You have become a different kind of boy."

"And what kind of boy is that?" I asked, feigning boredom. I spent most of the important moments in my life feigning boredom.

"I guess you can't help becoming the places you go," she said. "I think of you now as a San Francisco boy."

Teresa and my mother hugged like long-lost sisters, one apologizing into the other's hair for being so late.

"This traffic is unbe*liev*able!"

"I thought I told you not to make anything," Teresa said, taking the *boreg* and placing it on a little side table, a safe distance from the dining area, where I could smell the homemade tamales waiting for us.

We followed our noses to the table, where Watts's father, Seth, had already taken a seat. "Welcome," he said in his jowly, graveled voice. He didn't stand. He was an enormous man with thick brown sideburns, which he stroked and tugged at in an anxious display of impatience. Clearly he was ready for everyone to sit down and eat; when he twisted open a two-liter bottle of Coke, he released its hiss like a starting gun.

"Lena," Teresa said to my mom once we'd all taken a seat, "I'm sorry again your husband couldn't join us."

"Me, too, Teresa," said my mom. Because of their accents, they pronounced each other's names better than Americans could, and therefore did so as often as possible. *Lay-na,* not Lee-na. *Teh-reh-sa,* not Tuh-reesa. "I'm disappointed, too, Teresa, and so is he."

"I'm not," said Seth, scooping beans onto his plate. "More for us, right?"

Teresa asked everybody to hold hands while she said grace. As a nonbeliever, I always dreaded these exhibitions of group prayer—I feared my disbelief was palpable. Seth, who had to put down the tortillas he'd just peeled from the basket, was the only other person who didn't seem eager to join hands. But we did: I was sitting between my mother and Watts, and held on to them while Teresa spoke. We bowed our heads and closed our eyes.

"Bless us, O Lord, and these, thy gifts, which we are about to receive from thy bounty. Through Christ, our Lord. Amen."

"Amen," came the chorus. Even from me.

I reached for a tortilla, but Teresa said, "Daniel, would you like to—?"

Then Watts repeated the prayer in Spanish—I knew this only when he got to the cognate for "Christ." I caught Seth rolling his eyes. We chorused again, and this time I paid special attention to the big man, the only one of us not to say "Amen." He started to eat.

I, too, reached for the food, but my mother asked if it wouldn't be too much if she said a prayer in her native tongue, as well. Teresa said, "That would be great," and we chained our hands together a third time. This time I let out a little laugh-groan, and Seth gave me a wink.

When we finally released hands, Teresa said, "I hate to say it, but Seth has some work to deal with tonight, too, so he'll be leaving us early. It'll just be the mothers and sons."

"I've got employees coming in and out," Seth explained, grabbing two tamales at once with his bare hand. "We got a lot of paperwork to do with them. When you're in the landscaping business, you've got to deal with a lot of forged documents. Some of these guys, it's my fourth or fifth time checking their information, because the government's been cracking down, and you can't be too careful. See, back in the day, when people like my grandparents were coming in from Wales, when Teresa's parents brought her up here as a kid, when Lena here was coming in from—where was it, again? Romania?—people got in line and waited their turn. Not anymore. People think it's a racial thing, but it's really not. It's generational."

Teresa sneezed thunderously, startling everyone. After blessing her, my mom took the opportunity to change the conversation by asking Watts how he felt to have his old friend back in town.

"It's cool," Watts said. "I'm just glad he came back even though he's kind of outgrown this place."

"You say that like it's a compliment," Seth said between chews. "But look at it this way. That truck of yours, Danner, was given to you when I got too big to fit inside. I upgraded to a bigger truck, and on paper, that looks like I'm doing pretty well for myself. But really what it means is, I'm obese and on the freaking verge of death." He laughed, wiping his mouth. Teresa clicked her tongue, and Seth put his hands up in mock surrender. "I'm going, I'm going," he said. Then he stood, shoving back his chair to make room. He apologized for dominating the conversation. "Hate to leave you guys," he said, "but *yo tengo mucho trabajo.*" The accent was so awful, I thought he was playing it up.

"The food is *so* delicious," my mom said once he was gone. "You know, Mexican food is so different from Armenian cuisine. Everything in Armenian cuisine—even the heavy stuff—is just *lighter.*"

"Well," Teresa said, "flavor does tend to make things heavier. . . ."

While they debated, Watts leaned over to me and said, "How's it been, being back?"

"Fine," I said. "Didn't do much this trip. I went to that rally on the Boulevard today, and that's about all."

"The American Popularity Party," Watts said. Apparently, his dad was a member. "What did I miss?"

"Well," I said, "I saw Roxanne."

Teresa dinged her glass with a knife. "Boys. Lena and I want to make a toast."

The two women filled their glasses with wine and gave us—underage, as we were—a tiny splash each. "It's a special occasion," Teresa reasoned. "And it's bad luck," my mom added, "to make a toast with an empty glass."

The four of us raised our wine.

"To you boys," Teresa said.

"And to your long, great friendship," added my mom.

"We're so proud of you both. In only one generation, look at our great boys in this country."

"And we can't wait to see what your futures hold. What your own sons and daughters, who won't be the children of immigrants, will be able to do."

"And also to Robert—"

"Who we all wish could be here with us tonight, but he's making us safer."

"And we're praying for him, to keep him safe, too."

"And for all of you boys. We're so proud."

"*Salud.*"

"*Abrés.*"

We clinked glasses to loyalty and sacrifice, though nobody said so, exactly. Karinger's name had been breathed into the room, though, like grace in another language, and I regretted avoiding his sister at the rally. She had always been kind to me. If I earned her trust again, I thought, I could eventually regain her brother's. I'd see her again. Next time, I thought, I'd catch her eye and walk over to her—

"What?" I said. Watts had been saying something to me.

"Was she with a guy?"

"Roxanne? No. She was with Linda."

Watts pondered this. He knew I had nothing to gain by telling
him of my sighting. But he also knew why I'd done it: I was from
here, a place where gossip—not ambition—served as the driving
force of stories.

"She looked good," I said.

"Of course," he said, hanging his head so his curls covered his
face. "Of course she did."

Just as my mom called off a second glass of wine, telling Teresa
we ought to be going, Watts flipped his hair back and punched me
lightly in the thigh. "You owe me a favor."

"Oh, God," I said.

"Stay here tonight."

"What?"

"Just don't go home."

Our mothers were hugging. They made plans to see each other
again, soon, just the two of them.

"Shit," I whispered. "It's my last night in town. You know I
promised my mom I'd stay with her."

"Look, I'll take you back to the airport tomorrow, free of charge.
But you have to help me tonight."

"Daniel," my mom said, coming over to hug him. "So good to
see you." Then, to me: "Ready?"

I rubbed my thigh where Watts had hit me. He'd been kind to
pick me up from the airport, and generous to offer another ride in
the morning. But that's not why I owed him my loyalty. I owed him
because he was still here. I owed him my loyalty because he'd given
the Antelope Valley—and me—his.

"Actually," I told my mom, "I thought I'd stay the night with
Watts—with Dan—if that's all right with you? And with Teresa,
of course. We've got a lot of catching up to do."

"But you leave tomorrow," my mom said, maintaining her smile. "Don't you think you should come home tonight, get a good night's rest?" She put her hand on Teresa's back. "They've got workers coming in and out, too, remember, so it's better if you're not in the way."

"Oh," Teresa said. "We can handle one more boy, no problem."

"And we were going to have *hatz banir* tonight." She fiddled with the Band-Aid on her thumb. "And I made all that *boreg* for you."

"I'll have some of the *boreg* we brought here," I said.

"But who will eat all the ones we have at home?"

I didn't have to answer that—my mom knew she was beginning to sound desperate. To cover this up, she offered a little laugh to our host and said, "I guess it's already been decided."

When we hugged, my mom said she could call off work again tomorrow, if I wanted, to spend another hour or so together before she drove me to the airport. But I told her I already had a ride, and plus, she couldn't keep doing that, calling in sick. What I meant was she couldn't afford to, but speaking of money always embarrassed her. So I made a joke instead. "Stop pretending to be sick," I said, "or karma's gonna catch up with you, and you'll get sick for real."

I arranged to swing by the house later to pick up my bag and say good-bye. Any pain I felt for choosing Watts over her was swept aside by the conviction that my mother and I had decades more to spend together. For another fifty years or so—an impossible amount of time to imagine—I would sit in traffic with her, run errands with her, taste-test her cooking. And eventually, once the drought ended and the town exploded into a true city around us, we would huddle together in the crammed aisle of a bullet train and reveal to each other the various occasions on which we'd sacrificed for each other in the name of loyalty. All the times we'd survived more than a cut.

———

The truck his father had outgrown started on the second try. It was just after midnight. In the hours since dinner, the only idea Watts had come up with was to head over to Roxanne's house.

"To do what?" I asked.

"I don't know," he said. "Karinger would've had a plan. Even you might have something in mind. But my motto's always been, 'Just be there,' and usually whatever needs to happen will happen."

At this time of night, the roads were unlit and empty. The Antelope Valley seemed to revert back to the town I knew as a kid, and the drive toward the Karinger house seemed less like a distance to traverse than a stretch of time.

We arrived at a streetlight that had been switched to a flashing red, and Watts came to a complete, unnecessary stop. Nobody else was around. The rosary hanging between us reflected the red light, on and off, in perfect time. Watts didn't move the car. Instead, he started to talk.

"It sucks being here without you guys," he said.

I wanted to tell him that the word "here" was unnecessary, that I felt the same way in an entirely different place. But the truth was, leaving and being left produced two distinct species of nostalgia, and I could speak to only one. So I said, "Go on. I'm listening."

He checked the mirrors constantly while he spoke, making sure we were alone on the road. "I lied the other day," he said. "I know why Roxanne stopped talking to me."

"I knew it," I said. "It's because of me. She hates me and doesn't want you keeping in touch with me."

Watts laughed. "Dude, not everything's about you. Roxanne likes you a lot, actually. She thinks her brother was an asshole to you. She's always trying to get him to apologize. No, this is about me, for a change."

"For a change?" I asked, though—considering how badly I

wanted to ask for more information about Roxanne helping me and Karinger be friends again—I knew he had a point.

"I don't know if you can get how hard it is growing up in a place where all your friends look alike except for you. Like, nobody's blatantly mean or anything, but there were a lot of times with you and Karinger where I felt kind of invisible. I don't know if you knew that about me, but there it is."

"No," I said. "I didn't know."

"What I mean is, I'm trying to figure out how to tell you this story. I guess the best way is to just come out with what I did, which is I ratted out one of the workers at my parents' company. For months I heard this guy—our age, maybe a little older—talking shit about my dad to another worker. He must've thought I couldn't understand Spanish or something. My dad can be a prick, but he's a good guy. He treats his employees fair, is what I mean. So I was pissed at this worker, who kept saying petty things about my dad—making fun of his weight, for example. Then one day I heard him mention to another worker that he was undocumented, and I sort of filed it away. I told myself, the next time he makes a joke about my dad, I'm going to—and, the next time he did, I went straight into my parents' office and ratted him out."

He paused. Then he said, "He's always called me Danner, you know."

"What?"

"My dad. He calls me Danner."

We laughed, sort of.

"When I fucked up in school or something, he'd say, 'Danner, you got that from your mother's side of the family.' He's always wanted me to be more—"

"White?" I said. "So you told your dad about the undocumented worker because you wanted him to know you weren't just your mother's son, but his, too? You wanted to make your dad proud, and you didn't care if you hurt someone along the way."

"I don't think so," Watts said. He turned to look at me, and the already cramped cab of the truck seemed to shrink. I rolled down my window to breathe.

"Like I said," he went on, "I think it was more about me, for a change. I think I wanted to feel that kind of power, the power of having somebody's life in my hands. I also think I wanted the worker to know I wasn't invisible. That I'd been there when he was talking, that I'd heard what he'd been saying and understood him. That I was like him, in a way, and also not. That I had something he didn't have, which is that I could be two things at once. I think that's why I had him deported."

I wanted to punch him in a friendly way, let him know I was still listening, still someone he could talk to. But I feared Watts would understand my hitting him as an indictment of what he'd done, and I knew he deserved much more than a punch. The haloed headlights of an oncoming car grew ahead of us. I asked Watts how this had anything to do with Roxanne.

"The whole time my dad was on the phone with the immigration officer, he kept saying that his son, Danner, was the hero. I'm not going to lie, Kush. I felt proud. For a few weeks, I felt like a fucking patriot. Only later did I start feeling sick. I fucked up a man's life—and his family's, too—because he called my dad fat. Jesus. I was really sick with guilt, man. I started going to church more and more, tried to atone, but I couldn't tell some stranger what I had done. God, I wish you or Karinger were around, because I was crying like a fucking idiot and ashamed and I needed someone to talk to. In person, I mean. So I went to Roxanne. I picked her up and we drove to the aqueduct, and I told her everything. After a while, she just stared at me, like she'd never seen me before. Then she told me to take her home. We haven't talked since."

The oncoming car passed, flooding us momentarily in white light.

"She's the only reason I still love being here," Watts said. Then he said it again. "I really love her, Kush. I really do. And I need her. I need to fix this. I don't know how, but I need to fix this."

I looked at my friend beside me, the one who stayed, and I knew what I had to do. I wanted to believe good men could do despicable things and remain good men. I wanted to believe this place was better for having him.

"I can fix it," I said.

"You can?" he said.

"I think so."

"What can I do to help?"

"Nothing," I said. "Remember your motto: Just be there. Then we'll see what happens."

One of the poems Robert Hass read the day I stole the wine began, "In one version of the legend the sirens couldn't sing." That's how I felt that night, just being there with Watts at the Karinger house, unable to lure the story closer. We parked across the street, knowing we couldn't do anything but watch the unlit windows. This wasn't a movie. We couldn't get out of the car and call Roxanne's name. We couldn't perform a grand apologetic gesture. We couldn't even apologize, simply. We couldn't predict the future, which was that Watts would go on to save more lives than he damaged. We couldn't reverse the deportation of the undocumented worker. We couldn't do what Karinger would've done, concoct an extravagant plot to prevent further deportations by splashing bleach across the lawns of the Antelope Valley, heightening the demand for workers. We couldn't continue to demonize Seth Watts, and I couldn't balk when his son, understanding how flatly he'd portrayed him, began reciting a litany of genuinely redeeming qualities. We couldn't say another word about mothers, though we thought about ours constantly. We couldn't spend all night parked at the Karinger house, waiting for a girl to emerge and absolve us of our sins, and we couldn't regret turning the truck around eventually, back through that flashing red, to get some rest before my departure.

All we could do was return to our lives. Only then, from the distant *Oakland Tribune* offices, could I go through with my plan. I wrote an email to Roxanne Karinger explaining how Watts had taken the blame when in fact the deportation was my fault. I'd been doing research for an article, I lied, calling out small-business owners exploiting illegal labor. I'd been the one who discovered the undocumented status of the worker, and Seth Watts deported him on my notice. Why Watts would cover for me, I wrote, I couldn't say. Why do friends do anything for each other?

Roxanne never replied to my email, but the plan worked. Watts, grateful, kept me informed. Roxanne thought what I had done was disgusting and inhumane. Journalism, she concluded, was nothing but self-promotion. At last she understood why her brother stopped talking to me, and would never take my side again. Still, she could see why Watts would stay in touch with me after all these years—she admired his loyalty. Anyway, the truth was she hadn't been that upset about the deportation in the first place. She could see now that she'd used the opportunity to take a "much-needed break" at a "difficult time" in her life. Later, with her brother visiting between deployments, and with the inception of her new, adult life fast approaching, she felt ready to stop keeping her love for Watts a secret, which was the true issue at the heart of their struggle. Watts agreed. And the nameless worker who'd been arrested and deported soon became simply another part of their story, important only in the most fleeting way: that he had been there, and then one day, he wasn't.

THE COSTS AND BENEFITS
OF DESERT AGRICULTURE

———— ◆ ————

For a brief but memorable time I belonged to an organization at my high school called, ridiculously, the Future Farmers of the Antelope Valley. Ridiculous, because I believed at the time that neither farmers nor the Antelope Valley had much in terms of a present tense, let alone a future. But I needed a noncompetitive extracurricular for college applications. So, twice weekly after school, I met with the group, led by an actual, visiting farmer, boots and hat and all, named Reggie Nelms.

Reggie spoke to us about farming in general, but desert agriculture in particular. You'd be amazed at how many of the kids appeared legitimately shocked when he informed us that water was hard to come by in the Mojave Desert. We were the product of the population boom of the late '80s and early '90s; our neighborhoods were so paved over with shopping centers and tract homes, we sometimes forgot about the biblical ecosystem lying beneath all that concrete. Reggie said, "When you shower or flush, do you think for even a minute about the finite source of that water?" We didn't. He accused us of not seeing value in anything we couldn't scan under a price-checker. Then he handed out black permanent markers and told us to draw bar codes on our faucets at home.

I immediately trusted Reggie, who looked like a baseball manager in the wrong costume, eyebrows all bristled like misplaced mustaches. He was a workingman in his late fifties, which meant people had begun to feel for him again after a long drought of sympathy, and since no one else on that first day seemed interested in asking him a question, I threw him a softball.

"Where does all our water come from, Mr.—?"

"Just Reggie," he said. Then: "Aside from the all-too-occasional rain, my alfalfa farm is run on a combination of what are known as aquifers—pumped underground—and imported water via the aqueduct."

A number of us recognized the man-made river in the hills above town not as a source of water, but as a destination, grinning at one another as if to say, *Remember that time at the aqueduct. . . .*

Eventually, in the most casual of tones, as if he had no idea how mystifying all of this was to a group of suburban desert kids, Reggie arrived at some general dos and don'ts about farming alfalfa. Starting out, for instance, make sure your pH is over six and a half. Keep an eye out for armyworms and weevils and—if you've got horses—blister beetles. They'll come for the alfalfa and stay for the hay.

The other bit of advice he offered at the end of every meeting: Cultivate a large family. I always thought he was talking shop here, too: children as indentured workers. But he meant otherwise. I learned later that he and his wife, Allison, never had children, and he didn't realize until she'd passed what a mistake that was.

In May, Reggie told the administrators he could no longer make the trip to the school. Instead, he asked that they send the students to his farm. He blamed his health, though my guess is he just didn't want to drive across town anymore, having reached the time in his life when he relied on a consistency in scenery.

Despite knowing that most of the Future Farmers had chosen not to take part in the field trip, Reggie might have imagined a cavalcade of school buses wobbling in the heat off the paved road from town. As soon as he saw the lone purple minivan heading his way, however, he set aside his fantasy. He waved his cowboy hat to let us know we'd come to the right place, even though he knew the driver didn't need any help.

I was one of five students—three boys and two girls—to scoot out the back of the van, followed by the driver, a bald man with a neatly trimmed red mustache. Reggie recognized him not only as Mr. Peterson, the parental advisor of our club, but also as his brother-in-law, Keith.

By now, Reggie had put back on his hat, which he tipped, and said, "Welcome, boys, girls. Keith."

"Hey there, Reggie." Mr. Peterson—Keith—reached out and pumped his hand.

After a moment, Reggie wiped his palms against his sand-blasted jeans and said, "All right, then. Let's start the tour."

He lived in a two-bedroom house on a small alfalfa farm east of town, not far from the golf course I used to sneak onto a few years earlier. We all expected cows and pigs, but all he had were three acres of alfalfa, a horse, and six chickens in a coop along the northern edge. The farm was more for personal use than business, although he did make some money off the hay and never had to pay for eggs. The horse, Genie, had been his wife's. Reggie, he told us plainly, had never learned to ride.

Throughout the tour, the other two boys kept clearing their

throats intermittently, trading secret, profane messages in their coughs. I tried to make severe eye contact with Reggie, nodding up a sweat, in order to make amends for their attitude. One of the girls ended up doing what I didn't have the courage to do myself: She confronted them. In her blond hair she wore a red headband, which brought out the pimple on her chin. I'd seen her on campus before—her name was Jackie Connolly, and her family ran a farm themselves on the other side of town—but I had never heard her speak until now.

"This trip is voluntary," Jackie Connolly said. "No one forced you to be here."

Although I appreciated her for scolding the boys, I found myself resenting her strict advocacy of the rules as if I were among the scolded. I understood her eagerness for the opportunity to reprimand the boys as a kind of disrespect toward the farm itself; only someone absolutely bored with an experience would use that fleeting time making sure others weren't squandering it. I trusted Reggie felt the same.

The other girl in the group was Mr. Peterson's—Keith's—daughter, Charitye. It took me a moment to do the familial math and realize Charitye Peterson was Reggie's niece. Through this new lens I watched her on the farm. At school, in her stylishly unstylish denim jackets and bloodred lipstick, she'd always seemed out of place—tall and stoic and urban like a beautiful door at the top of a New York City stoop. Everywhere she went, she carried a green spiral notepad, which complemented her long orange hair. She was a year ahead of me, a junior, but she still had the two-dimensional body of a boy—a fact that reminded me she was a swimmer. I watched Reggie ignore the bickering boys and the pimpled Jackie Connolly, studying Charitye, some distance from the rest of us, kneeling at the alfalfa. She wedged her pen between her thumb and palm so she could feel the leaves with her fingertips. Then she wrote in her notepad and stood, skinny and nearly as tall as Reggie in his boots, and faced the San Gabriel Mountains to the south like a statue engraved, *WOMANHOOD.*

Reggie returned to the finer points of fertilization, though I suspected his mind was elsewhere. Later I found out—though I might've known by the awkward handshake earlier and the way Reggie seemed unwilling to let Mr. Peterson out of his sight—that he was remembering the vague plan his brother-in-law had relayed to him over the phone earlier that day: *The wife and I could use some time alone.* Mr. Peterson had asked Reggie if it would be all right for Charitye to spend some time—a few days, maybe—at the farm.

Reggie's wife, Allison, had died two years earlier—and so for two years, Reggie had been listening at night for the wind rattling the chains of the realty signs flanking his property. Sure, he told his brother-in-law. He could use an extra pair of hands.

At sunset, while we followed Mr. Peterson to the van at the edge of the road, Reggie pointed to the sky and told us the clouds at this time of day always reminded him of peeled tangerines. We boys and Jackie Connolly fought our way into the backseats of the van. Mr. Peterson unloaded a single large duffel and hugged Charitye, the only one of us to stay. Again the two men shook hands, and Mr. Peterson said to his brother-in-law: "I don't mean to repeat myself, but please make sure she's careful around that horse." To which, Reggie smiled his cowboy's smile and said, "We'll be extra, extra careful." Then we were off, and the dust behind the diminishing van rolled east with the light but influential wind. As Mr. Peterson's van carried us away, I watched Charitye shrink in my window, scribbling in her notepad, craning her neck to the page, straining her eyes against the twilight.

In the van, Mr. Peterson said, "Kind of a kook, huh?" And when the boys laughed and the pimple on Jackie Connolly seemingly doubled in size as she chided them, I felt a deep, strange respect for Reggie, and a longing to have known him better.

So although I couldn't see them any longer, couldn't even see the farm—we were well on our way back to town—I imagined Reggie, a man who had always respected a person's right to privacy, ask as gently as he could what Charitye was straining so hard to write in that notepad of hers.

"Lines," she said, "for a poem."

"Ah," Reggie said, more a breath than language. "A poet. I once wanted to be a poet."

"I figured," she said, "what with the clouds and the tangerines."

Reggie expected her to ask what had changed. He wanted, stupidly, to tell her that farming was a kind of poetry you got to do with your hands. He even had a little joke lined up about the two professions, how steeped they both were in anachronism. But by the time they made it back inside the house for dinner, the thread of the conversation had already been lost.

Since boyhood, Reggie had always appeared more confident than he actually was—lifting his chin when he spoke, projecting his voice, exerting little energy and displaying little patience with those who could not keep up—and for this reason, many of us Future Farmers believed he was born and raised on that little alfalfa farm of his. Sometimes, late at night, when he looked out at the silhouettes of Joshua trees dancing black against the deep blue between the stars, he bought into that story himself.

The truth was his father-in-law had owned the farm, and Reggie didn't move out there from town until he and Allison had been married for sixteen years, when her mother died and it became clear the old man was soon to follow. Allison and her kid brother, Keith, fought about selling the land to the proprietor of the nearby golf course, a man named Knickerbocker, who wanted to build a new driving range on the property. Keith argued for the money—at the time, his daughter, Charitye, was an infant, and the money wouldn't have been useless. Allison must have said something about keeping the farm *in the family,* because Keith, lifting his daughter in his arms as if she were a smoking gun, said, "I'm the only one *with* a family, Allie."

Which is when Allison Nelms reportedly removed her wedding ring—she was a lefty—and punched her brother clear across the nose.

At dawn on Charitye's first morning at the farm, Reggie expected a fight to get her out of bed. He slipped into his jeans and boots, snapped the buttons on his shirt, and clacked along the hardwood hallway to the spare bedroom she'd sidled into after dinner the night before.

After four increasingly loud knocks, he let himself in. Both the twin-sized beds (as kids, Allison and Keith had shared the room) were made. The large black duffel—unpacked and deflated—lay folded in the corner, the only visible evidence that Charitye Peterson had visited at all.

Reggie left the house to find his niece knee-deep in the alfalfa field. Again she was scribbling in her notepad.

"Surprised you're up so early," he said. "Took me a few months to get used to waking up with the sun."

"Sleep's not my thing," Charitye said, not looking up from the paper.

From the coop, the chickens clucked.

"I'm also surprised you're out here," he said, "as opposed to feeding the horse. Your dad told me I'd have to work my ass off to keep you away from her."

At this she looked up. "Same horse that killed her, isn't it?"

To that, Reggie didn't say a word, just hummed an affirming hum.

"I prefer plants anyway," she said, returning to her notes. "Smell nicer."

"That what your poems are about? Plants and flowers?"

"Poems aren't about anything," she said. "They *are* things."

"I see. What kind of *things,* then, do you write?"

She exhaled into her own mouth, making little zeppelins of her lips. "I'd rather you just read one and decide for yourself. At the end of my time here, I'll leave a poem on your kitchen table. How's that?"

"Poetic," Reggie said. "I'll look forward to it. In the meantime, why don't you follow me to the chickens. They sound hungry."

"A few more minutes."

"I think you'd be remiss not to come along now."

Charitye laughed, irritated. "Those chickens can wait a few more minutes, can't they?"

"I'm sure they can," Reggie said. "But you'll want to cover your notepad, at least."

"What do you mean?"

"I mean—"

The sprinklers sputtered to life. Charitye, shrieking, slid her notepad under her shirt and hopscotched her way out of the alfalfa.

She tilted her head to twist water out of her hair, a deeper red now that it was wet. "Well played," she said, fighting back a smile. "Well played."

———

Reggie had to drive Charitye to class and back four times before the school year officially ended, at which point, he taught Charitye how to bale hay. "Might as well learn something while you're out here," he said, helping her into the tractor.

"With alfalfa," he explained, "it's all about the leaves. Two-thirds of the plant's protein and three-quarters of its digestible nutrients are in the leaves, and when you're selling alfalfa hay to feedstores, that's what they're paying for. No leaves, no cash. Not even for a pretty, teenaged, redheaded poet, okay?"

He showed her where he parked the equipment: mower, tractor, swather, baler. "Once the plant's mowed, you attach the swather to the tractor, which you drive—carefully, carefully—dragging the swather behind, until half the cut alfalfa is arranged in neat windrows."

"Halfalfa," she said when they got back on solid ground.

"What?"

"Half the alfalfa, halfalfa, is arranged in cornrows."

"Whatever helps you remember it," said Reggie. "But it's *wind*rows, not *corn*rows. Like 'windows,' but with an *r*."

"We ready to bale, or what?" she asked. "Should I attach the baler?"

"Not yet. You bale the day *after* you windrow."

The next day, they dragged the baler by the tractor, producing small rectangular cubes of hay. The heat that afternoon must have been in the three digits. Sweating and desperate for shade, they stacked the bales near the stable.

"Keep enough here for Genie," Reggie instructed. "The rest will go to the feedstore."

Charitye asked how much a bale of hay gets you nowadays.

"About six dollars apiece."

She wiped at her forehead, burnt pink and shining in sweat and sunlight.

"Allison's got some old hats in the house," Reggie said. He suggested she wear one with a large brim, like his. For the sun.

"Thanks," Charitye said, "will do." But first she loaded the last of the bales onto its stack with a grunt and offered her own advice: "You know what you ought to do?"

"What's that?"

"Invest in a swimming pool."

During the years Reggie and Allison lived on the farm, Keith asked on a number of occasions if his daughter could visit. Allison never said yes.

"Why should I?" she'd ask Reggie in bed at night. "Keith was the one willing to give this place up, and now he wants to use it as a day-care service?"

One night, Reggie decided to risk an argument. He said, "Forget about Keith for a minute. Think of the girl. She'd love it out here. She'd love Genie. You could show her how to ride."

"That's just what he wants," Allison said. "He'd train her to fall off the horse. Get hurt on purpose so he can sue us for the money he's wanted from the start."

"You really believe that?"

"You don't know him like I do, Reggie." She felt the need to provide an example. "Growing up," she said, "he used to call me Frecklestein. Like Frankenstein, only uglier."

Reggie waited for a *there's more* that never came. "That's it?"

Allison remembered the farmer next door—long dead now, house demolished, land for sale—how he'd asked her over the fence line to tighten a small screw in one of his sprinkler heads. He needed her tiny fingers for the job. While she worked at the screw, he slipped his hand up her shorts. His fingers were as cold and wet from the sprinklers as a slice of bologna. There was her brother, eleven or twelve years old, watching from the safety of the alfalfa field. Why hadn't Keith helped? Well, he was a child, she supposed. Still, she never trusted her brother after that—maybe she never loved him after that, either—and she'd never told her husband, or anyone else, the reason why.

"Yeah," she said. "That's it. You calling me petty?"

"Forget the horse ride," Reggie said. "Wouldn't it be nice to have a young person out here for a change? Someone seeing the place for the first time?"

"Everything children see, they see for the first time."

"But we're talking about family," said Reggie.

"You're my family," she said, and kissed him on the forehead. "You, and no one else."

In the second week of her stay at the farm, Charitye drove her uncle's truck into a ditch. She'd asked for a driving lesson—her dad had only taught her on an automatic—so Reggie took her out in the red Ford to an unpaved but leveled section of the desert, where he'd seen kids with dirt bikes and paintball guns spend their weekends. This early in the morning, no one was around except for the wind, which, despite the time of day, was already going strong. Still, the sand under the tires was packed tight enough so that, if she timed the clutch right, they wouldn't go skidding into a sandbank. Unfortunately, her timing was off.

She'd left the engine running and was standing in her straw hat—Allison's—over Reggie at the front of the truck, where he'd kneeled to inspect the buried front wheels. "God, I'm really sorry," she said, genuinely embarrassed.

"Hand me a plank out of the bed," he said, reaching out for it prematurely, the way Charitye had seen doctors do in hospital dramas.

After she'd handed him the plank, Reggie wedged it behind the front right tire—the one more deeply embedded—and told her to stand clear as he backed the truck out.

"Wait," she said. "I got it stuck, so let me back it out. Please?"

A gust of wind nearly knocked Reggie off-balance. The straw hat on Charitye's head went tumbling into the bank. She chased the hat down and, when she caught it, pressed it to her head. Sheets of sand slapped their faces. Reggie tongued granule after granule in his teeth. "Okay," he said. "Give it a try."

Charitye looped around the truck and stepped in behind the wheel.

When she'd backed the truck out far enough, Reggie heard her crank the gear into neutral, as he'd shown her. She leaned over the seat to punch open the passenger-side door.

Tipping her hat, she said something Reggie couldn't make out over the noise of the wind and the engine.

"What's that?"

"I *said*," she said, "Need a lift, cowboy?"

In the afternoon, Keith called.

"Yeah," Charitye said into the phone. She spun in place, wrapping herself with the helix of the cord, and then spun the other way to unleash herself. "It's fun," she said. "We're having fun. I'm getting a lot done. I've learned a lot."

Reggie tried not to eavesdrop. He sat down at the table near the window and looked out at the sun damage growing white across his truck's red paint like a beard. I'll have to get a new truck soon, he figured to himself, if I plan to drive into town for groceries or to lecture the Future Farmers at the high school for much longer. The truth was he didn't want to leave the farm ever again, for any reason. He could get some livestock, he thought, plant new crops for food—he could learn how to self-sustain. The Future Farmers could meet here if they really wanted to learn about farming, which he doubted more and more every session. If he stayed put at the farm, he could give his truck to Charitye. He enjoyed the pun, inscribing it to his memory for when he'd make a speech at her next birthday party or at her graduation ceremony. He'd be welcomed into the family's celebration, having wrapped one of those giant bows around the truck. Someone might click a knife against a glass: Uncle Reggie wants to say something! Then he'd stand up and tell the story of how he first came up with the idea: *You know, originally, I planned on giving this truck over to charity. . . .*

The sound of the phone meeting its cradle broke his line of thinking.

"How're your parents?" he asked from the window.

"Sounds doomed," Charitye said. "I think they're getting divorced."

"Sorry to hear that."

"Maybe it's the best thing for my poems," she said, joining him at the table.

"That's one way to think about it."

"I know," she said. "I'm trying too hard to *seem* like a poet to actually *be* a poet."

"Sometimes," Reggie said, "you've got to act the role before you can reach the goal."

"I've been doing that with swimming," she said. "Getting pretty good, too. My mom's been making fun of me, though, so we'll see if I stick with it."

"What'd she say?"

"Said, '*Sweetheart,* you'll *never* grow breasts.'" She impersonated her mother in a vaguely European voice, laughing in a way, and then: "I've been meaning to ask you, Reggie. How come you never had kids?"

"Oh," Reggie said, drawing it out like a sigh. "The short version of that story is your aunt didn't want them. And I hope I'm not spoiling the surprise by telling you it takes two."

"What about adopting? I mean, now? I mean, after she passed?"

"They don't look at farmers as foster parents so much as employers."

"That's sad," Charitye said. "You're acting the role well. Of a dad, I mean."

For a moment, Reggie let himself feel pride, the steam of it, before cooling. "You know, I've got the kids at your high school. I get it out of my system with them."

"You deserve better."

He let out a little laugh. "They do act up a bit, don't they? Especially when I mention the aqueduct. What's so funny about the aqueduct?"

"Well," Charitye said, "for one thing, it's the closest thing we've got to an adventure out here. The river's man-made, obviously, but there's fish, so there's fishing. People spread out on the cement slopes so they can tan. A lot of couples go out there to do, as you've said, whatever they can with each other that they can't do by themselves. And then, there are the swimmers."

"That current's pretty strong, though."

"That's the point. It's a dare. If you can swim from one side to the other without getting dragged to Long Beach, you win."

"What do you win?"

"The prize of not dying."

"See," Reggie said, "a benefit of not being a parent: I never have to worry about my kid doing something so stupid."

"I've always wanted to try it."

"Don't, please."

"I bet I could," she said. "I don't know if I've mentioned how I am a prih-tee good swimmer."

Again the phone rang.

"Hold that stupid thought," Reggie told her, leaving to answer the phone. For the second time that afternoon, it was Keith.

Charitye took the phone. After a minute, she put her hand against the receiver so her dad couldn't hear her. "Apparently, he's coming to pick me up now," she told Reggie.

Reggie felt a brief but unshareable disappointment, like being alone the one time you see a UFO zigzag between the clouds. Before Charitye arrived, he'd just gotten used to living alone, and now he was just getting used to having someone else around. For how many people, he wondered, was life only a succession of moments you were just getting used to?

"Keith," he said, having taken the phone from Charitye.

"Sorry," Keith said, "for the sudden change of plans. Lucy's decided to leave for a few weeks in the morning. She's come around to the popular opinion of women everywhere of hating me. She wants Charitye home tonight so they can leave together first thing."

"Hate to hear you couldn't work it out."

"Tell him I still have work to do here," Charitye said from her tiptoes, loud enough for her dad to hear.

"Look," said Reggie, "the girl wants to stick around for a bit longer. She's getting some poetry written out here, is the thing."

"I respect the arts, Reggie, I do. But she can jot down her feelings anywhere, so poetry's not the best excuse you could've come up with. Anyway, Lucy's got this plan—"

"What about one more night?" Reggie said. "Her mother can pick her up first thing in the morning, no hitch in the plan."

Charitye nodded approvingly.

From Keith: "Hold."

"Reggie?" A woman's vaguely European voice.

"Hi, Lucy."

"She can spend the night so long as you promise me she'll be packed and waiting for me outside at seven in the morning. If I have to so much as honk, I'll crash my car into your house and drag her out of the wreckage."

"Okay, Lucy, thank you."

"Oh, and Reggie?"

"Yeah?"

"Do I have to tell you again to keep her away from that horse?"

Reggie lived far enough from what we call society to feel sorry for himself with neither shame nor showmanship. His thoughts on the matter were: If the only person you love gets a fatal kick in the head from a horse, you've got that right. Feeling sorry for yourself is a problem only if you do it around other people who don't feel sorry for *you* (as you intended), but start feeling sorry *for themselves*. It turns out self-pity *is* contagious, but not in the way you want it to be.

For this reason, Reggie preferred to feel sorry for himself in the privacy of his own bedroom. On Charitye's last night, he stayed awake in bed, staring up at the stray hairs in his eyebrows, remembering Allison. This was an insomniac pastime he'd grown to resent and rely on.

One thing he resented: the beginning, the time spent waiting behind her in the small (God, how short the lines used to be in the Antelope Valley!) registrar's line at the community college. Allison kept turning around, this sunburned and goofy farm-girl-turned-student. Certain freckles on her face were illuminated by the holes in her straw hat. Nineteen eighty, and he was wearing a Reagan button on his denim jacket. Allison said, "Reagan, huh? Plays a cowboy on TV, but he's too goddamn slick to be good for farmers." She reached out and unfolded the list Reggie had been carrying at his chest so she could see which classes he was signing up for. Skeptically, she said, "Beginning Poetry. Next semester you'll take the course on finishing a poem, that how it works?" Reggie started to correct her, but Allison interrupted. "A joke," she said. "I know you Republicans ain't heard many, but they're called jokes." Later, over coffee, she described her father's farm, and Reggie asked her to repeat the word "weevils" a hundred times—"Way-vulls, way-vulls, what's so funny about way-vulls?"

He was resentful, too, of the end. He'd found her in the stable, her eyes open and crossed like a child's funny-face. A surprising lack of blood (flooding, as it did, to the inside of her skull). The seat of her pants was covered in shit—he'd figured, wrongly, that she fell in horse dung. She'd gone to the hospital then, alive in no way but a technicality, until her body made the decision for everyone and just quit. When he returned home, Reggie thought of nothing so much as beating Genie to death with a shovel. He must have held the spade so tight, it bruised the back of his hands. How long did he look that animal square in its enormous, intelligent eyes before telling it—out loud, like he'd just realized—"You're a fucking horse." He resented the end because Allison's death brought with it a severe loneliness, a reminder of his own impending death, of not having children in the world to sweeten the tasteless batter of mortality.

It occurred to Reggie that every time he thought he was remembering Allison, he was actually remembering the way she'd made him feel at different points in their entangled lives—that anytime we try to remember anyone we've loved, what we're really remembering is ourselves.

Of course, a man can think in this way for only so long before it becomes tedious. So Reggie willed himself out of bed. The sun wouldn't be up for another three hours or so. He felt his way along the dark hallway into the kitchen, where he opened the fridge, searching for juice. The light from inside the refrigerator hurt his eyes. To let them adjust, he turned away. That's when he saw the sheet of paper—frills along the left edge where it had been torn from the spiral notebook—on the kitchen table:

Uncle Reggie,

Here's that poem I promised. It's called "The Costs and Benefits of Desert Agriculture," and it's a draft so don't judge it too harshly.

> *Men built a river so that desert girls can finger*
> *the nutrient-heavy leaves of alfalfa*
> *in the summertime. Chickens clamor*
> *while horses eat six-dollar bales*
> *of hay. If men built the river so that water*
> *flows west, can the water change its mind*
> *and flow east? Can the desert girls swim*
> *against the current with nothing on*
> *but the lights of a carjacked pickup?*
> *Can the horse tiptoe into the widower's*
> *bedroom & whisper apologies before daylight?*

I know, I know. Ending a poem on a question. I had a bunch of lines about wearing Aunt Allison's hat at the end, but that seemed less poetic and more trying-to-be-poetic, you know? Thanks for letting me stay here, and for everything you've taught me. By the way, I'm borrowing your truck for a trip. It's time I took that dare. Love, your niece, and forever

Yours,
Charitye Peterson

Reggie ran to the spare bedroom to check if she was pulling a prank. She wasn't. He ran outside, and, sure enough, his truck was missing. Considering his options, he found a flashlight and made his way to the stable, out of breath. He mustered a hello to Genie. Careful not to stand behind her, he lugged Allison's old saddle over Genie's back and whispered into her ear: "I'm going to learn how to ride you tonight, okay?"

Atop the horse in his boots and hat, Reggie looked the part. But no matter how high he lifted his chin, the rest of his body's posture—crouched low to Genie, one shoulder higher than the other for some twisted sense of balance—proved how ridiculous a man he'd become. For miles and miles he rode, speaking in a low, cinematic voice into Genie's ear: "In the middle of the night, a man and his horse ride out of the farmland and into the suburbs, past the fast-food chains and used-car lots and community college, into the foothills above Avenue N, upward, upward to the aqueduct where he suspects to find and rescue his runaway niece." He laughed at himself. He said, "Genie, babe, we're almost there." Genie, out of shape from years of disuse, spat her breaths. They'd been riding for an hour, maybe more; the sun was getting ready to rise. Charitye's poem was the poem of a teenager, Reggie thought, but he knew it was better than anything he'd ever written. He especially enjoyed those last lines: "Can the horse tiptoe into the widower's / bedroom & whisper apologies before daylight?" He enjoyed imagining what else Genie might whisper to him in the nighttime. Maybe she'd have a toothpick-in-the-mouth drawl, and whisper: "Let's go someplace new, cowboy. That girl ain't gonna be up there at that old waterin' hole. I reckon she's long gone by now, way out past these parts. It'll just be you and me and the aqueduct. What are you planning, Reggie? You aim to kill us tonight? Walk me right into the river? You know the sayin' about leadin' a horse to water. Hey, why don't we drop this nonsense and go someplace new? Because all I know is, that young girl's mother's gonna be knockin' at your door pretty soon here, Reggie. How 'bout let's not be there when she gets there. How about it, huh? Promise me. Let's be anywhere but there."

Wherever Reggie went, I never saw him again. Charitye I sought out recently. She's a server at the Bunker Burger off Knickerbocker's golf course, and during her break, we spoke for a little while. About five years ago, she said, they expanded their driving range. Lushest Bermuda grass in town.

HOW TO REVISE A PLAY

—————— ✦ ——————

First, attend one. After all, if you're not willing to spend the sixteen dollars to see, for example, a modern, gay, Spanish adaptation of *Romeo and Juliet* titled *Ramón y Julio,* how can you expect anyone to see yours? If the production you've chosen to attend is in, say, your hometown, some 350 miles south of your San Francisco apartment, rent a car. Take the weekend. Remind yourself that this is why, as a blogger, you've sacrificed workplace companionship and a consistent reason to dress yourself in the morning—this mobility.

Take more than the weekend. Take your boyfriend, Lloyd. Understand that the five hours on the road might be tense. Lloyd, despite a tearful heart-to-heart between the romance shelves at Dog-Eared Books, still may not have totally forgiven you for not letting him meet your mother. Now it's too late. Understand that the only way to make up for this is to introduce Lloyd to your father, and that this is the real reason the two of you are going to the Antelope Valley. Lloyd knows this, too, of course, but neither of you should mention it. Instead, continue talking about the modern, gay,

Spanish adaptation of *Romeo and Juliet,* and tell yourself you've made a leap in maturity, that you feel so ready to share your family with another person that a conversation about bringing Lloyd home would merely seem self-congratulatory.

Make sure, however, to call your father to inform him that he'll have company. He's a Midwesterner by birth and doesn't enjoy surprises. When he, too, acts as though this—his only son bringing a man home for the first time—is not a big deal, continue to play along. One way to do so is to replace the word "you" with the word "ya," as in, "Love ya, see ya soon." Hang up the phone and chat incessantly with Lloyd about your hometown. Explain how surprising and uplifting you find it to have a modern, gay, et cetera, et cetera being staged in the conservative desert death-hole you so desperately attempted all your life to escape.

Drive. Allow Lloyd, whose laptop contains thirteen hundred pages of a novel about whaling, to be the poet. Let him call the I-5 "the yellow spine of California." Let him describe the Joshua trees in the desert as dancers striking poses or deformed hands or barnacles—barnacles bunching from the smooth hull of a ship. When you're this close to home, it's vital you focus on the concrete—literally, almost—on, for example, watching for potholes and observing traffic signals. At a red light beside CAMACHO'S AUTO SALES, ignore the tiny triangular flags beating against one another in the wind. Keep your eyes on the light. When it turns green, feel the wind's hold under the car and hear Lloyd say it feels as though you're in an enormous, swirling glass of wine.

Turn right onto Comstock Avenue. Your destination is on the left. When Lloyd jokingly asks how you can tell your house apart from all the other nearly identical tract homes on the block, point to the only palm trees in town, which a neighbor had transplanted from Los Angeles, and say, "Mine's the one across from Hollywood Boulevard."

Recognize the bent old man examining a sprinkler head in your summer-dried front lawn: that's your father. Pull the rental into the driveway alongside your mother's burgundy Corolla, which, judging by the white splotches of oxidation, hasn't been moved since she last parked it there. Do the math—almost a year. Before opening the car doors, answer Lloyd's question. He's had five hours on the road but waits until now to ask what he should call your father. Tell him Ed will be fine. Make that Edward.

When your father hugs you, remember the funeral at Forest Lawn. Your mother's brother Gaspar paid for the coffin, the flowers, the space, and the alcohol. You and your father were the only men in cheap suits, and the hug between you—jackets lifted and bunched—was awkward. Afterwards you slalomed between your Armani-clad extended family to the gold-fauceted, marble-floored, ridiculous bathroom and sobbed. "You okay?" asked the towel-dispensing attendant, a Filipino man your father's age you pretended not to see. "How about these Middle Easterns," he said, trying to lighten the mood. Other than your long eyelashes, you look nothing like your mother, and this wasn't the first time someone talked about Armenians as if you weren't one of them. The attendant must have mistaken you for a member of the waitstaff, frustrated after dropping a tray of wineglasses. When you asked what he meant, he said, "That's a lot of money to spend on the dead, no?" He passed you a hand towel, thick and soft and slippery, like a cashmere sweater. On the way out, to demonstrate that you hadn't been affected, you tipped the attendant a dollar. As you hug your father now, allow yourself to feel angry at that man, for making that one dollar what you think of when you think of your mother's funeral.

Get over it—you have work to do. Introduce your father to Lloyd, and take a look at them as they shake hands to see what kind of first impressions they make. Your father is in his early sixties, hair the blond-gray of mummies. Otherwise, he looks healthy: he's lost weight, and he's wearing a new (creases still intact) polo shirt tucked into slacks. As for Lloyd, you'd convinced him to shave his green-dyed goatee and to discard his usual "à la David Foster Wallace" bandanna, but the rest was his choice—tight white jeans tucked into '90s-style high-tops; a forest green deep-V; a decorative, light-weight navy scarf sporting white polka dots in the shape of terriers. The pale skin on his face is purple in the two spots where the sun comes through his tinted glasses. You hate those glasses. Hold your applause when he removes them. As he introduces himself, notice his lisp—"Greetingss, Misster Kushner"—for the first time in years.

Examine your father's tone as he compliments Lloyd's terrier scarf.

Follow the men into your childhood home. The living room is decorated almost exclusively with porcelain angels, the one exception to your mother's hatred of the gaudy. Female angels in ballet poses, baby angels lifting children over a fallen bridge, male angels farming wheat—from the glass-encased shelves of curio cabinets, from the white-flecked bricks of the mantel, and from the sills of windows narrow and wide, the multitudes sing.

On the coffee table sit three plastic bottles of water and a bowl of pizza-flavored Chex Mix, the extent of your father's efforts as host. Your mother would've sliced and salted cucumbers, tomatoes, and cheese. Flat, skinlike bread would splay in the belly of a wicker basket. Mention, in a light mood, your father's relative ineptitude, and listen as your father agrees that yes, your mother was better than he, in more ways than this.

When Lloyd says the scene reminds him of a novel called *The Left-Handed Woman,* try to change the subject immediately. Your father is in the business of selling furniture. He does not want to talk about literature. Still, try to remember why you're here. Have compassion. Take a seat with Lloyd on the floral couch you once wet as a child, and listen.

Watch Lloyd scoot forward on the cushion. "Well," he says, "it's about a couple—a hetero couple—and the woman, you guessed it, is left-handed. When she leaves, the man has to go to his cupboard and turn all the mugs so that the handles are on the right side. Isn't that something?"

Now you're depressed, but your father, having fallen into his favorite recliner, calls the image "lovely." Conceal your confusion. Avoid asking aloud why this trip is going so smoothly.

Brace yourself when your father asks Lloyd about his novel, which you neglected to notice Lloyd mention just a moment ago, while you were busy concealing your confusion and avoiding et cetera, et cetera.

Watch Lloyd scoot even farther forward on the couch, so that the cushion comes up at a forty-five-degree angle behind him. As you listen to him talk, imagine the world of his novel entering the living room—Ottoman whalers, Argentine pirates, a Dixieland jazz band lost at sea after a New Orleans flood (working title: *Moby Dixie*). See these figments rush into the living room alongside the chorus of angels presiding over the father, the son, and the ridiculous boyfriend.

When your father responds by praising "the mind of a real writer," resist the urge to defend blogging. Instead, offer an inquisitive smile as Lloyd asks your father if he's ever done some writing of his own.

You're surprised to hear he has. He understands the two of you are out this way to see a play. Well, a million years ago, when he was a member of his high school drama club in Dearborn, Michigan, he happened to write a few plays himself, believe it or not. Choose not to believe it, and then doubt your doubt as he goes on to say he probably has an old typewritten script stashed in a box somewhere in the garage.

Smile, smile, smile while Lloyd suggests the three of you spend the remaining daylight digging for the manuscript. Keep to yourself not only your skepticism regarding the prospects of finding the play but also your questions regarding what will be done with the play if it were, by some miracle, to be found.

Go along with the plan. Watch Lloyd open the garage door while you back the rental car out of the driveway into the street, making room for your father to back his car out of the garage. Join Lloyd there. Take note of how utterly full of boxes the garage has become, how the only free space is in the shape of your father's car. Realize this is because your mother's stuff has been added.

While your dad is in his car in the driveway, ask Lloyd quickly if he's sure this is a good idea. And when Lloyd says looking for the play would make your father "probably happier than he's been in a long while, Daley," kiss him on the cheek. Think of the only time you met his parents, two years ago. You met at an expensive vegetarian restaurant in San Francisco. They were visiting from Denver, and Lloyd, an only child, called them by their first names. Remember the stilted conversation you had with Rayne, a ballet instructor, and Lloyd Senior, a lawyer. You knew they were paying Lloyd's share of the rent, and this knowledge made you a bitter and unpleasant dinner guest. At the time, you didn't feel as though you could be honest with your parents about your relationship with men. Your mother's reaction, especially, concerned you. She was an immigrant, a devout Christian, and you feared her as much as you loved her, which is to say, as much as you've felt anything before or since. At dinner that night, you saw Lloyd's friendliness with his parents, and you wondered enviously if money, the flow of it, served as some sort of conduit for their ease, and whether you might've been more honest with *your* parents if only there had been money—like a string between paper cups—keeping you tethered.

Return to the boxes. Begin unboxing. The three of you together can rummage through nine stacks of boxes per hour. No need to search through the top boxes—these are your mother's things. Remind yourself that there is nothing for you to do with her clothes, her records, her wigs.

Drag the boxes you've already checked out to the driveway. When passersby slow down, anticipating a sale, wave them pleasantly along.

Find a strange box of clear liquor, and, because you've never known your father to be a drinker, ask about it. When he explains he'd been gifted the alcohol from your uncle Gaspar, examine the bottles more closely. Recognize the Armenian label. This is arak, a clear, absinthelike liquor. With water, the arak takes on a murky white color. Remember what Uncle Gaspar, at wedding receptions and engagement parties, always called it: *aratzi gat,* "lion's milk."

During the third hour, when Lloyd proclaims he's found the play, allow yourself a moment of genuine, surprising joy. Your father wants to fact-check the discovery, and when he does, be sure to give each of your hunting partners a dusty high five.

Go inside. Bring along one of the bottles of arak, uncap it, and select three glasses. Find Lloyd and your father sitting in the backyard at the patio table near the swimming pool. Make a note to mention to Lloyd how pools in the desert don't mean wealth, and often, because of maintenance, can actually lower a house's value. Watch the sun set behind the tops of houses. A bright motion-sensor bulb gives enough light to read by, provided someone waves an arm every now and again. Lloyd has spread the manuscript across the patio table, using rocks as paperweights on each sheet. Glance at the title page: *Snow Easy Way to Say It.* Giggle. Hand out the glasses of lion's milk, and make a small toast: To Dad, the Shakespeare of Dearborn, Michigan. Touch glasses.

Leave them to work on the play, and find canned soup and sandwich fixings for dinner. Make another note: to go grocery shopping before heading back to San Francisco.

Leave the patio door open as you slap mayonnaise onto six slices of Wonder Bread at the counter, and listen to them talk. Your father says his protagonist has just enlisted in the navy, which is why he's in such a rush to see Geraldine. Lloyd says the snow itself can't be the only obstacle between them. Maybe the bus is late because of the weather, and he's waiting there at the stop, freezing to death, debating whether or not to go on foot. Note that your father likes this idea—hear the pencil scratches. Lloyd wants to know what Geraldine wants. Other than Teddy, the protagonist, your father doesn't have an answer. Lloyd says Geraldine needs to want something other than Teddy. Something concrete. Like, like a . . . car! A car, to pick Teddy up at the station, where he's waiting, freezing, et cetera, et cetera. Hear your father say that Geraldine wanting a car is "a definite maybe."

Bring them food, bring them drink. Of the latter, a little will go a long way: your dad wants the cup for any further toasts, but won't drink a sip of the arak. Remember to wave your arm periodically to keep the light on. When Lloyd excuses himself to use the restroom, wait a beat, and then ask your father how the revision is going. Nod along as he says the word "progress." Then he tells you, quickly, knowing Lloyd could return at any moment, that although he is happy to see you happy, et cetera, et cetera, he would still very much appreciate it if you and Lloyd would sleep in separate bedrooms. Cut him off to say "of course." Thank him again for his hospitality, but don't stop there. The lion's milk has kicked in, and you've summoned the courage to ask him a question.

"Why are you being so nice?"

"That unusual?" he says.

"No, but don't you think Mom would've disapproved? Don't you still want to be loyal to her?"

When Lloyd returns, he compliments the hand soap in the bathroom. "What'd I miss?"

Your father says, "I was just about to tell Daley about the first time I met his mom's family."

At that point, her family had been in the country for just over a year. The only person aside from your mother who spoke any English was her older brother Gaspar.

"Her father invited me over for a glass of arak," your father says. "I was never a drinker, but I agreed to the visit anyway, expecting the meeting was more important than the drinking. But when I got to the apartment, I saw twelve men—every man in the family, cousins and brothers and uncles—sitting in chairs arranged in a semicircle, with her father at the center. Everyone had a foggy glass of arak and a pack of cigarettes within reach, and the room was full of smoke. One empty chair sat facing the jury. Her father said something in Armenian, and Gaspar translated for me: 'Ed, have a seat.'"

Notice how Lloyd's jaw looks unhinged. He looks at you and says, "How have you not told me this story before?"

You've never heard this story. Say, "I've never heard this story."

"They passed me a glass of arak, and even though I had no intention of drinking, I held on to the glass, trying to keep my hand steady enough so that the ice didn't rattle. One by one, each of the men asked me a single question, with Gaspar translating. Most of the questions were easy: 'Are you a Christian?' 'What is your job?' 'Why do you love Lena?'"

Lloyd, beaming, says, "What was your answer to that?"

Your dad doesn't have to think: "The first time I met Lena, I forgot the name of every woman I'd ever known. Hell, I barely remembered my own name. I knew—I swear, I *knew*—hers was the only name I needed to know from then on."

Lloyd grabs at his heart.

"And then came the final question," your dad says. "Her father was a tailor, and until he was in the hospital at the end, I never saw him out of a suit. At that point, I'd never even seen him wear a smile, let alone a T-shirt. He sipped his drink seriously, took a thoughtful drag from his cigarette, and asked his question. I looked to Gaspar for the translation."

The light switches off. You've forgotten to wave an arm. In the brief moment of darkness, remember the name of the first boy you loved, Robert Karinger. He used to take you to the desert and show you how to siphon water from plants. He'd pinch the prickled flesh of an ugly cactus at just the right spot, and you'd kneel to catch the stream in your mouth like a wanderer in the holy land.

Lloyd waves his arm, and the light returns. "Her dad was asking you the final question," he says.

"Right. And Gaspar translated. Only it wasn't a question. Her father had given me an instruction: 'Drink the arak.' I explained to Gaspar that I didn't drink. I'd made a vow, because my father had been a drunk, and I didn't want to be anything like him. Gaspar listened to me and slowly relayed my message. And then her father stood up and shook my hand. Gaspar said the old man respected me for my convictions. I had his approval."

"Bravo!" Lloyd says, for both young Ed's victory and for old Ed's telling of the story.

So your father had to pass a test to join the family, and he's being nice because he doesn't want to put Lloyd through the same wringer. Why does this make you feel uncomfortable? Call it an early night, and stand up from the table. Brush your teeth, and head to your childhood bedroom, which, aside from a new futon your father probably brought home wholesale from the furniture store, looks and feels eerily well preserved from your high school days. Glide your fingers along the glossy surface of the poster of John Lennon. Scan the colorful spines of the Goosebumps novels and volumes of *Encyclopædia Britannica* lining your old desk's oak shelves. Pick up the baseball signed by Mike Piazza and Eric Karros. Karinger always envied you over that baseball, and you would've given it to him if he'd asked. He was the only person who could teach you—a boy obsessed with escaping—to love the desert. He was the only person who'd taken you past the tall fences of the driving range to hunt for golf balls, the only person who'd convinced you to brave the aqueduct's currents and risk your life only to prove you could.

A long time ago, that boy rapped his fingernails against this window. You were sixteen, and you opened it. Maybe you hoped he'd shake the world that night by coming into your bedroom and touching you. Instead, he told you that Dan Watts, licensed driver as of noon that day, was parked in his dad's pickup at the end of the block, waiting for you to join them on their way to a strip club in Los Angeles. You hesitated—you'd never sneaked out before. You were nervous to break the rules, even though your sister, the only person who would've heard your window slide open, had already moved away for college. You were nervous, too, about your ability to mask your apathy for naked women. Your friend promised to have you back soon, and so you climbed through the window thinking, you remember, of that Beatles song.

Later, after failing to convince security to let you into the club, you all three packed into the cab of the truck and drove back home—un-sexed, yes, and un-glittered—but exuberant still, aware for the first time of what you thought would always be true: that you could leave home, return to it, and nothing would be different except for you.

Now, when Lloyd pushes open the bedroom door and peeks in

on you, pretend to sleep. Wait until he steps inside, and then say no. He doesn't say anything, but comes closer. He bends down to kiss you. Smell the black licorice on his breath—lion's milk. When he asks why you don't want him, realize you don't know the answer yourself. Do not lie. Do not improvise. Simply wait for him to step back until he's out of the room and the door arcs slowly to a close.

In the morning, wake early and find, in the kitchen, a pot of coffee already brewed. Pour yourself a mug. At the counter, look out the window onto the backyard, and see your father and Lloyd at the edge of the pool, acting.

Join them outside and mumble a good morning. Your dad tells you to take a seat—they're at the climactic scene. Ask how late they stayed up the night before, and feign surprise when they say, in unison, they still haven't gone to bed. Listen to them recite lines they've spent all night revising.

"Love transcends language" is just another way to say love's a bad listener.

But can love be frozen and thawed? [TEDDY picks up a fistful of snow.] Like snow?

And all this time I've been standing out here, freezing half to death, my life was driving right at me in a 1969 Buick LeSabre.

Ignore that these fragments of dialogue fall short of great literature. Instead, choose to love them. Not the particular words, really, and definitely not their delivery, but the simple fact that they exist. Love that you can walk out onto your back patio and spot

the two most important men in your life building something together. Think, again, of your mother. Imagine her sitting next to
you at the edge of the pool, feet in the water. For the first time, admit to yourself that you thought less of her for being religious, superstitious, for having an accent. You were ashamed of her. Regret
that you were ashamed of her.

And know that clichés in English weren't clichés to her. Know
she would've been able to do gracefully what you're working so hard
to do now: love.

Realize you're not capable. You may have been able to love Lloyd
in San Francisco, but you can't love him here. You can love only
one man in the Antelope Valley, and Robert Karinger is gone. He
always treated you like a little brother—someone to mock, someone to protect, someone to instruct. Bringing Lloyd home has
helped you see that you've been using him to fill that role. Decide
to break the pattern. Decide you don't need an instructor. In fact,
start instructing yourself, Daley. Instruct yourself.

Get Lloyd alone, away from your father and the script. Tell him
the truth: you need to stay home for a while. When he says he
doesn't understand, say nothing. Grief transcends language, too.

When your father comes into the living room to find you and
Lloyd crying quietly on the couch, let him do the talking. He's put
aside his discomfort and has treated Lloyd like a son. He's earned
this monologue.

"When Gaspar sent me that case of arak after your mom passed,
he attached a note. He said he'd been lying to me all these years.
Apparently, when I'd given that answer of mine about my father
and my vow never to drink, Gaspar knew I'd be doomed. How
could I handle a wife if I couldn't handle a single drink? So he im-
provised. He told his father and the rest of the men that I'd given
a speech about courage. About how I was already a brave man, and

that my children—his grandchildren—would grow to be the smart-est and strongest and bravest Armenians in the world, raised not on lion's milk but on Lena's milk."

He lets out a single laugh of nostalgia that moves all the air in your lungs up to your throat. This is the most your father has ever said to you without asking a question. Now that your mother is gone, he has become the verbose, explicit man you'd wanted so badly as a boy. Now you have taken on the role he'd played, the man who asks questions, the man whose job it is to listen.

"Your uncle Gaspar lied," he continues, "and that's the only reason I was allowed to marry your mother. You owe your entire life, son, to the greatest lie ever told. And I guess that's what my old play, or Lloyd's novel, or any kind of fiction is trying to be—a lie that lets love exist. But I was a kid when I wrote that damn thing, and as much fun as I've had revisiting it, the kind of love between your mom and me was beyond what a kid—even a sensitive, tuned-in kid like me, like you two—could've got down on paper. A lie might allow love, but it can't create it."

After a moment, Lloyd wipes his eyes with his terrier scarf and asks, half crying and half laughing, if he can take the case of arak back with him to San Francisco. Laugh-cry along with him. When you help him load his suitcase and the box of liquor into the rental, arrange to meet in a few days or a week. Once back together in the city, you will get to the work of love. For now, tell him you need some time at home with your dad, who shakes Lloyd's hand and tells him to drive safe in the same way he used to tell you: Stay above your tires.

At night, after Lloyd's gone, your father falls asleep in his favorite recliner. Remember the reason—the false one—you are here. You almost forgot, didn't you? Find your mother's old car keys hanging by a pink plastic lanyard by the door, and take them into your bedroom. Take care to be quiet. Slowly, slide open the bedroom window and, as you did a million years ago, heave yourself through.

Feel the warm night cup your elbows and pad the back of your neck. Get into your mother's old Corolla, and count it as a blessing to hear the engine start on the first try. Before you know if your father's heard you, take off.

By the time you make it to the play, they're in the third act. Ramón and Julio have just awoken. They argue about what type of bird is outside their window. Be sure to look around to count a surprising number of people. Many seats are still open, but many—more than you'd have guessed—are filled. Understand maybe a quarter of what is said onstage, and piece together the rest. Most of the play you remember from high school, when star-crossed love felt not only real but inevitable, too. Stop thinking so much and listen to the actor playing Ramón as he says something about wanting to stay in bed with Julio. He doesn't care if the guards barge in. *"Ven, muerte, y bienvenido,"* he says, preferring death to leaving. Fool, you think. You will leave *and* you will die. There is no choice to be made.

SHELTER

———————— ✤ ————————

We each carried a plastic grocery bag and a club. Karinger's was an old 3-wood—so old, it was actually made out of wood, except for a little metal plate across the top of the head that had the number *3* painted on it in red. Mine was an impossibly long 2-iron that had a face as flat as a ruler. Karinger said even pros couldn't use it right. Sometimes when the wind was low and if I got a ball that wasn't cracked or yellowed, I could hit it pretty well. Problem was, the only golf balls we found in the desert by the old course had been lost there for a while. Some looked so old, they seemed just as natural as the California junipers. Good white golf balls were so rare, Karinger made me feel bad for using them. "We can sell them," he'd say, but we never did.

We'd been ball-hunting out there for ten days straight. Karinger said he hadn't seen anyone on the old golf course in a year. He had the idea to collect balls and take them to the new golf course on the other side of town, where crowds swarmed and the grass was kept nice. With the balls we collected in the desert and the clubs Karinger's dad left behind, we could hit on the range there for free.

It was something to do. The walk was a slog, though, and some-times I'd pretend I didn't see balls in the tumbleweeds that I nor-mally would've gone for, just because my bag had already gotten so heavy. "I'll get them tomorrow," I'd tell myself, but it was always harder to find a ball I'd already found and let go.

One time, Karinger reached into a dry bush for a ball that was lodged in there. From about a hundred yards away I heard him scream, so I ran over. I was going to ask what happened, but I saw it myself. Craning over a sharp yellow bush, a rattlesnake sat up like they do in movies. Karinger said in a whisper he didn't get bit, but it was close. We got out of the way, just in case. Karinger took his 3-wood and nudged the snake until it hissed. "Let's leave it," I said, but Karinger didn't listen to me. He took a huge backswing and almost hit me in the face with his club. Next thing I knew, he was drumming the snake's head and body into the hard white dirt. I felt bad for the snake, but I hit it, too, once it stopped moving.

On the way home, Karinger straddled the yellow dashes of the empty highway. I walked in the dirt on the side of the road, using my club as a walking stick. Lizards raced before my feet, and once in a while I crushed a Pepsi can with my shoe or else knocked a plastic water bottle into the tumbleweeds with my 2-iron. The plas-tic bags, filled with old golf balls, hung from our wrists.

At one point, Karinger said, "You know we did more than kill a snake, right?" He kept moving forward, but now he looked right at me. "We'll never get credit for it. But in the future, we just saved somebody's life."

Before I met him, Karinger walked five miles home from school. Mom would pick me up, and every day on the drive back we'd see this chubby blond kid walking in the desert with a big backpack

and a huge T-shirt darkened with sweat around its collar. One day
after school, Mom drove me to a clothing store on another side of
town. There he was, still walking, slower now, an hour and a half
after school got out. Mom pulled the car over and told him we
would give him a ride. From then on, we drove him home after
school.

Of course I knew who he was: we were in seventh grade together.
He wore old oversized T-shirts every day. From his face grew the ugly
blond beginnings of a beard, a feat at school accomplished only by
a Filipino eighth-grader. Karinger never talked in class, and I'd
never seen him talk to anyone outside of class either. He was always alone. I usually spent my time at school alone, too, but at least
people knew I could speak because I raised my hand a lot in class
and answered questions.

In fact, in the beginning I heard him talk only when my mom
asked him questions in the car. Once she asked him why he walked
home in the heat. Karinger didn't tell her it was because his mom
worked all day and his dad was gone. He told her he liked finding
things in the desert.

He started to come over to my house to play video games. We
jumped on the trampoline in my backyard, jumped from the
trampoline into the pool and swam all day. One time we'd been
floating out there for a long while without saying anything to each
other. I surprised myself by asking if he was jealous of my house.
My parents both worked full-time; we weren't well-off. But I knew
he lived in a trailer.

"Jealous?" he said. "No way."

"But you live in a—"

"Yeah," he said. "So?"

"So, don't you get bored?"

He dipped himself low into the pool so that the water came up to his nose. Without his oversized shirt on, he didn't look so chubby. When he came back up, he asked me, "Have you ever hunted lizards?"

"No," I said.

"You ever drink the water from a cactus?"

I hadn't.

"My backyard is the whole desert," he said. He formed a cup with his hands and guided a dead yellow jacket along the edge of the water. "I've got this knife that used to be my dad's, from the army. You take it to the cactus at just the right angle, you can get this really sweet water out of it."

He went on and on about the desert and all the equipment his dad had left behind. He told me about the golf clubs and the abandoned course. By the end of his speech, I was so excited, I asked my parents if I could go to Karinger's place after school. Later, his mom called mine and said, "You've got no idea how important your Daley is to my Robert." Then it was summer, and I was at Karinger's all the time.

Karinger's mom, Linda, did two things: She worked fifty-five hours a week at Antelope Valley Animal Shelter, and she entered sweepstakes. Scattered all over the floor of the trailer were losing scratch-off tickets. Walking between them on the carpet, my feet picked up their shavings.

If Karinger had shaved and worn a long blond wig, he'd have looked just like Linda. She even wore baggy T-shirts, too. After working at the shelter all day, she'd come home to Karinger, his younger sister, Roxanne, me, and the three cats living in the trailer. I couldn't tell if the shaggy brown carpet smelled like the cats or if the cats smelled like the shaggy brown carpet. Either way, Linda had that smell, too.

One time, Karinger and I cleared a patch of that spotted carpet and sorted our golf balls. We put newer balls in one pile and scratched or warped ones in another.

That's when Karinger told me we should sell the good ones.

Linda was standing in the room, rocking a big brown cat named Potato in her arms. "Why don't you tell Daley your real plan," she said. She had a smile on her face like a kidder.

"That *is* my plan," Karinger said. "We can sell them and spend the profits on better clubs. Then we'll get really good at golf and be rich."

His eleven-year-old sister—who, like my own sister, and therefore like *all* sisters, as far as I knew, had an amazing ability to disappear and reappear without my noticing—suddenly stood beside her mother. Roxanne Karinger said, "That's not a bad idea, but me and Mom like your other idea better."

Karinger slapped his hands together and nearly shouted: "Goodbye, ladies."

Potato leaped from Linda's arms and into our golf balls. She batted them between her paws and messed up the neat piles.

Karinger hissed at the cat. "Get out of here," he said.

Roxanne stepped over and scooped Potato up from underneath. She flattened the cat's face with her open palm and made funny noises. "You're mashed, Potato," she said. She giggled and squeezed the cat tight. I laughed, too.

Karinger rolled his eyes. He made a gun with his finger and thumb and pulled the trigger at the side of his head. "Boom," he said, and flopped dead on the floor.

A few times a year, Linda brought kittens home from the shelter in groups of six or seven. They'd stay at the house until they no longer needed to be bottle-fed. Sometimes the batches overlapped.

Sometimes there'd be thirteen or fourteen kittens living in the yellow bathtub. Once in a while, one of the kittens would die. When this happened, Linda wouldn't bury the kitten nearby, even though Karinger asked her to let us bury it in the desert out back. "I can make a cross out of some twigs and we can say something nice," he'd say, but his mom wouldn't budge. She'd get rid of the dead kitten some other mysterious way.

She told us not to name the kittens. No use in getting attached, she'd say. Karinger did anyway and named them based on their colors. Black kittens were called Midnight or Oiler. He called orange ones Tangerine or Carrot. One time, Linda brought home a black and orange kitten and I suggested we call him Halloween, but Karinger said no. "That's too easy," he said. I wanted to point out that calling a white cat Snow White wasn't exactly difficult, but I just shrugged. After a little while, Karinger said we could call the kitten Halloween, just until he thought of something better. He never did, and Halloween, like the rest of the kittens who survived, eventually went back to the shelter with Linda.

We carried our golf balls and clubs to the new course across town. We walked for an hour before we came to the place, a lush green oasis with a big parking lot full of cars. A large boulder sat at the gate between the parking lot and the driving range. The words KNICKERBOCKER GOLF CLUB were engraved on it and painted red. When we walked past the boulder, Karinger slapped it with his hand and said, "They use these fake rocks to cover up electric boxes and things like that."

The boulder looked real to me, but I didn't argue.

Toward the end of the packed driving range, we found two empty slots. When we set down our bags and clubs, Karinger knelt down and brushed his hand against the grass. "Not Astroturf," he said.

Real golfers, he said, have to stretch before they start hitting. He put his 3-wood behind his neck and across his shoulders and hung his arms over the club's shaft. He twisted his body left and right for a long time. I didn't know what to do. I cracked my knuckles and rolled my ankles. Karinger said, "We need tees."

In the grass we collected broken tees. They were wooden and colorful and left behind by real golfers. Some of them still had enough length to stick into the ground. A few of them had tops that were still intact enough to balance a golf ball. Once we found enough, we emptied our plastic bags onto the grass. Karinger had about fifty old balls and I had maybe half that. I got through mine with one swing per ball. My shots rarely got off the ground, but some of them rolled pretty far, spitting up dust like a car in the distance. I turned to see how Karinger was doing. I expected him to have a few more left to hit, but he hadn't even made a dent.

"I'm taking practice swings," he said. "Don't get mad at me because you rushed through yours."

He teed up and took a few more slow practice swings. He stepped up to the ball and placed his club behind it. He looked out into the targetless field for a long while. Then he brought the club back and around. He lost his footing on the way down and barely made contact. The ball dribbled a measly fifteen feet into the grass.

"Redo," Karinger said. He jogged out into the field to re-collect his miss-hit. Just as I was about to tell him he needed to hurry up, a man a few slots away in a Crocodile Dundee straw hat yelled out, "Kid, get back behind the line!" I hated being scolded, and even though Karinger was the one getting yelled at, the fact that I was with him made me nervous.

"Sorry," I said to Crocodile Dundee.

When Karinger got back, the man came over with a huge metal

driver in his hands. "You guys have got to be careful," the man said. "I'm not a good enough shot to guarantee I won't shank it in your direction next time."

"Sorry," I repeated. Karinger didn't say anything. The man tipped his hat and went back to his slot.

"Can you believe that?" Karinger asked. "Old farts like that give golf a bad name."

"I thought he was pretty nice about it," I said. "You really shouldn't have gone out there. It's dangerous." I pointed to a sign that said so.

Karinger was quiet.

"You need help finishing your pile?" I asked. I hoped he would say yes so we could get on our way.

"No," he said, "I'll be quick." He went over to his slot and without much of a wait started hacking at the pile of golf balls. Some of them shot out at strange angles, but most of them hardly moved. He was chopping at them with his club. The 3-wood ripped hunks of grass out of the ground, leaving wet, muddy holes. Chunks of turf and mud splattered all over Karinger's pants and T-shirt. Crocodile Dundee and a few other men ran over, yelling. Karinger, holding his weapon, grabbed my wrist with his free hand and we fled.

"Sorry!" I yelled out as we ran. On the way home—through the desert, to avoid roads—Karinger didn't say a word.

When we got back to the trailer, Linda told us she had a surprise in the bathtub. We went into the bathroom and opened the sliding door of the shower. A yellow kitten, alone, roamed. It had huge eyes, one blue and one green. Roxanne, toying with her single blond braid, appeared behind us and said, "Her name's Kallie. Isn't she cute?"

Karinger said, "I thought we weren't supposed to name them."

"Well, this one's not going back to the shelter," she said. "Mom says there's something special about her."

"What kind of name is Kallie?" Karinger said. He looked at the kitten while he asked his sister.

"It's short for Kaleidoscope. She sort of looks like one." She bent over to put her face near Kallie. "Don't you?" she asked the kitten.

"That's stupid," Karinger said. He let the word hang there for a second, and then left the bathroom.

I stayed behind and played with Kallie. She made small squeaking noises by opening her mouth as wide as possible and shutting her eyes tight. Her head was too big for her body. She nibbled on my fingertips. I'd forgotten Roxanne was still there until she said, "Cute, right?"

"So cute," I said.

"Guys?" Linda peeked around the door at us. "Where's Robert?"

"Being a baby in his room," said Roxanne.

"Go check up on him," Linda told her daughter, who, groaning, obliged.

Linda and Roxanne traded places, and before I could feel the awkwardness of our standing in a small bathroom together, Linda began to talk.

"Robert can be sweet," she said. "You should have heard his original plan for the nicer golf balls you guys have collected. He came into my bedroom one night with the saddest, reddest face, like he'd been crying for years on end. He'd be embarrassed if he knew I'd told you, you know. It's just that he can be so sweet, is all. I told this story to your mother."

I thumbed between the kitten's eyes.

"He came in all sad and I asked him, 'What's the matter, baby?' And he didn't even get mad when I called him that. He just inched his way to my bed and flopped down into it with me. You have to understand how sweet this all was. When I told your mother, you should have heard her voice. 'Really?' she seemed like she was asking, and I said, *Really*. It was just so sweet."

I was nervous that Karinger was going to come back into the bathroom and discover his mom telling me his secrets. I decided I could only stay another minute.

"So he's in bed with me and he's just so red—I've never seen anyone so red—and he asks me, so quietly, *'Mom'*—and he said it just like that—*'Mom?* You think if I get enough of these nice golf balls—' "

She paused for a moment. When she continued, something in her voice had changed.

"He said, 'You think if I get enough of these nice ones, Dad'll come back and teach me how to play?' "

I kept on with the kitten, afraid to look Linda in the eyes. The year before, I'd been a businessman—a neighborhood landscaper. I'd negotiated wages, for God's sake. Now I'd regressed to the point of looking to a kitten for strength. Karinger was to blame, but I wasn't sure how.

"Sure," Linda continued. "I told him, 'Sure, your dad will come back. Of course he will.' But Robert's not a child anymore. He knows I can't promise a thing like that. He could tell I wasn't being honest, and he's been upset ever since. You should have heard your mother when I told her this story. 'How sweet,' your mother said in that cute accent of hers. And it was. It was really, really sweet."

That night, when Linda was asleep, I joined Karinger in his bedroom to play video games. They used to be mine. For my birthday that year, I'd been given new games on the condition that I hand my old ones over to Karinger. While we were playing I asked, "Why'd you freak out earlier?"

Karinger kept playing. His mouth was open and his eyes were watering. He hadn't blinked in a while. I asked him again.

"I didn't freak out," he said. "Those old men are why people hate golf."

"You were kind of stupid."

"Look. Can we play this game or what?"

"Sure," I said. "But can we go back and apologize tomorrow?"

"Wow," Karinger said. "Are you serious?"

"You messed up their grass pretty bad. It's not easy to grow grass out here, you know."

That last part was true. In the desert, it takes a certain knowledge and work ethic to keep a lawn green. One skill my dad taught me was how to maintain a desert lawn, how to keep the mower's blade high. Too short and you can burn the grass at the roots. I never told Karinger any of that. I felt guilty talking about my dad when I was with Karinger, so when I was, I pretended our dads abandoned the Antelope Valley together.

Karinger paused the game and looked at me. The random yellow hairs on his face had multiplied since the morning. "You're going to leave, too," he said. "I can see it in your face. One by one, I'm going to watch everyone leave this place, aren't I?"

"You can leave, too," I said. "Don't you want to?"

And as soon as I asked, I knew the answer was no.

"Let's go make that apology," Karinger said. He stood over me, backlit by the lamp in the ceiling.

"What time is it?" I asked. Outside, the sky was still dark.

"Don't worry about that," he said. "There's no wrong time for an apology."

"Robert," I started, but I didn't really have anything to say. I didn't want to walk over to the golf course in the middle of the night.

"The groundskeepers will be around," he said. "They're the ones who have to fix the holes in the grass we made, right? They're there all night, and we'll apologize to them directly."

"Your mom—"

"Sleeps through everything. Besides, you were right last night."

"I was?"

"Yeah. I feel really bad about the grass thing. I can't sleep until we go out there and say sorry."

I got up and put on a sweater. I was about to leave the room when I noticed Karinger had his 3-wood and his grocery bag in his hands. I asked him why he was bringing his equipment.

He said, "After we say sorry, we'll be able to hit balls while no one else is out there. We'll have the whole place to ourselves."

I thought of Crocodile Dundee yelling at us for retrieving bad hits. I had to admit it would be fun to be out there alone, with an infinite number of chances to hit a good shot.

"Don't forget your stuff," he said, and I didn't.

Under the stars, the gate looked like the entrance to an old zoo. It was locked. Karinger tapped his club between the gate's metal bars. He was thinking. I suggested coming back in the morning. He wasn't listening to me. He was listening to the rhythm he was making with his club against the gate. Finally he slid the 3-wood between the bars and did the same with his plastic grocery bag. "Here," he told me, and he took my club and bag and put them through the gate, too. He went to the KNICKERBOCKER boulder. He knocked at the rock with his knuckles and listened to the sound. "Guess I was wrong," he said. "It *is* real." He pitched himself up onto it. The baggy shirt made his stealth a surprise, and I watched the secret muscles in his forearms press against his skin. Karinger latched on to the top of the gate and heaved himself up over it. He landed on the other side with a thud that sounded painful. Immediately, though, he said, "Your turn."

"I can't," I said. What I had meant to say was: *What's the point?* There was nobody there. No groundskeepers, no Crocodile Dundee.

"Your turn," he repeated.

I climbed onto the rock and up to the top of the gate. Falling from there to the cement on the other side was the hardest part. Karinger reached up and I reached down. He helped pull me to the pavement. When I landed, I still held on to him. My feet rang like my hands sometimes did when I hit a ball in a weird place on the club's face. It stung a bit. It didn't hurt as bad as I thought it would.

Some of the smaller lights were still on, but the large stadium lights down the field were all shut off. Huge sprinklers showered the grass two hundred yards out.

"No one's out here," I said. "Let's just go find someone. And if we can't, let's go home."

"We'll go hit a few balls," he said. "Someone is bound to come find us. Then we'll apologize, and all will be right with the world."

"I'm going to leave now," I said.

"Don't," Karinger said. I thought he was going to continue. I thought he was going to try to bully me into staying. I thought he was going to call me weak or lame or gay. But he didn't. He just said, "Don't," and stopped there.

We found the giant muddy divots he'd carved out of the ground earlier. In them was a sandy mixture of seeds and dirt one of the groundskeepers must have planted. Karinger put down his grocery bag and took slow practice swings with his 3-wood. I did the same with my club.

"Let me have a ball," he said, and I tossed him one from my bag. I didn't even ask why he didn't use one of his own.

He put his club behind the ball and took a quick swing. The impact sounded solid. The ball shot off into the dark, disappearing among the stars before we could see it land.

"Wow," I said. "Great shot."

Karinger was still holding his stance, the club over his shoulders.

"Really," I said. "That was awesome." I shivered even though I was wearing a sweater. Karinger stood there in a T-shirt like a trophy.

Then he pulled his club over his head and hammered away at the grass again with everything he had.

"Robert!" I said. I whispered it as if there were people around to hear us. "What is wrong with you?"

Karinger threw his club away into the field past the safety line and fell to his knees. He started clawing at the mud and grass with his bare hands.

"Stop," I said. I looked to see if anyone was around. "Robert, please."

He stretched his arm out to snag his plastic grocery bag. He started to dump its contents into the hole he'd made. Whatever was in that bag, he planned to bury. I thought, Kallie could fit in a bag like that.

With both hands, I lifted the 2-iron over my head. For a second I believed I might actually bring it down on Karinger's skull.

But he emptied the bag, and what fell out—all the good white balls we'd collected—toppled into the hole, one on top of the other.

"Oh," I said, dropping my 2-iron.

Karinger gathered the strips of mud and grass he'd unplugged from the ground. He placed them over the golf balls in the hole. He pressed with both hands and all his weight.

"Help me," he said. He was crying—the first and last time I'd ever see that. I put my hands over his and we pushed the mud down together. For some reason I started crying, too, and the shame of that only made it worse. No matter what we did or told ourselves for the rest of our lives, this moment revealed the truth: We were not tough boys.

When the ground was as flat as we could make it, Karinger got up and walked over to pick up his wooden club, which he broke over his knee. Out of the broken shaft he made a cross and laid it over the mound. He said, "This is the last I'll ever mention him," though that wouldn't, of course, turn out to be true. Then Karinger spoke to his father under his breath, and I couldn't make out the words.

The sprinklers came on and we dashed out from the grass toward the gate. It didn't take long for us to realize that without the boulder, we wouldn't be able to hop over the fence and make our escape. The night was cool, cold because we were both dripping wet. Maybe we could have laughed, but we didn't. Karinger stood with his head down and his eyes closed. I stared at him. In his baggy shirt, which was even bigger now that it was soaked, he looked like a kind of monk. We were quiet for some time. Then the east lit up, and we waited for men to open the gate.

THE MISSING ANTELOPE OF
THE ANTELOPE VALLEY

✦

Of course, they weren't antelope at all, but *pronghorns*—
pronghorns that looked, to the treasure-seeking settlers of the
California high desert, like antelope. Upwards of eighty thousand
pronghorns grazed the outer valley's tussock grass before the completion of the Southern Pacific Railroad line in 1876. The pronghorns, which had coexisted with native human populations for
eleven thousand years, refused to cross the railroad tracks. This con-
finement, along with a growing number of fur-hunters and, at the
turn of the century, a series of bizarre weather patterns, all but killed
off the valley's misnomered namesake. The few that survived mi-
grated inland and north, and nearly a hundred years passed before
anyone in town saw an antelope—a pronghorn, that is—again.
That person happened to be my sister.

We—Mom and Dad and I—called her Jean, as in denim, but she
went around pronouncing her name as if it were the last syllable
in "parmesan." Everyone at her high school who'd seen a map of

California was taking Spanish, but Jean found herself among the four seniors who'd kept with French, the other three being: Colette (Colleen Ditzhazy), Bertrand (Bert Strife), and Jean's best friend, Amélie (Emily Goodson). Not until year two did Jean's teacher mention that pronouncing her name "the French way" actually made it male, but by this time, Jean—as in parme*san*—had already stuck.

Meanwhile, I was enjoying the eighth grade. My parents were so distracted by my sister's college applications and general entanglement with what my mother called "womanhood" that I was left, by and large, to my own devices. Said devices were few but important, and consisted mainly of my best friend, Robert Karinger, and the expanse of uncultivated desert that stretched from the stone wall behind Karinger's trailer park to the back loading zone of Albertsons, some three miles away. Outside my parents' purview, we finished our homework and ran off into the wilderness. We hunted lizards. We studied the carcasses of feral cats. We searched the makeshift dumps for treasure. We slept, on warm nights, on his roof. We woke early and eavesdropped on Karinger's mother and little sister through the EPDM rubber roofing. "Ethylene propylene diene monomer," Karinger told me on our first night atop the trailer. He waved his open palm across the surface like a game show model. "All spread out over a layer of wood decking." We pressed our ears against the bottoms of empty water glasses. All we could hear was the running shower and the occasional violence of the blow-dryer.

A decade after her husband left, Karinger's mother, an avid lottery player, won a sweepstakes for a new tract home on the west side of town. Soon, Karinger would be living in a big house with stairs and a rec room, and I made him promise I could stay over as much as I wanted. "Sure," he said, "but we'll have to make a concentrated effort to continue spending time outdoors."

"True," I said. "When you're right, you're right."

Jean was preparing to hear back from colleges just as Karinger's mother made plans to move from the trailer park into the new house. While the movers did their business, Karinger spent nights at my place. "It's decision week," I warned him as he unfurled his sleeping bag on my bedroom floor.

The day Jean was accepted to UCLA, the college of her choice, the French Club had a study session at the house. Colette hugged her, thinking probably of her own mailbox at home. Bertrand, aware of my father's presence in the room, offered a neutered high five. Amélie—Emily Goodson—who'd been coming over to the house since I was a baby, grabbed Jean by the wrists and jumped up and down with her, squealing, for a full minute and a half. She had enormous breasts, and Karinger nudged me to pay attention. I *was* paying attention to Amélie, but for different reasons. Of all the French Club, I knew her to be the only one staying in the Antelope Valley after high school. I studied her for any signs of envy or devastation, and, when I found none, returned to watching Karinger watch her bounce.

Then came summer. As far as I knew, Amélie and Jean were spending every day at the mall. That was true of most teenagers in the Antelope Valley. Karinger was proud to say we were the only ones wise enough to understand the desert. "You can find a mall anywhere, can't you?" he said. So when, after a long day of digging trenches and bunkers between Joshua trees for a game of paintball, we spotted a parked car reflecting the orange sun next to our dismantled bicycles, we were—at least I was—afraid. But I vaguely recognized the car, and when the doors opened to reveal Jean and, on the driver's side, Amélie, my fear was replaced by a kind of bitterness. The one unspoken rule between my sister and me—keep your worlds separate—had been violated, and I was ready to call foul. However, Robert—"Karinger," he reminded me with an elbow to the side—was all charm and accommodation. "Ladies," he said. "What can we do you for?"

To hear them say it, Amélie and Jean hadn't seen an antelope but a ghost. Karinger kept asking for details.

"Where, exactly?"

"Way east, down by the 138."

"When?"

"Just now—drove the twenty minutes over here right after spotting him."

"*Him*—you sure it's a male?"

"How do you tell?"

"Well, horns or no horns?"

"Horns, small ones."

"How big?"

"I said small."

"Not the horns, the animal."

"Big, real big."

I took a different line of questioning.

"What were you and Emily doing out in the desert in the first place?"

"It's *Amélie,* and we were just going for a drive, that's all."

"How'd you know where to find me and Karinger?"

"Didn't—just saw your bikes on the side of the road by accident."

"So what'd you stop for—what is it you want from us?"

"I'm beginning to ask myself the same question, jerk."

Karinger convinced Amélie and Jean to drive back to the place of the sighting, but couldn't convince me to leave our bikes behind and join them. I rode home, maneuvering Karinger's bike alongside mine. The next day, I asked Karinger how the search went, if they saw the antelope. "Negative," he said. "Waste of time. Should've rode home with you." And that was the last we said of the matter.

At the end of summer, Jean moved away to college, and Karinger and I started high school. Four years later, my sister had gone back to Jean, as in denim, and moved East for law school. Karinger and I celebrated our diplomas before he left for boot camp. Then we had our last conversation, and time passed indifferently.

The unspoken rule: Keep your worlds separate. But once Jean finished law school and decided to stay in New York, and once I moved to San Francisco after college, the rule became enforced not by us, but by the width of a continent. This—we preferred self-enacted divisions—we didn't like. So as we got older, we grew closer. We called each other more often, and Mom got sick and passed away, and I went back to the Antelope Valley temporarily, and Dad was doing fine, selling more furniture than ever, he said, though we had a hard time believing him. He was sixty-two and still nowhere near retirement. He didn't need me at the house, but I ended up moving home anyway to keep him company, and made some money

writing for the internet, which almost anyone can do. Jean kept saying how she felt bad for us—bad for Dad, mostly, which I joked
sounded like a gloomy book by Dr. Seuss. Jean didn't laugh. She
was the kind of person who cried in the parking lot if the cashier
at Target was over the age of forty. So one day she called and told
us to pack our bags. "Family vacation," she said, and when I asked
her where she was taking us, she just said to start calling her *Jean*
again.

Dad refused to get a passport. He didn't want to be in Paris without his wife. He insisted we go ahead, and Jean asked a million
times if he was sure.
    He was sure.

Naturally, Jean did all the talking. Having not taken a French class
since high school, she must have spoken at a ninth-grade level. Still,
I listened to the most basic French words fall out of her mouth, and
something about the familiarity of her voice combined with the
strange music of her speech carved out of me so much respect for
her, I almost cried when she ordered, at a sidewalk café, two slices
of quiche.

We scaled the Eiffel Tower and took selfies on the Champs-
Élysées, which I stupidly hadn't known was a street. (I'd thought
it was a hotel.) This was my first time outside of the country, and I
clung to Jean everywhere we went. People must have mistaken us
for lovers. Jean looked beautiful—heavy lashes and eyebrows
framed her big hazel eyes, and she had this naturally layered brown
hair and year-round summer skin, and a wide mouth with lips so

full, it gave her the look of a woman always on the verge of correcting something you're about to say. People like a large mouth on a woman—even in Paris, I bet, and they probably looked at her and thought, why is this beautiful large-mouthed woman with *him*? Why is she with this young American boy with pale skin and an incomplete beard and skinny jeans unfashionably and unseasonably worn with boat shoes? Why is she with this idiot, who keeps calling her by a man's name?

The flight the next day wasn't scheduled until the afternoon, so Jean took me to a queer club that night and said, "I don't know if there's a place on earth more diametrically opposite to the Antelope Valley." We ended up getting a table in the corner beneath large floating paper orbs of green light. I enjoyed watching the men dance, but the sheer mentioning of the name of our hometown seemed to tether our conversation to it, and our attention stayed there, and we spoke about home over the swelling *wub-wub-wub*s of the music. I told her about the name of the town, how the antelope weren't really antelope at all. She seemed upset—she was drunk, to be fair, and so was I, and I said, "Sad, right? Even in Paris, we're talking about the fucking Antelope Valley."

Jean thumbed the water on the outside of her glass. "Have I ever told you the story of when Emily and I went out looking for one of those antelope-whatevers? We were with a guy." I told her I knew; the guy she was talking about was my friend Robert Karinger. I reminded her about our meeting in the desert. "Weird," she said, "I don't remember that."

Here's what she remembered: She and Emily and a guy Emily brought along drove out at twilight to the eastern edge of the desert. The sky was the beautiful sky you hope for during a sunset, blue and orange upstrokes from behind the mountains. And there, on

its hind legs, gnawing at the flower of a Joshua tree, stood an antelope. A pronghorn. Its black nub of a tail swatted yellow flies you
could make out in the last of the light. When the animal landed
on all fours, it turned to look at the car. Then the pronghorn came
walking right up to the road, sauntering, and put its face up against
the passenger window, the one by Jean's face, as if saying hello.

The animal waited there for a while, its black eye staring dumbly
into the car. Jean and Emily and the boy in the backseat spoke
in the reverent tones of witnesses. Jean was the only one afraid.
"Emily wanted to open the window and stroke its nose," she told
me. "The boy in the backseat, well, he got out of the car on the
opposite side, and walked slowly around the back of the car to
where the antelope was standing. He came up behind it, real slow.
The antelope knew he was there, and put out his back leg. Not a
kick—just slowly put out his leg, I swear to God, like a hand. And
this boy, he held on to the hoof. First he just had one hand on it, as
if they were greeting each other. Then he wrapped his other hand
around the ankle. He just held the leg for a long time, started pet-
ting it, until Emily went out of the car and stroked the antelope's
nose. And the antelope—the pronghorn—let it all happen, back
leg out, nose down. And I just watched and watched, afraid that as
soon as I opened the window, he'd dart off. Eventually I did open
the window, and I was right. The antelope shook free of the boy
and ran off into the desert. And the boy—I can't believe he was
your friend—he kept saying on the ride back how the antelope must
not have liked something about me. Emily was fine, and he was fine.
But something about me scared the animal off. And the boy kept
saying we shouldn't tell anybody about this, like it was a secret between us. I think both Emily and I had a little crush on him. He
was young—I didn't remember he was *that* young—but he was a
beautiful, white-haired, serious boy. And so, yeah, we agreed that

we wouldn't tell anyone, that we would keep the antelope—the pronghorn—a secret."

The green light of the bulbous lanterns sharpened her features, lengthening the shadows of her cheekbones and nose. She had the look of something between a Halloween-store witch and our thinning mother toward the end of chemotherapy. The *wub-wub-wub*s seemed to increase in frequency and in volume, and although Jean continued to speak, I stopped straining to hear her. Soon we would catch our flights—Jean to New York, me to the Antelope Valley—and I didn't know when I would see her next. Suddenly I imagined this was the last moment we'd ever share, and because I knew she would go on to remember it differently than I would, I ached to do something so spectacular and unordinary that, if every other memory of Paris were to be corrupted, at least we'd have this.

I stood, accidentally knocking one of the green orbs into a sway, and held out my hand. *"Jean,"* I said, the French way. And soon, while everyone else in the club beat their bodies against the thick air between them, I held her—my sister, depending on the swinging light, or my mother, or Karinger—and danced, slowly, to another kind of music. *"Je t'aime,"* I said through her hair, into her ear.

"I love you, too," she said into mine. *"Moi aussie, je t'aime."*

When you spend a life leaving a place, only to return to it again and again, the returns become increasingly shameful. One way to deal with this shame is to create theories, theories that either justify your returns or else allow you the possibility of leaving—actually leaving, once and for all.

This time, my theory is this: The antelope—the pronghorn—somehow knew that Emily and Karinger were different from Jean. Emily—married, pregnant with twins—continues to live in the

Antelope Valley, just off Avenue N where the water tower looms in the foothills. Karinger became a husband and a father after joining the marines, and I'm convinced he would have lived in town the rest of his life if he hadn't gone off and died in a different desert. My theory, I guess, is that the pronghorn knew Emily and Karinger were meant to stay, and Jean was meant to leave. All places, maybe, bear these two kinds of people, and ours just happens to have a way to tell the difference.

It's a hypothesis, anyway. In order to make it a theory, I have to run a test. So, in the late afternoon I tell my dad I love him, I'm heading out. I drive my mother's old car east, away from the light and the railroad tracks, far out into the desert. I leave the road and go as far as the Toyota's tires will take me before they fail, settling for good in the soft grip of the dirt. The headlights I leave on and the keys I throw thirty feet into an enormous heap of tumbleweeds. I remove my shirt and shoes, and sit. Far off, the sun falls—slowly at first, and then as quickly as a dropped coin—behind the San Gabriel Mountains. This is death country, and I am either going to survive it or not. Under the bleeding sky, I wait for the antelope, the pronghorn, the god of staying and the god of leaving, to show me what kind of man I am.

ACKNOWLEDGMENTS

How can I thank enough:

Clark Blaise and Bharati Mukherjee, my mentors and friends and greatest advocates, for all the brilliance and confidence over the years.

Rick Moody, an unerring adviser, and Robert and Peg Boyers for introducing us at their wonderful New York State Writers Institute.

Scott Covell, for teaching literature with humor and enthusiasm and high expectations, and for assigning books written by the living, which gave me the courage to try.

The Helen Zell Writers' Program at the University of Michigan, which changed everything for me, and the program's namesake, Helen Zell, for the financial and creative freedom granted by her extreme generosity and dedication to the arts.

The faculty and staff who looked out for me at Michigan, especially Peter Ho Davies, Eileen Pollack, Doug Trevor, Michael Byers, Sugi Ganeshananthan, Keith Taylor, Andrea Beauchamp, and the legendary Nicholas Delbanco.

All the writers I lucked my way into befriending including my mythically great cohort at Michigan, but especially Brit Bennett, fellow country mouse, for help on this book at every stage.

My earliest reader and closest comrade, Ezra Carlsen.

Jenna Meacham, a true artist and friend, and the unstoppable Suzy Chandler, both of whom stuck with me through the awkward phases.

Jenni Ferrari-Adler, my agent and trusted guide, for seeing through the haze before I could, and for motivating me to move forward.

Everyone at Picador, especially Anna DeVries, hyper-sagacious editor and *deus ex machina* of my life, who turned a book I was proud of into a book of which I'm prouder; Elizabeth Bruce, synonymous in my mind with good news, for working so hard to smooth the publication process; Stephen Morrison, kind and inspired publisher, for providing safe passage for this book and so many others into the world.

My family, for enough to fill another few books.

Mairead Small Staid, who came into my life like an RKO outta nowhere, for making this book and its author so much better.

And all my fellow desert kids, especially Bob Kniepkamp, Anthony Galura, and Nick Reuter, for being there.

ABOUT THE AUTHOR

CHRIS McCORMICK was raised in the Antelope Valley. He earned his B.A. at the University of California, Berkeley, and his M.F.A. at the University of Michigan, where he was the recipient of two Hopwood Awards.